The Philanderer's Wife

Katharine Trelawney

A Bright Pen Book

Text Copyright © Katharine Trelawney 2012

Cover design by © Elizabeth Fitt

All rights reserved. No part of this publication may be reproduced, stored in a retrieval system, or transmitted in any form or by any means, electronic, mechanical, photocopy, recording or otherwise, without prior written permission of the copyright owner. Nor can it be circulated in any form of binding or cover other than that in which it is published and without similar condition including this condition being imposed on a subsequent purchaser.

British Library Cataloguing Publication Data.
A catalogue record for this book is available from the British Library

ISBN 978-0-7552-1463-1

Authors OnLine Ltd
19 The Cinques
Gamlingay, Sandy
Bedfordshire SG19 3NU
England

This book is also available in e-book format, details of which are available at www.authorsonline.co.uk

Prologue

"She's pregnant." Paddy spoke the words slowly, looking directly at his wife.

Joscelyn was shocked; terribly shocked but not surprised. She had sensed something from the arrival of that letter. The news seemed to confirm something that she already knew. This didn't ease the pain, the intense terrible pain. This is, she thought, the worst thing that could ever happen to me. It is the worst thing that could happen and now it has happened. How foolish I was, she thought, never to have anticipated this moment. She had accepted that Paddy sometimes had sex with other women, but she had never, ever thought that any other than herself would bear his child. Paddy had always assured her that it would not happen. Besides, it just wasn't right. She was his wife. It was she who should be the mother of his child.

The pain that flooded in, with the news, was just too awful to bear. She didn't know how she was ever going to bear it. But she was going to have to.

At the same time she looked at her husband's face. His eyes were searching for contact with hers; she immediately felt the pull of his need for her. He was lonely. He looked desperately unhappy. His feelings flooded in, where hers had been. Oh, what a relief that was!

She felt sorry for him.

"Oh Paddy," she whispered. "Are you all right?"

"I feel dreadful," he said.

Chapter 1

Paddy Gregory came home late on Friday evening, to find his wife Joscelyn already in bed, with her head buried under the duvet. He could tell, though, from the pattern of her breathing that she was not asleep.

"I had a good evening." He sat on the bed next to her, and gently pulled the duvet off her face, wanting her to rouse herself and listen to his news.

"Good," said Joss in an entirely neutral tone. Her eyes opened, but her gaze wasn't quite directed at her husband.

"I took Hilary out for a drink. I had some news for her. I had the go-ahead on that short, the one on Celtic folk music. She's going to direct it; she was delighted."

"I expect she was." Joscelyn was sounding noticeably grumpy. With a reluctant air, she sat up a little, resting her head on her pillows, and revealing a shock of hair, which grew down to her shoulders.

In his late thirties, Paddy showed little sign of impending middle age. Even sitting on the bed, and concentrating on his wife, he displayed a slight restlessness, which spoke of the impatience of youth rather than the complacency of achievement and experience.

"She's such a nice girl; and so talented. I'm sure she's got a great career ahead of her."

"I thought she was a theatre director?" Joscelyn was finally looking intently at her husband's face. She was a bit concerned. Paddy's judgement was normally good, and his instinct to put himself first strong, but infatuation has a special way of magnifying a woman's talents.

Joscelyn, eleven years Paddy's junior, and very pretty, had a much more settled presence than her husband.

"Oh, a good director can do either," Paddy said confidently, and he stroked his wife's cheek. "Of course she's got a bit of a thing about the theatre, but I'm not sure that her talents aren't better suited to film."

"So this is still a business relationship then?"

"Certainly, although I think that she's getting quite fond of me. And you know that does matter to me. I don't chase girls to score points, or to boost my ego, like some men do."

Joscelyn looked at Paddy with steady eyes.

"I know you don't do it to score points. But it does boost your ego."

Paddy conceded that one. "Of course; but I do like them to care for me."

He swung his legs up onto the bed, so that he was lying on top of the covers, but next to his wife. Even wearing casual clothes, corduroy trousers and a shirt without a tie, he had an affluent air, which contrasted with the shabby look of their rented flat, where the bed had a battered headboard, and the carpet was ancient, brown and bare.

"I know," said Joscelyn. "You do." Then after a pause, she said, "I care for you."

"Absolutely, more than anyone. And I for you, Joss; you mustn't ever doubt that."

"I don't."

This was a conversation they had had many times. The exact phrases might vary, but the same words were re-used each time. It was the tone that would change, and it was from the tone that Joss could judge with almost exact precision what her husband was telling her. They might be celebrating their mutual strength against an outside threat. Sometimes, like this evening, Joss would use the opportunity to convey a little concern. And today Paddy was also pointing out that the reservations his wife had weren't going to alter his plans.

Paddy took one of Joscelyn's hands in his two, and held it firmly. She softened towards him. He had just had considerable professional success and she knew that this only activated his underlying sense of insecurity. He was daily haunted by the realisation that it could all go as quickly as it had come. Perhaps he felt that women had the capacity to be more faithful than fame.

Joss might have to deal with the anxiety, even sometimes the pain that Paddy's girlfriends caused her, but she could cope. She smiled at him.

"Will you come to bed?"

"Of course I will."

Paddy pulled off his clothes, but folded them, as he always did, quickly and neatly on a chair. In bed, he put his arms round Joscelyn, who still had something to say:

"You will be sensible, won't you? You won't waste too much time on ten minute shorts and lunches with Hilary rather than lunches with directors, backers and other useful people?"

"Of course I won't. I'm working all hours of the day. I only spend a tiny bit of time with Hilary, and that's all work as well."

"Paddy, I don't mind if you're not a great success. But I know you mind and that's why I care about it."

Paddy laughed. "Listen, you must stop thinking about Hilary. I've stopped thinking about her. I'm thinking about you, and how absolutely wonderful you are. I'm thinking that in a few weeks time we shall have a house of our very own, and won't have to wake up looking at that awful purple wallpaper. I'm thinking that today was your very last day slaving away at Slater, June and Warbeck, and that tomorrow we are going to our favourite place in all the world for a perfect night away."

He hugged Joscelyn even closer, and finally she put her arms around him, so that they were closely entwined, under the duvet.

* * *

"Number 53. That's the room we had last time."

Paddy held their key, with the number prominently displayed, for his wife to inspect, then leaned forward very slightly, and kissed her.

As they were in a cramped lift, and surrounded by rather more luggage than was necessary for two people spending one night away, they were squashed into the space between their suitcases, and clinging on to each other to avoid toppling over.

"Do you really remember the room number?" Joss was laughing, and she looked at her husband with mock admiration.

"Of course I do." The lift doors opened, revealing the two of them, still wrapped in each other's arms, wedged in by bags, to a small polite queue of people waiting on the second floor.

Joscelyn blushed, and Paddy smiled broadly.

"Good afternoon," he said to their little audience. He waved Joscelyn forward out of the lift, shifted the luggage quickly and efficiently, and ushered a grey-haired lady from the front of the queue into the lift, before heading confidently into room number 53.

Paddy was right. It was the same room they had had on their last visit, earlier in the year. It was a smallish space, because you couldn't expect large rooms in a fifteenth-century coaching inn. Most of it was filled with a large dark wooden double bed, which had a billowing chintzy canopy.

Out of the window you could see the garden, a little bare in the winter months, but on a table in front of the window was a huge bunch of red roses.

"And you remembered the roses," Joss said, reaching up to give her husband a kiss.

"Would I forget?" Paddy replied.

Dinner started at seven-thirty. The Gregories had booked an early meal, with the idea that this would give them longer to savour the excellent food in the hotel restaurant. In fact the four and a half hours between their arrival and dinnertime had slipped away very easily in the comforts of their hotel room. It was eight o'clock when quiet but determined-looking Joscelyn led a slightly grumpy Paddy into the dining room. He hadn't been quite ready to dress and come downstairs, but she had insisted that they shouldn't antagonise the hotel staff by being more than half an hour late.

"They have oysters!" Paddy looked up from the menu, and immediately caught the eye of a passing waiter. "Do you have oysters this evening?"

"Yes, sir, we do."

Paddy's temper changed instantly and he looked triumphantly at his wife.

"It's a good job we weren't down any later. They'll only have a limited supply in the kitchen, and might well have run out."

He managed to sound as if it was only his foresight that had brought them there before the oysters were all eaten by other people.

"Yes, it was." Joscelyn's equable tone had nothing in it that might dent her husband's satisfaction.

Joscelyn looked down and studied the menu, while her husband watched her. She always took several minutes to choose her food. It was one of those idiosyncrasies that had seemed sweet when he first knew her, and now, after five years of marriage could sometimes be a little irritating. Tonight, however, he was all indulgence as he watched the serious expression on her face. She had a difficult choice between duck or salmon.

"Big decisions, ah?" Relaxed as he was, he didn't like the silence going on too long. Those long moments, when her attention was focused so intently away from him.

"Yes." Joscelyn nodded, calmly, but without looking up.

Paddy was going to have to be patient, and perhaps for thirty seconds more.

Paddy, large, and physically confident, ran his broad hands through a mop of dark curly hair. He was dressed with only just enough formality to conform to the rules of the Bear dining room, with an expensive but chunky green sweater, on top of a shirt and tie. In 1980s Britain, it still wasn't exceptional for a smart restaurant to demand a tie. His wife, by contrast, was elegantly dressed, in a long blue silk gown.

Joscelyn had long fair hair, not Scandinavian blonde but a rich Teutonic dark yellow colour. It was her most striking feature, and tonight it was, apart from being regulated by an Alice band, allowed to fall loose over her shoulders.

In due course Paddy's oysters arrived, as did some mushroom soup for his wife.

"This is really nice," said Joscelyn.

"Certainly is." Paddy was looking at his food with wholehearted appreciation.

"Just the two of us."

"Absolutely."

There was a pause, and they both ate. Then Joscelyn said, "I'm very glad that Barbara has gone to Hong Kong."

"Well, you've no need to be." Paddy smiled at his wife, but there was a hint of irritation in his face. Why did she have to bring that up all of a sudden? They were just about to have a really good meal. That was one of the annoying things about women, they harboured all sorts of resentments which just came out, without warning, and often at the most inappropriate times.

He held her hand briefly. "I'm very glad to be here with you. Especially as they have oysters."

As Paddy ate his oysters, Joscelyn thought about Barbara, the woman who had gone to Hong Kong a couple of weeks before, and Paddy's thoughts turned to Hilary.

She was young and serious-minded. Straight from university, she'd directed a play in one of London's better-known pub-theatre venues. Then Paddy had helped find money to stage another one, which was currently in rehearsal.

"You should come with me to Cannes," Paddy had told her last week.

As director and producer, the occasional lunch had been

almost a professional obligation. They had taken to going to a small vegetarian restaurant, where Hilary ate heartily and Paddy normally insisted on paying the bill.

"I'll be there for the showing of *Terrible Beauty*, and of course I've got a number of other projects to discuss with people. Everybody goes to Cannes. You have to go."

Paddy's recent big success, *Terrible Beauty*, had started off as a stage play, and was now a film. He had told Hilary, over one of their lunches, how he had left his job as a commercial lawyer to work at getting it onto the big screen. How it he had done it, by sending the Hollywood actor Patrick Doyle a crate of Guinness on St. Patrick's Day, and Doyle had agreed to play the leading role. The film was already doing well in America, and it was about to open in London. It was a good story, and Paddy had become well practised at telling it. Hilary had been impressed, despite working hard not to show it.

Hilary looked worried. "Surely not?" she had said.

But Paddy noticed that she wasn't absolutely appalled by the idea. He'd been winning her round. It was his help on her play that had done this, slowly. He had, gently and unobtrusively, supported her, and now she was responding to him.

"Why surely not? We'd go as two colleagues. It would be a business thing. We'd enjoy ourselves and get lots of work done."

Hilary put her head on one side, as she had a habit of doing, her dark eyes solemn and unblinking. Then she had said,

"I am grateful to you for your help on this production. You're so good with everybody. The way you always seem to turn up just as we're getting tired and cross, and creating a bit of a party atmosphere to help things along."

"I admire the way you cope," Paddy replied. "There are some difficult people, even by theatrical standards, and you manage them magnificently."

This was not just flattery. Hilary had a way of accepting and negotiating the various large and fragile egos on set with a quiet authority that was unusual in someone who couldn't be more than twenty-two.

She'd smiled a brief smile.

"We make a good team then."

Hilary hadn't responded to this one, but Paddy had sensed his chance.

"You see, you should come with me to Cannes."

Hilary frowned. "Well perhaps," she'd said. "I'll think about it."

Paddy looked up from his thoughts and across the table at his wife, and just caught the end of a frown on her face.

"Penny for your thoughts."

"I was thinking about Barbara, and how she took me out to lunch that day to try and frighten me away from you."

Paddy grinned. He was soothed by the meal and a good bottle of wine, and prepared to indulge this little bit of upset from his wife. "She didn't succeed, though, did she? I'm not even in touch with her these days."

"No, she didn't succeed." Joss looked at him archly.

"You are made of sterner stuff than that, Joss, and that's one of the many reasons why I love you. And when we are back in our room, I'll tell you a few more of them."

* * *

On Monday morning, refreshed from the weekend with his wife, Paddy was in work early. Hilary was still in bed in her rented room when the phone started ringing about a quarter to nine.

"I don't want to put any pressure on you," he said, "but I've just been asked to confirm my dates for Cannes. I'll probably be fixing everything up in the next few days. I'll need to know for definite whether you're coming with me."

Hilary hadn't expected this. Paddy had talked about her going to Cannes with him, but she hadn't expected him to ring up first thing in the morning and talk about dates as if it was virtually settled.

"Well, if I do come along, I can make my own arrangements. You sort yourself out, for the time being. I haven't had the chance to think about it yet."

"Yes, but I've got a chance to get two rooms in the best hotel in town, both with views of the sea. I'm getting such a good deal, they're practically free, so you wouldn't need to pay anything. I'd put it down as a business expense."

"I'd prefer to pay for myself." In fact, Hilary was thinking that the whole trip was probably beyond her budget.

"Why waste the money? As long as I confirm the booking today, I can get them for almost nothing and then charge them against tax. You can buy me a meal while we're there."

Hilary wasn't quite sure what she felt about Paddy Gregory. He had a reputation for being a dreadful philanderer, but (and Hilary wasn't sure whether or not she should be offended about this) he hadn't tried anything on with her. She thought about her father, who now lived on his own in Provence. She could combine a trip to the festival with a visit to her Dad. And Cannes would be fun.

"Thanks for the offer. I'll think about it and call you back."

* * *

Joscelyn felt that next year was going to be her year. Paddy had definitely had his, with his film not only being produced but doing so well. Her achievements would be more modest, being at last able to give up a job she disliked, and study. It would be enough to make her very happy, and very proud. At least, until they had children.

Her contented mood was shattered by Paddy, who came home a little early. He was in transit, having another meeting that evening. Joss didn't mind him going out, but she was shocked when her husband, over a cup of tea and in the course of relating the day's events, told her calmly that he had arranged to go to the Cannes Film Festival with Hilary.

Joscelyn looked at him for a moment. This was completely out of the blue. Last time she had heard, it was just the odd working lunch.

She was outraged, and turned on Paddy.

"Didn't you know that I wanted to go to Cannes more than anything else in the world?"

Paddy was taken aback by his wife's reaction, but he didn't hesitate more than a second before responding.

"No," he shouted back. "Because you didn't bloody tell me! I'm not psychic."

Surely he would have known she would want to go to the Film Festival?

"Tell her you made a mistake. That I want to go, and you didn't realise." Joscelyn stood up in the small kitchen of their rented flat, and glared at her husband, who sat with his mug of tea.

"Don't be ridiculous, Joss. This is work. That's why Hilary is coming with me, because it will be work for both of us. She's made it clear to me that this is strictly professional. She'll have her own room and will be paying for herself. There's no need for you to react in this way. It's completely over the top."

"But I wanted to go. I really did. I deserve it. I was the one who put up with our flat being sold to finance a project that might have been a total flop – that might not have happened at all. I kept on working for the awful Mungo Muggins when you gave up the law to try your luck in films. And now it's paid off – which of course I'm delighted about – I want to share in the rewards. And you take a young thing who's taken your fancy and is directing a short on Celtic folk music!"

"May I remind you," Paddy used his stern, lawyer voice, "that 'our flat' that was sold was *my* flat paid for before we got married by my very hard-earned bonuses when I was a partner in Slater, June and Warbeck."

"It was our home," Joss interrupted, but Paddy carried on,

"And as for rewards, you will get plenty of them. A new house in Fulham; time off to study, paid for by me. You're already going to the premiere in London, and you're coming to the one in Dublin."

Paddy looked at his wife, standing by the oven, still looking angry. He changed his tone:

"I'm going to need you at the Dublin one, as you know. Only you can keep me sane when I have to spend more than a day at a time with my family. I shall be absolutely relying on you then."

Joss said nothing. Paddy finished his tea and went out to his meeting. By the time he came home, it was very late, and his still angry wife had finally gone to sleep.

Chapter 2

Realising the sheer impossibility of venting her feelings on Paddy, Joscelyn turned to her friend Philippa who, despite two of her three children having chickenpox, was happy to see her if she came round in the evening.

Philippa was a tall, athletic-looking woman, who normally dressed in practical clothes in tasteful, muted colours. Her main concession to vanity was her hair; naturally mousy but highlighted to an almost completely convincing blonde, and cut sharply and expensively. Joscelyn was a few inches shorter, softer-faced and a little rounder.

Philippa listened patiently to a long history of the details, and her friend's fury and disappointment.

"I really did want to go to Cannes. I don't care if I don't see much of Paddy, because of all his business meetings. I wanted to see what it was like; feel the atmosphere. We've been married for five years; he should know what I like by now."

"He should have asked you. He should never have arranged something like that without your consent."

"And if he'd asked," Joss wavered a bit, "I'd probably have said yes."

"And missed out on the trip?"

"Possibly. After all, I'm going to the London premiere and the Dublin one."

Philippa looked at her.

"But as it is, you're very upset and Paddy isn't really taking account of your feelings."

"No."

There was a moment's silence, and then Philippa said, rather abruptly, "Have you thought about taking a stand?"

"What kind of stand?"

"Something that makes it quite clear that you're not happy. He may be telling himself that you don't really mind, that you're just suffering from hormones or some such and will come round."

"He is taking exactly that attitude. That's why I feel I have to keep telling him. If I keep telling him, he'll have to listen."

"In my experience, the more you tell men something the less they listen." Philippa spoke quite matter-of-factly. "I think you would have to make it clear some other way."

"If I threatened to leave, he probably would take me to Cannes instead of Hilary. But I don't want to make that threat. It isn't that serious. I need to save that one for when I really do mean it."

"Do you think you ever will mean it?"

Joss thought about this one. "I hope not," she said.

They had finished eating their take-away meal. Philippa stacked the plates, and the little tin foil cartons which had contained their food, but she didn't clear away. Instead she said,

"When Tara was a baby I insisted that Alistair came with us on a family holiday. He'd been a partner for six months and of course he didn't want to go. I insisted. It took all my energy. Actually I did threaten to leave, and I meant it.

"Paddy was very good about it, I remember. I shall always be grateful for the support he gave us both at the time. He explained to Alistair that assistant solicitors are supposed to belong to the firm body and soul, but partners need to pace themselves a bit, and learn to delegate. So I won the day, or rather a week, because it was a week in Devon we were fighting over. Alistair came, and by the end of the week he was quite cheerful."

Paddy had been a colleague and partner of Alistair's at the

time. The two men, although very different, had got on well. That was how Joscelyn came to know Philippa.

Philippa frowned, slightly, as she recollected, "I found it a bit odd, to be honest. All that togetherness, I wasn't used to it, at least not with him. In some ways, I think once he made that big concession he found it easier than I did. But that was four years ago, and he's not come with us since."

Philippa got up, and put the dishes on the side, and put on the kettle for coffee.

"If I wanted to get him away every year I'd need to be prepared to fight and keep fighting, although if I did, I think eventually he would come round. Maybe I just don't want it enough," she looked at Joss, and her face was sad. "Maybe I've decided to bring the children up on my own and be by myself."

Joscelyn felt sorry for her friend. They both had difficulties, and that bonded them. But they were of very different kinds. Paddy, affectionate and exuberant, just unable to contain himself, was a very different kettle of fish from Alistair Hardwick.

Philippa interrupted these thoughts,

"If you want to be truly assertive with Paddy, you'd need to really show that you weren't going to accept certain things. Make it clear to Paddy that he's just going to have to do better if he wants to keep you. Or you could do what I do; let Paddy go his own way, and look for your own happiness elsewhere."

Joss sensed her friend's loneliness, and felt compassion for her. "I can handle Paddy," she said. "I don't think I need to take a stand, at least not now. And I admire you, being so strong and brave."

Philippa smiled, and said, "Talking of holidays, will you come with the children and me to the cottage sometime? At half-term maybe?"

Alistair and Philippa had recently bought a very pretty cottage in Hampshire, which Alistair had been very much happier to finance than to visit. Joss was glad to accept. It would be something to look forward to.

* * *

Hilary Mackay came home in the late afternoon of a warm spring day to find that the daffodils in her window box had finally flowered. She found a message on her answer machine from Paddy.

"Terribly sorry," Paddy's voice said. "I can't make drinks this evening. Something's come up, which might be very useful to me on the Popeye project. Speak to you soon. Bye!"

Hilary wasn't sure whether she was disappointed or not. She and Paddy had been going to have a drink with two of the actors from the play. Now it would be just her, and the actors. That was OK, although it would have been easier if Paddy had been there.

But perhaps it was better this way. She had agreed to go to Cannes at the same time as him (of course strictly as a professional colleague) and she had an idea that word had gone round, and people were beginning to link them in a way that wasn't appropriate. If they were too much together, that would just fuel the gossip.

Altogether, Paddy was hard to place, hard to explain. He wasn't exactly a friend. He was married, which none of her friends were. Although Hilary had not met his wife, Paddy talked quite freely about her. Hilary remembered when she had first had lunch with him, and he'd told her the story of doing the deal on *Terrible Beauty*. She'd asked,

"Were you married, then?" And Paddy had laughed, and said,

"Yes, I was, and to the same wife as I have now."

"And so what did she think of you selling your flat and your car, and going off to America to try and sell a film?"

"Joss was tremendous. She's a great support to me. I couldn't have done it without her."

Paddy had brought Hilary a lot of work. He admired her talent, and often told her so. And he had brought into her life not just work, but excitement. He was intelligent, and enthusiastic, and had knowledge of the arts, which was really very commendable in someone who had been a lawyer for ten years. Hilary still felt that he was basically a businessman. She had once tackled him about this, and he had happily agreed, and refused to accept that this was a waste.

Hilary felt that ultimately art and business were not compatible, which was difficult as Paddy had found the finance for her play. But he was more than just a money man. He would call by, at rehearsals, and have an almost magical capacity to raise morale, by having a laugh with people, and buying them drinks. Actually he always seemed to be buying things: drinks, the rights to film and theatre scripts, flowers, and the other week a shiny new sports car. Hilary felt that people with money should either share it with the less fortunate or spend it, thoughtfully, on things that were really worth having. She feared that there was a thoughtlessness about Paddy which would prevent him from ever being truly successful as a creative person.

There was an unpredictability about him, too. The day after he cancelled their drink, he'd phoned her, and asked her, at the very last minute, to join him, with Oscar Peterson, the famous writer, and several other people at a Chinese restaurant near his office.

* * *

Joscelyn was also phoned and invited, impromptu, to dinner in Chinatown. Unlike Hilary, she wasn't already in central London.

"I'm in the bath," she said, "and it will take me at least three quarters of an hour by tube."

"Get a taxi. Order it straight away as soon as you're clean and then get changed. You must come. We'll have a drink first, and if you're very late I'll order for you."

Joscelyn arrived at the restaurant just as the first course was being put on the table. Everyone else was sitting down, and there was a space left for her. Paddy got up. Large, and smiling, he spread out his arms as if he was going to embrace everyone.

"Wonderful timing, darling." He introduced her. On one side of him was an elegant woman, aged about thirty-five, and on his other side was Hilary.

Hilary got up, the only one besides Paddy to do so, and came and shook Joscelyn's hand.

"I'm so pleased to meet you," she said. "I have heard such a lot about you."

"And I have heard a lot about you," Joscelyn replied.

Hilary blushed, slightly. She was dressed all in black, with chunky flat shoes. She wore a large silver necklace, and Joscelyn guessed that the addition of this rather striking piece of jewellery to her normal outfit had been Hilary's gesture towards dressing for the evening out.

Well, Joscelyn thought to herself. At least she's no Barbara.

Politely, Joss started taking to a man called Steven, who was sat next to her. It was difficult. He was not very chatty, and she had long ago learned not, at such meals, to say to people "And what do you do?" Once she had failed to recognise the hero of a very popular soap opera, and had asked that very question. He had not found it amusing.

So it was with some relief that she caught Paddy's eye, and on cue, he said,

"Joss loved your performance as Seamus in *Terrible Beauty*. She agrees with me, it was the best bit of acting in the film."

Paddy had seen her predicament, and was helping her, but still for a brief moment, Joscelyn felt adrift. This man Steven did not look remotely like any character in the film that she could remember.

Steven smiled, briefly, and at last she recognised him.

"Oh, yes, I loved it. You did it so well. In just those two short scenes, I completely knew that you were the right man for Irene, and it was so sad that it could never be."

Steven frowned and began talking very quickly.

"I was the only real Irishman in the film. You would have thought that this might give me a bit of status, as they say, a bit of dignity, but not a bit of it."

At first, she wondered if he was joking; but pretty soon it was clear that Steven was a very serious man.

Out of the corner of her eye, Joscelyn was watching Hilary.

Despite sitting next to Paddy, Hilary gave no hint of any proprietorial feelings towards him. She didn't touch his arm, or over-use his first name. That was a good sign. Women easily started feeling that they owned him.

"But you did it splendidly," she told Steven.

"They made me wear those dreadful green trousers. Quite dreadful. I did try, you know, I made it quite clear that they were quite wrong for the scene. Quite wrong. How I ever managed even to speak with those awful trousers on I really don't know. I thought it was going to be impossible. It was virtually impossible."

"I really think that you transcended the trousers," Joss said soothingly. "I didn't even notice them. I was only looking at your face, and listening to what you were saying."

Joscelyn looked at Paddy flanked by two very different women. The elegant woman on the other side from Hilary was called Eugenie, and was an American. She had striking green eyes, and her clothes, hair, make-up and jewellery were all perfect. She smiled a good deal. Joss couldn't help thinking that she looked like the kind of person who would have no scruples about an affair with a married man, but fortunately Paddy showed no sign of being attracted to her.

Steven was mollified, but only by a millimetre.

"Transcended the trousers; that's exactly what I had to do. It took a tremendous effort of will. Of course I am a professional and I did my best, as always, but at what cost to myself! I'm not recovered, even now."

"No," said Joscelyn, suppressing a smile. "I can see that."

It was a long evening, talking to Steven, and she liked him less when he began ordering more bottles of wine, without so much as acknowledging that it was her husband who would be paying for them. Paddy was a generous man; too generous sometimes. He had no need to invite Steven that evening. Steven would never be of any professional use to Paddy. It would have been done out of simple desire to offer friendship to a fellow-countryman. This was fine, but she would have liked the recipient to be a little more appreciative.

On the way home, in a taxi, Paddy squeezed his wife's hand.

"You have to say one thing for me, don't you darling, I give people a good night out. We could hardly have had an odder lot together, could we? But they all enjoyed themselves."

Joscelyn hoped this was true. She hadn't particularly enjoyed herself, although for the purposes of that evening, she did not count.

"What did you think of Hilary?"

Joscelyn paused. "She seems nice. Rather serious, and very young, although she can't be very much younger than me."

"You're just more mature. Which you had to be, to take me on."

Joscelyn looked at her husband.

"Why don't you take me to Cannes? If it's just a business thing between you and Hilary I can go as your wife and she'll be there in her capacity as a director."

"Joss," Paddy spoke with studied patience. "It is just a business thing between Hilary and me. I need to be there on my own. I'll be working, and shall need to concentrate. That's why I shan't mind Hilary being around, she won't distract me. If anything, she'll be helping me."

Back in the dismal rented flat, Joss looked at her husband, and wondered if what he had been telling her in the taxi was actually true. Paddy didn't lie, directly. At the moment, his relationship with Hilary was business, and maybe a friendship. But with Paddy and women, the boundaries between business, friendship, and intimacy could easily be crossed.

She knew that, and he knew that. He knew that she knew. But at the moment he wasn't going to acknowledge it.

Paddy put his arms round her. "We're both tired, now. Time for bed."

For a while, Joss still felt unhappy. She lay on the edge of the bed, clinging on to the side. Then she relented, rolled into the dent in the middle of the ancient mattress, and bumped into Paddy. They made love, and afterwards Paddy was very tender. He held his arms tightly round his wife's waist, and told her, as he often did in those last dozy moments before sleep, that there was no one quite like her.

In the early hours of the morning Joss was dreaming. She and Hilary had been having lunch, just the two of them, when Hilary turned into Barbara, and she found herself awake and thinking. Thinking about Barbara and a lunch they'd actually had, before she and Paddy were married.

Barbara had never been Paddy's mistress. She'd been a junior colleague of Paddy's, before he had changed career, from lawyer to film producer. Then he had been a partner in large London firm of solicitors. Joscelyn had worked in the same firm as a secretary. Paddy still believed that (whatever she might say to the contrary) Joscelyn's dislike of his former colleague stemmed from the difference in status between her and Barbara at the office. Back in the 1980s, there weren't many women solicitors, especially not in City firms. Women like Barbara had needed to fight to succeed, and they liked to keep the distinction between them and the secretaries very clear indeed. It was understandable, Paddy thought.

Barbara had definitely been in the running for Paddy before his engagement to Joscelyn. But she had been very discreet about it. She was not the kind of woman who would ever risk public failure. Paddy had responded to her overt charm, and had rather enjoyed playing the game of courtship by Barbara's rules. These had involved very strict and formal behaviour in the office, and rendezvous which had to be well away from any convenient haunts where the two of them might be spotted. This had been the form even before Paddy showed any interest in Joscelyn.

Once Paddy's engagement was announced, Barbara had behaved with great dignity and her usual smooth manner, which, when it was directed towards Joscelyn, masked a complete fury.

But after a few weeks, Barbara had called to see Joscelyn, bearing a cup of coffee.

"I was just making myself one," she said, "and I know that you've been busy this morning so I expect you could do with some refreshment."

"Thank you." Joscelyn was surprised.

"Milk and sugar, that's how you take it, isn't it?"

"Yes." Joscelyn wondered how Barbara knew.

"I thought we should have lunch. I know Paddy quite well already, and it seems a shame that I don't know you too. Of course I could do the dinner party bit and invite you both, but I never get away in the evenings before seven, so you can imagine that my domestic life is pretty basic."

"You're certainly very busy." Barbara was so immaculate, so in control, it was difficult to imagine any part of her life being basic.

"And this way we'll be able to have more of a chat."

Perhaps Barbara is human after all, Joscelyn had thought. She just isn't very good at expressing it.

They had gone to a moderately smart restaurant where the firm's lawyers (but not the secretaries) quite often went to lunch, especially if there were office-related matters to discuss away from the constant interruption of the telephone. The waiters knew Barbara.

Joscelyn chose pasta, which proved difficult to eat with any pretence of elegance. Barbara ordered steak, and tucked in heartily.

"I never eat breakfast," she announced, as if this were a virtue, "and by this time of day I'm quite ravenous." It was amazing. She was so slight and delicate-looking.

Barbara was always very neatly, although never ostentatiously dressed. Joscelyn noticed that she always wore very expensive jewellery. Today she had on a pair of huge diamond ear studs, set in platinum that sparkled when she turned her head.

"You really could be something a bit better than a secretary, with your qualifications and abilities."

Barbara spoke rather as if she were a career adviser at an interview.

"Well...." Joscelyn was just about to go on to say that she hoped to do a teacher training course one day, when her companion ploughed on, "But you must know that yourself. Do you lack a bit of confidence? Or maybe," she smiled a charming smile, "you simply chose an uncomplicated life. And why not?" The smile returned.

Joscelyn felt her throat tighten. Barbara had got her on a bit of a raw spot here. This was not the moment for confidences. No way could she explain to this hostile audience about her father, a domineering man, who could have come out of a Victorian novel. He had declared that his daughter (despite her more than reasonable success at school) was not university material and that he would pay nothing for her if she went. Joss had decided to work for a couple of years to earn some money, and although she had intended to apply to university, when she had some money in the bank she had somehow never got round to it. Had she, perhaps, never quite mustered the courage?

She opened her mouth, and got a few words out. "I wanted to be independent; to earn some money. I do have plans…."

Barbara showed no sign of wanting to listen. "Of course you aren't a fool, so you'll be aware that everybody in the office was gobsmacked to hear that you and Paddy were actually getting married."

Joscelyn sat bolt upright, recognising a challenge. "I suppose they thought that Paddy wasn't the marrying kind."

"Well, the stupid ones might have thought that. But most men do marry eventually, even if not for very long." Barbara was smiling again.

"That's between Paddy and me. And if either of us thought it wasn't going to last, we wouldn't be doing it." Joscelyn was conscious that her sulky, defensive tone made her seem childish. But Barbara was being horrible, and she couldn't just let it go.

"Of course." Barbara had stopped talking, and was waiting for Joscelyn to respond.

"Perhaps we should get the bill?"

"Actually, I haven't finished my coffee, but you're right that we shouldn't be much longer. I have a very important client who is likely to phone just after two, and you mustn't get the reputation of taking liberties now that you're engaged to one of the partners."

"I don't think I have that reputation."

"Of course you don't. And I mustn't lead you into bad ways. But I just wanted to let you know that I'm concerned for you. I know Paddy quite well; as I'm sure he's told you. And I think that you might be taking on someone who will make you upset."

Never was such a statement less convincing, thought Joscelyn.

"I think that Paddy does need a wife. He does need to settle down. He obviously thinks so. But as his friend - and as his friend I care about him as well - I wonder whether he isn't making a bit of a cautious choice with you. I know I'm speaking out of turn, but I think that he might benefit from a bit of a firmer line than you might be planning to give him."

"You are speaking out of turn." Joscelyn looked straight at Barbara, who turned her head away, flashing the diamond studs.

"Can we have the bill please?" Barbara said to the waiter. She turned back. "Of course," she spread out her hands with a dismissive gesture, "it's always been a fault of mine to speak my mind. It's got me into trouble loads of times. And even I have to admit that I haven't always been right. There have been occasions when I have had to eat my words. So perhaps you shouldn't take any notice of me."

Joscelyn had said nothing to that. It was quite clear, from her tone, that the occasions when Barbara had had to "eat her words" had been very few and far between, and that she did not have any anticipation of being wrong this time.

Anyway, that had been five years ago. If Barbara had married Paddy, as she had so clearly wanted, they wouldn't have lasted five months.

Joss turned over, restlessly. Paddy, still asleep rolled over and reached out for her. He put his arms around her, and held her tightly.

"It will definitely work," he said to her, still in his sleep.

Joss snuggled into the comfort of her husband's familiar body. He must have been dreaming, too. She would ask him in the morning, and see if he could remember.

Chapter 3

Hilary had found herself in a rather unexpected state of emotional turmoil since agreeing to go to Cannes with Paddy. It was something she had not planned for, or thought about, and the decision (which had somehow seemed so decisive a decision) had been made so quickly. Hilary would have liked to have more time to consider. She had to accept, however, that the only person to blame for this was herself. She had felt (at least in retrospect) rushed, even pressurised into the decision, and this made her cross. But the option of saying no had been available to her.

She could still change her mind, and if she were going to, sooner would clearly be better. Several times she had considered telling Paddy that she had been offered some unrefusable subsequent engagement, or simply that she had accepted hastily and no longer wished to go. But time went on and she did none of these things. She still met Paddy regularly. Her play was running now, and Paddy had come not just to the first night but to several other performances. There was so much to talk about; they rarely mentioned Cannes. He had given her various details, and offered to book her a plane ticket. She'd refused, and said that she would come separately by train.

The disconcerting thing about him was that week by week, even day by day, she felt differently about him. He could be fun, and charming, and he could be very kind. This meant that sometimes she suddenly liked him ever so much more, but there were also plenty of times when she liked him less. He was (as his name implied) Irish, but he was a Protestant from the South, born in Dublin. He had some shocking views on the political situation, and was very hostile to the Republican movement in the North; views he had defended very aggressively from her disapproving English liberal sympathy.

"There is sometimes a bloody good reason why some groups are underdogs," he had said. "My lot are a minority in the South, but we've never set off bombs all over the place. And I don't like getting lectures on the subject from the English."

Hilary had liked Joscelyn when she had met her at dinner, and she'd noticed that Paddy was clearly very fond of his wife. Joss seemed to be a calm, patient person, who had dealt quite charmingly with the actor Steven, who was known for being socially awkward.

She had asked Paddy if Joscelyn was coming to Cannes, and he had said no. "She's going to be very busy around that time. She'll be sorting out the new house, and working hard on her Open University modules."

"But she does know that I'm going?" Hilary ventured.

"Oh, certainly," Paddy had replied. "I've told her."

Even so, she had felt a little uneasy during that conversation and had wondered whether she really felt sure about what she was doing. At one moment she had been on the point of expressing her doubts, when Paddy, who, like a large male Cinderella, had an effortless ability to make an exit from anywhere at any time, disappeared.

Joscelyn found the start of her Open University course a bit daunting. It was quite exciting, going into libraries and bookshops to get equipped with all the books she needed, but reading them – and being expected to have an intelligent response - was quite a worry. Her French A level just hadn't prepared her for reading the likes of Racine, and she might well have given up the French option had it not been for Philippa.

"Don't be silly," Philippa had said. "You'll be fine. It just takes perseverance and faith in your own ability to crack it over time." Philippa had a degree in French and German. "My French is probably a bit rusty as well. I'll read your set texts and we can go through them together. It'll be good, I'll enjoy it."

Philippa got out her diary, and Joss found herself arranging extra tutorials, with her friend. They were kindred spirits in that way, both organised and orderly people who liked to make a plan for the future and then work to it.

Joss and Paddy's friend Ben also offered to help. Ben had known Paddy at university, and he was now something called a venture capitalist. Paddy would joke about "Ben the Venturer" because Ben, despite doing a risky job where he put together multi-million pound deals, was quiet and precise. He wasn't like all those flashy City types the 1980s were so full of. This was probably why he'd set up on his own. He had an office in Wardour Street, the office consisting of two rooms, one large and one small. He sublet the small one to Paddy, so the two men worked next door to each other.

"I read history at university," he told Joss, when she told him about the help Philippa was giving. "I'm not sure I could commit to anything as structured as monthly tutorials, but we can have lunch sometimes, if you like, and see if anything I learned for my degree lodged anywhere in the brain."

Every so often, Ben would ask Joscelyn out to lunch. She never quite knew why. True, she liked him, and he seemed to like her, but this could hardly be a sufficient reason in itself. On the first occasion, Ben had asked Paddy's permission, and on every subsequent one, Joss did. Paddy would always be deliberately magnanimous about it.

"Of course," he would say. "Just make sure he takes you somewhere nice."

As Ben was single, Joscelyn inevitably felt a keen concern about his love life. He had been known to have girlfriends, but they never lasted long. She had only ever met one of them, a very quiet, slightly sullen-looking girl in her early twenties, who had soon got a job in Manchester. This seemed to bring the relationship to a complete and immediate end. Joss would sometimes ask Paddy to join with her in speculating about Ben's private life. Paddy's standard response, "Why don't you ask him?" always infuriated her. Ben was just not the type of man one asked. This was one of the intriguing things about him.

Anyway, they always did go somewhere nice for lunch, and today they were in a small, friendly restaurant, which served convincing French food. Joss told Ben all about the new house. Contracts had been exchanged and the move date had been set. Ben surprised her by knowing exactly where it was.

"Oh, yes, I know," he said matter of factly. "It's parallel to Burchlere Road, near the Italian delicatessen."

"So you know the area?" It was always such a surprise to think that Ben led an ordinary life.

"Yes, actually, I do."

Joscelyn knew that that was the most information she would get out of him. She knew too, that one reason why she was given the honour of Ben's friendship was that she had the instinctive discretion not to ask too much.

"It's very nice. And no more than you deserve. Do you have a garden?"

"A lovely one; it's walled, and South facing. And it has a magnolia tree."

Ben looked at her. "I imagine that you like that very much," he said. "In the summer you will sit out there with your cup of tea and your book, safe in your own private domain. Is the magnolia tree like the one in your parents' garden, in Wiltshire?"

Ben had never been to her parents' house, but she had once told him about the tree, with the lovely pink and white blossom in the spring. She had actually forgotten about telling him, until he mentioned it again. Ben remembered such things, and it left her with a warm glow of being appreciated. Paddy did not, or at least not any longer. Joss realised that this did not make him any different from any normal husband. Except that he did have that facility with women he was courting. It was part of the phase of mutual appreciation, to remember little details, and to make a point of telling the other person that you had remembered. Immediately Joss felt angry about Hilary. Hilary, who was going to Cannes, and whose choice of flowers, shoes, or novels would currently be right at the very top of Paddy's brain, the bit that could be accessed at a moment's notice.

Joscelyn told Paddy about this as they ate scrambled eggs in the kitchen, that evening.

"So Ben is a memory man, is he? I'm surprised that you find this attractive. I thought that us poor men were dreadfully annoying because of our wearisome ability to remember actual facts. Dull matters like the name of the Chancellor of the Exchequer, or the right exit to take from a motorway, instead of being intuitive and sensitive like you women."

"Ben is intuitive. And he doesn't remember facts just for the sake of them. That's the whole point."

"Well, I wonder why he hasn't found a better use for his remarkable talents."

Joss said nothing.

She saw Ben again the next day, when she called into the office. Paddy had asked her to call and collect his post, as he would be away all day. She put her head round the door of Ben's office, but he looked harassed, and sadly not at all intuitive. But he did have a neat pile of letters to hand to Joss. She took them home with her, and, true to her secretary's training, placed them in an in-tray in the bedroom. In the rented flat, there was no place for a study. She looked through them, in the way of a professional wife, to be sure that nothing needed her husband's urgent attention.

One them was from Barbara. It was from Hong Kong, in Barbara's elegant, round, slightly over-large hand. In the office, Barbara had been famed for her hand-written notes. She liked to impose her distinctive presence whenever possible, and her notes reverberated with finely presented ego.

"My job here has been a bit of a disappointment, so I leave at the end of the month," she wrote.

Damn, damn, thought Joss, just when I thought I might have got rid of her for good.

"I've decided to make something of it now that I'm here. Somehow I never managed a gap year or any kind of real me time, so I plan to reward myself with a few months off."

Self-satisfied cow, Joss thought. No one was better at rewarding herself than Barbara.

"A trip to Australia and then a long cruise home," the curly, imposing script went on. "I intend to arrive at Southampton, later this year, thoroughly pampered. A Something is winging its way to you. Don't imagine you've changed. You'll have to see if I have. Barbara."

Joscelyn stood for a while and glared at the over-neat over-satisfied handwriting. Even the handwriting had the capacity to make her boil with fury. She put it with the others, in her bag, and left the room, shutting the door rather pointedly, although there was no one present to witness.

On the way home, Joscelyn found herself re-running the memory of that lunch with Barbara through her mind. She remembered how for a few days after their tête-à-tête Barbara made a special point of being friendly to Joscelyn when they met in the office. As time went on, she had reverted to ignoring her completely, something that was infinitely preferable.

Paddy had also been ignored by Barbara for quite a while, but she did speak to him the day before the office party to celebrate his forthcoming nuptials. Unfortunately, she explained, she would be unable to come.

"Never mind," Paddy found himself saying to her, "We'll have a little celebration, just the two of us."

And so they did. It was just a drink, in one of their regular wine bars, some way from the office. This made the occasion, in fact, neither more nor less than most of their encounters had been. But Joscelyn had been furious when she found out that the drink took place the last night before Paddy took leave before the wedding. Joscelyn used to refer to the occasion as Paddy's "stag night", and to the elegant silk tie she gave him that evening as,

"Our wedding present from Barbara."

Chapter 4

Joscelyn and Paddy moved house, on a rainy April day. The whole process had gone remarkably smoothly, but even so the last few weeks had seemed an unbearably long time to Joscelyn. After many months of willing self-sacrifice, she now realised how desperate she was to have a home of her own. She woke up early, even before her husband, and started listing, in her head, all those useful kitchen appliances, comfy chairs, and books to read in them which would finally be coming out of store.

At eleven o'clock the keys were handed into Joscelyn's eager hands. Philippa helped her friend oversee the men, make cups of tea (she had arrived with her own picnic bag with a kettle, tea, sugar and milk for the purpose), and do some sterling work on the cobwebs which were revealed behind the last owner's outgoing furniture.

After the men left, Joscelyn looked around, pleased, and slightly dazed. "It will look nice when it's decorated," she said to her friend.

"It looks nice now," Philippa said. "And it will be quite lovely when it is decorated."

After a late lunch of ready-made sandwiches and fizzy water Philippa went home to collect her children from school. Joss was just making herself a cup of coffee when Paddy arrived, carrying a bottle of champagne and a large bunch of flowers

"What are you doing here?"

"I've come home to my wife," he said.

"Perhaps we had better put the champagne in the fridge for tonight," Joss said.

"Nonsense. It's cold now. We are in our new home. This is the beginning of what we've been waiting for."

So they drank the champagne and made love on the bed with its specially firm mattress, which had been in store for so long. There were no sheets, of course, because they had not been unpacked yet, but the room felt quite warm with the heating on and some bright spring sun through the window. They drank some more champagne, and Joss, suddenly overcome with the effects of all her anxiety and exertions, fell asleep in the warm sunshine. Paddy found a rug to cover her up, and then he got up and dressed, took the last glass of the champagne downstairs with him, and set to work.

When his wife appeared, bleary-eyed, a couple of hours later, Paddy had unpacked most of the boxes of kitchen equipment and crockery and was devising a system for the kitchen. Paddy was very good at thinking up systems. He was not always so good at implementing them. That usually became Joscelyn's job.

Joscelyn put the kettle on, to make tea.

"The first thing we need is some new kitchen cupboards. Some nice wooden ones like we had in Victoria Road," Paddy said.

"I thought we'd make do with these for a while. They're not too bad, and new ones are so expensive. I thought I'd make a start on the garden room. It looks so awful and it ought to be the best room in the house."

"The kitchen is the most important room in the house. Then the bedroom. If you have Sunday morning breakfast in the right surroundings, the whole week will go well."

Joss reflected that it was the kitchen and bedroom where Paddy was likely to spend most time. She had imagined herself in every room in the house, reading in the garden room in the afternoon sun, laying the table for a dinner party in the small dining room, preparing the guest room for her brother and his family when they came to stay, and who knows, perhaps the dining room would one day be full of toys and double as children's play room. Paddy was a kitchen and bedroom man.

But it was her house. Paddy kept saying so. She would start on the garden room. Paddy's kitchen could wait, for a little while.

The next day was Saturday, and Paddy had to spend some time in the office, and so Joscelyn went to the supermarket, and carried on unpacking. Paddy was home by two o'clock, a sure sign that he had not lingered or had lunch with anyone. The two of them went for a walk down the high street, and found a fishmongers where they bought prawns and sole for dinner. Paddy was the fish cook. His meals were done with great panache, and used every knife, fork and saucepan in the house. Joss would make a pudding of caramelised oranges.

On Sunday, the sun was still shining, and the first weekend in the new house was a clear success. After breakfast, Paddy went out to buy the Sunday papers, and he came home with an armful of newsprint and a pot of extra large magic bubble mixture.

"What is that for?" Joscelyn asked.

"For Kevin MacAteer's children. Didn't I tell you? I told him we'd have him around as soon as we moved in. I've invited him to tea, and he is bringing his wife and their two children. Girl and a boy I think, both quite young. I want to talk to him about his new script. I'm thinking of buying an option on it. A little bit of speculation. I could have done the usual restaurant lunch, but now we have a house, I thought that we should start being sociable again."

"You could have told me," Joscelyn protested, although she wasn't really cross.

"I'm sorry, darling. I thought I had. You usually can read my mind, after all. And it will be fun, won't it? The two of us entertaining in our own home."

"Yes," said Joscelyn, smiling indulgently, "it will."

Kevin MacAteer had written the script for Paddy's film, *Terrible Beauty*. Joscelyn had met him several times, but did not realise that he was a family man.

"He doesn't look as if he has a wife and children." Joss remarked.

"Well, I suppose that wives and children are such popular things that the most surprising people have them. Look at Alistair. He's never out of his office, but he's still managed two, or is it three, with Philippa?"

"Do you mean children or wives?"

Paddy smiled. "In his case, I meant children."

"Well, I'd better make a chocolate cake then," Joss said.

Paddy sat in the kitchen with her as she weighed out ingredients in her old black scales, which needed to be washed before they could be used, and mixed them together in the mixing bowl that had been a wedding present. Paddy had found a large book with plain empty pages and a bold cover in a glossy William Morris print. It had been given to him by one of his girlfriends. He wrote "House Book" on the first inside page in his large black handwriting. Then he headed pages with the names of rooms, leaving three or four pages empty in between, and after that he began to write lists of "things to do" and "things to get" for each room. Joscelyn watched her husband lovingly.

At the same time she reflected on the fact that the book that had now become their house book had been the first present Paddy had received from another woman after their marriage. She had been rather upset at the time. She had of course known that there would be other women, but this gift, given to him by one of them, had seemed like a real intrusion. Now, at something of a distance, she reflected that Maria, the donor, had definitely been one of Paddy's better ones. She had only been indulging in a little flirtation; and she'd also had good taste. This was more than could be said for some. Joss reflected that there was, in those packing cases, quite a collection of tapes of music, cufflinks, shirts, ties, books, and videos given to Paddy by admirers, either before or after their marriage.

She voiced this thought to Paddy. "Maybe I should put them all together on a special set of shelves, so that we have the complete collection of mistress memorabilia together?"

Paddy laughed, and Joss could see that he was actually quite taken with the idea. But then he waved his hands dismissively:

"Well, you'd be the person to do it. You have an elephant's memory when it comes to exactly who gave me what, I've noticed. I'd quite forgotten that Maria gave me this. It just seemed to be right for what we needed."

It was true, Paddy would have forgotten. He lived so fully in the present, looked so much to the future, but the past faded quickly in his mind.

After their guests had gone Paddy went into the study to wire up the computer. Joss, still feeling a little churned up by the thoughts prompted by the new House Book, looked for and found several boxes containing mistress memorabilia. She put them all in one box. She and Paddy didn't need them; they could be kept packed away, in the cupboard under the stairs.

One item, though, did get removed from the box. It was a rather beautiful piece of Indian marble, inlaid with semi-precious stones. Minerva, the dumpy travel journalist, had bought it for Paddy. She was the first actual mistress Paddy had after marrying Joss. She had been a friend to both of them at first, and then had a fling with Paddy. Joss had tolerated the relationship, and she and Minerva had continued to meet, from time to time, alone. It had been an odd dynamic, because after the affair started, by tacit consent, they had never spoken about Paddy. This forced them to get to know each other better, and meant that they had forged a strange private intimacy.

Nonetheless, Joss had been very pleased when the affair came to an end, and relieved when Minerva, six months later, married a schoolmaster from a major public school.

Minerva was a lively, interesting person, but she knew Paddy was married, and should never have given such a beautiful piece just for him. If she had to give something, it should have been to them both.

Joscelyn put it in a bag. She would take it to the Oxfam shop tomorrow. It would sell for a good price, in Putney, and the money would go to a good cause.

Before sealing the box with the rest of the bits and pieces, she took out one particularly ugly watch (from an old girlfriend from before Joss arrived on the scene), and put it in the bin.

Supper was soup and some crusty bread. Paddy said little, so Joss made conversation.

"I'm enjoying my studies."

"Good."

"I feel more confident now. Pippa and Ben have both been ever so supportive."

"Excellent," said Paddy, who clearly had no intention of following her friends' example.

"You know I could do a module of law, at some point. Then you could help me."

"Goodness me no, Joss. You're not a lawyer. You'd have to learn lots of facts, and be precise about things. It's absolutely not your kind of thing. I'm sure you're fine with a literature course or Art Appreciation or whatever it is you do. You need something that doesn't too much tie down that magnificent free mind and spirit of yours."

Joscelyn looked at her husband rather sourly, and he laughed.

But Joscelyn had other thoughts about her future. Thoughts and plans that could be realised, now that things appeared more settled.

"It's only a part-time course, Paddy. I thought that in due course I could combine it with something else."

"Fine." Supper was finished, and as Joss cleared away. Paddy went and found his briefcase, and opened it on the kitchen table. He had a habit of doing this, sometimes, just as Joscelyn put a serious note into her voice. But it was a Sunday evening, and she was entitled to raise domestic and personal concerns.

"We ought to be thinking of having children. Now we have a home. Now that you're doing so well."

"Yes." Paddy was still looking in his briefcase. "But wouldn't it be better to wait until you are more settled?"

"Well, I was thinking of next year, maybe. Most of the people doing my course have full-time jobs, or children. I'm sure I could do both, especially if I had some help in the house, and maybe the baby went to a child-minder for a few hours each week."

"I don't think you'd want to be a part-time mum, Joss. I think you're thinking of taking too much on."

"We've always said we would have children."

"Yes, when the time was right."

"Would you support me?"

"Of course I would support you. I just don't think it's a good idea. You did talk about teacher training, at one time. Wouldn't it be better to do that before having children? It's much easier to go back to a career that to start one when you are a mother and have all those extra demands on your time. I think that you should ease yourself back into higher education by doing this course for a year, and then go to college full-time and train to be a teacher."

"But that would take me three years. And then I'd have to work for two years before I established myself. I'd be thirty-two."

"Women have babies into their late thirties, and beyond."

"Yes, but I don't want to. And plenty of women train for a career after having children. I would probably make a better teacher after I'd been a mother myself. And that's what I'd rather do. I don't want to wait five years to have children. I want them now. And I'd like to get the degree I didn't get when I left school. My way, I could do both."

"Teacher training is a degree. It's a vocational degree. It's much more you, Joss."

"Shouldn't I be the judge of that?"

"I think we should settle in here, Joss. And you should spend a bit longer at your course. You've only just started. One thing at a time."

"All right, but can we talk about it again?"

"Yes, of course we can."

Paddy shut his briefcase. He looked out of the window, looking outwards, from the space of his own dissatisfaction.

"I'm going to go out for a walk."

Sometimes in the flat, Paddy had seemed like a caged animal.

At least here, in the new house, he had a choice of floors to roam before he made his bid for freedom.

"Are you meeting anyone?"

"No, just a walk. I'll be back to watch the news with you."

He had been home for a long weekend already. It was pointless trying to keep hold of him.

"See you later, then."

But when he had gone, Joscelyn felt a little unnerved. Supposing Paddy kept resisting the idea of having children? Philippa had talked about her taking a stand. This was something that would be worth taking a stand over. She would definitely do it, if it were children at stake.

Joss thought about Hilary. Who already had a degree, and from Cambridge, not the Open University. Who was set on her career, and probably wouldn't think of having children for ten years, if ever.

What if Joss insisted on having children and Paddy left her for a career girl, like Hilary?

And then Paddy came home. He had only been gone half an hour. He was carrying a bag of logs.

"Are you still sitting in here?" He looked at his wife, at the kitchen table. "Come, I've got some logs. Let's light a fire and see if our TV works. It's nearly time for the News at Ten."

Chapter 5

Hilary had spent several winter months in her flat telling herself that her physical surroundings mattered little to her, because she could easily dissociate herself from them. This had always been her tactic in college, and she had rather despised those people who spent their time and money trying to make the small, neat, box-like rooms homely with plants, rugs and posters. In the neutral background of her modern college room, looking out as it did on fine old buildings and beautiful gardens of Cambridge, this had been an easy attitude to adopt. In her London flat, with its hideous yellow carpet, ancient (and once trendy, but before Hilary's time) brown hessian wallpaper, and the view of the local launderette, she could get a bit depressed.

She had confessed this to her sister over the phone, and three days later had received a telephone call from her mother announcing her intention of arriving the next day. Her mother was like that. As mother, she claimed the privilege of appearing virtually unannounced, and in her mother's way of thinking, she had been thoughtful by timing the visit for a weekend, when she presumed that Hilary would have nothing to do. Because she was making the long journey from Newcastle, she would have to stay at least one night, and, because it was part of the family tradition, she would have to be met at King's Cross.

"Don't worry," her mother had reassured her, "I know you

only have one room, so I have arranged to stay at a hotel round the corner from your house. It looks like quite a decent one, so I am sure I shall be fine there."

Her mother struggled off the train with two huge suitcases and an assortment of plastic bags, which struck terror into Hilary's heart. Normally her mother was a great advocate of travelling light. Was she really planning on staying only two days?

"Darling, I have brought you some things for your room. Victoria told me how absolutely awful it was. Of course you've been so lucky, only living in nice places all your life. But never mind, we'll soon get it looking better for you."

Hilary hoped that her mother would have the tact not to say such things in her flat, and especially not in the earshot of any of her flatmates.

Hilary's family came from Newcastle-upon-Tyne, and lived in a large Victorian house overlooking a little area of parkland. They also had owned (until her parents' separation) a cottage in the North York moors. Her mother and father's families were proud of their Northernness and their prosperity, both of which went back several generations. Consequently, in the Mackay family, there was no nonsense about regarding Southerners as posh. Mrs Mackay believed that out of well-off Southerners, only the tiniest minority were anything other than nouveau riche, "or upwardly mobile, as we have to call them these days."

"They may fancy themselves very grand because they eat goat's cheese and drink Earl Grey tea," she would say, "but that doesn't mean that they know which way to spoon their soup."

Hilary sat in the taxi with her mother feeling depressed. Was this going to happen all her life, she wondered? Would she be thirty one day and still be quite unable to prevent her mother just walking in and taking over? And what was in all those bags? The Mackay household contained some beautiful antique furniture and valuable pictures, all inherited, but her mother's own visual taste was frankly atrocious. There was no knowing what she would have brought.

Back in the flat, Hilary went to make a cup of coffee. She lingered over the task, practising some firm but polite phrases for the very worst eventualities. When she eventually took the coffee in, on a rather wobbly tray, she saw that her mother had wasted no time. Gone were the flat's own curtains, a faded William Morris print which had been the one part of the indigenous decoration that Hilary had quite liked. In their place was a bright blue velvet pair, which had once hung in the dining room of the Newcastle house.

"Oh, Mother," Hilary said, "don't you realise that I left home specially to get away from those curtains."

Fortunately, Mrs Mackay decided not to be offended.

"Nonsense, darling," she said. "They are very good ones. I bought them from Fenwicks."

That had been the low point of the visit, but things had got better. Amongst the rather weird assortment in the large suitcases were some thick towels, which would make bath-time much more comfortable, a useful lamp, a very handsome rug ("Your father brought it back from India. I never liked it") and one of Hilary's favourite vases. It was tall, made from plain glass, and Hilary associated it with the irises that her father used to grow in the garden every spring. All in all, Hilary had to admit that she was grateful.

In a quiet moment, over a cup of tea, her mother asked Hilary about her life in London.

"Your play is finished now, isn't it?"

"Yes, Mummy, it was quite a success."

"Victoria told me, she said it was very good and you had a full audience." Hilary's sister Victoria had come down to London from Durham to see Hilary's latest production.

"And I shall be directing a ten-minute film soon."

"Yes, darling, that sounds very good." Mrs Mackay couldn't keep the anxiety out of her voice. She tried to be supportive, but Hilary knew that her mother was very worried about the insecurity of her chosen career.

"And next week I'm going to the Cannes Film Festival."

As soon as she had said this, Hilary regretted it. She had wanted to impress and reassure her mother, but she couldn't give away much more.

"On your own?"

"Oh, no. I am going with some friends. We'll be networking."

"I see. Well, I suppose that's a good idea." Mrs Mackay sounded doubtful, but she had accepted her daughter's explanation without question. Hilary felt guilty. She rarely lied to her mother. But she just couldn't tell her about Paddy.

Part of her, though, would have liked to. She didn't often confide in her mother, but it would have been good if she could have. She would have liked to tell her mother, or perhaps anyone closely connected to her, the good things about Paddy. His enthusiasm and sociability, the way he concentrated on her. That was the most important thing. Hilary, although socially capable, often felt an emotional space between herself and other people, something that she regretted. Paddy, somehow – she just didn't know how, exactly – just filled that space. Warm, confident, compelling, he had a way of moving in, metaphorically speaking, and getting close.

But her mother would never understand.

Then Hilary had a phone call. It was Peter Saville, whom she had known at Cambridge. He was clever, and good-looking, and Hilary had sometimes wondered if he liked her, but he had never asked her out. He was now working for a large Italian car manufacturer in Milan.

"I'm in London for a few days," he told Hilary. "Staying with James. We are meeting up with Leonora and Jane, and wondered if you would like to join us. We thought of going for a pizza and then maybe a film."

Hilary had quite liked Jane, although not so much Leonora. It sounded fun, though.

"Well, my mother is here at the moment," she said. "Can I phone you back in a minute?"

"That was Peter, from Cambridge," she told her mother. "He lives in Milan now, but he is in London for a few days and he and some others are going out this evening."

"And are they inviting you?"

"Yes, but I don't need to go."

"Oh no," Hilary was surprised to see something like relief on her mother's face. "You must go darling. You must meet up with your friends. I shall go to my hotel. There is a very nice-looking bar there which sells light meals, and will be perfectly suitable for respectable woman eating alone. If anyone asks, I shall explain that I am visiting my daughter, who lives in a shared flat nearby, and that she is out for the evening with friends."

Hilary couldn't help thinking that her mother would probably tell several people these things whether they asked or not, but she didn't say so, and was pleased to be able to phone back Peter and arrange to meet.

In the weeks after the move, relations between Paddy and Joscelyn were generally harmonious. Paddy came home almost every evening, and helped Joss work on the house, or the garden. He was quite handy with a drill, and took great care over hanging pictures around the house. He put up some special shelves to take Joss's ever-increasing collection of books, and he drew up a plan for the garden. He and Joss pored over garden books and agreed (after some argument) on a plan for planting.

Philippa came round and admired it all, as well as Paddy's involvement. "I'd never get Alistair to take such an interest in the house," she had said.

There would be times, though, when Joss would remember the forthcoming trip to Cannes, which still felt like an unhealed sore to her. These times, she would harry her husband with remarks about arrangements being made "behind her back" and sad comments about how much she would have loved a trip away to the South of France. Paddy tended to ignore the former category, and respond to the latter with exaggerated reasonableness:

"You couldn't go away just now. You have got your course. You keep telling me how seriously you take it. You can't have it both ways, and just take off for a week whenever you feel like it."

"I wish you would talk to me about my course. You keep promising."

"Well, I shall when I have time. And maybe when there is something that I really can help with. You've got Philippa, and Ben. Ben seems to quite like playing the student again and speculating on the antics of medieval kings. I don't have time; I have a career to think about. Ben is one of life's dilettantes: a touch of business here, a little history there, and who knows, maybe a bit of flower arranging on the side. You should be talking to him, not me."

One long night Joscelyn slept fitfully, and thought endlessly and unproductively about how high-handed Paddy had been. In the long hours between two and four in the morning she wondered, over and again, what she could say or do that would make him realise how much he had hurt her this time. He was a good man. If only he could understand how she felt, he would not upset her in this way.

Tired and aching, Joss finally drifted into a deep sleep in the early morning. At eight, she woke, with a start. It was late. Paddy was no longer in the bed beside her: she had overslept and he would be on the way to his office by now.

But when she went downstairs, in her dressing gown and still bleary-eyed, her husband was in the kitchen. There was the smell of fresh coffee, and everything shone bright and clean.

"Look, I've cleaned out the teapot. It was all brown and filthy inside," Paddy held it out for inspection. "I thought we'd have a nice breakfast. I don't have to be in especially early today." He moved into a corner and opened a cupboard door with a flourish. "And these are for you!"

He produced a huge bunch of roses, tightly flowered, bright red and even-shaped, and handed them over with an exaggerated gesture.

"Oh Paddy! Where did you get these?"

"From the florist. It opens at 7.30. You were still asleep. Do you like them?"

"Of course I do." Joscelyn looked up at her husband whose eyes were turned towards her, like those of a little boy, longing but perhaps not quite daring to hope for approval.

Joss looked at the roses. Paddy always brought her red roses. Before she had met him, she had not much liked them; in her eyes there was something too glossy and unnatural about them. She loved irises, and tulips, and in the summer there was nothing more beautiful or romantic, in her view, than a bunch of blue cornflowers. But red roses, large and glossy, were Paddy's trademark flower.

"You are quite wonderful, Joss, quite wonderful."

Joscelyn, uncharacteristically, forgot to put the flowers in water, and they were beginning to look a little jaded in the evening when Paddy got home and pointed them out:

"You haven't put my flowers in water."

"Oh no, I haven't. I must have been distracted; the plumber came to put in the new sink. And I had to finish *Howard's End*, because I have an essay to write."

"So the plumber can distract you, eh?" Paddy was joking, but he looked a bit pained. Joss softened, and she kissed him.

"Don't be silly."

Serious argument was avoided, until the day before Paddy left. And when it finally came, it was not the subject of Cannes that brought it about.

Chapter 6

The day before he went away with Hilary, Paddy received a small brown parcel with foreign stamps on it.

It was from Barbara. She had sent him a tape of music, a compilation of short extracts of famous tunes, including Samuel Barber's *Adagio*, individual movements from well-known concertos, and arias from operas by Puccini. Paddy would never have bought such a tape for himself (he always said that the one thing of real value his upbringing had given him was a proper musical education) but he was touched that Barbara had gone looking for the type of music that she did not listen to but thought he did. She had also written a neat list, detailing each piece with a description of what each one "meant to her". A movement of the Bruch violin concerto reminded her of the wine bar where she used to meet Paddy, and the Barber *Adagio* "your more serious side, which I know you do have". In some cases, where she clearly hadn't been able to relate to the piece at all, she would say something like "I think that this represents complex emotions, which of course we both have."

This provided Paddy with a very welcome distraction. He had been thinking about Cannes, and feeling more than a little guilty about his wife. Poor Joss, she would genuinely have liked to go to Cannes, and really he could see that it wasn't a lot to ask. More than once he had thought of offering to take her. She and Hilary would co-exist all right. Besides, this thing with Hilary was just business. He would have to leave Joss to her own devices a lot, but she was quite self-sufficient, and could have taken some reading with her.

But just as he had been on the brink of relenting, Joss had always harried him with some sharp comment, some reproach, which had made him feel bad. No man wanted to be nagged into generosity by his wife. Naturally, he wanted the offer to be freely made. If only Joss could have given him a bit more space, over this one, he probably would have taken her.

Sitting in his office, and for the moment ignoring the rest of the day's post, Paddy mused over fond memories of Barbara. She had been quite magnificent. Pretty, efficient, good at her job, with that wonderful gift of concentrating all her attention on him, making him feel the most valued person in the world. True, she was rather inflexible in nature, and that might have been a problem had their relationship ever developed. Joss had been quite unreasonable in her objections to her. But this was because Joss felt disadvantaged by having been a secretary in the same office where Barbara had been an ambitious young solicitor.

Yes, he would have been quite keen on Barbara, had he not been distracted at the time that he first knew her by his courtship of Joscelyn. Then they had had little to do with each other for some two years after his marriage. But he and Barbara had ended up working together on a big case that went to trial in a court in the North of England. They found themselves, for purely professional reasons, staying in the same hotel, and eating dinner together. One night they had even ended up in the same bed.

Paddy felt slightly uncomfortable as he recollected that experience. He had said to Barbara, what he often said on such occasions, that they should just go to bed and "see what happened". Many women liked this approach, and in fact Paddy preferred it, too. But Barbara had not been happy to let things just happen. She wasn't a woman to go with the flow, and made it clear that she wanted to arrive at one predetermined place. This hadn't been very erotic. Barbara's intensity and concentration, wonderful as it was from the distance of a few feet across a dinner table, translated at a closer quarter into simple demands.

Paddy found himself remembering Joss's strong objections to the woman he was in bed with, and for a moment, even beginning to sympathise with them. He found himself suggesting that perhaps they were making a mistake.

"I was forgetting Joss," he said "she allows me a lot of freedom, but I know that she worries about me getting involved with anyone from the office."

Barbara had become very cross. She sat bolt upright in bed, breasts pointing angrily at him, and said:

"As far as I am concerned, Paddy, our relationship has nothing to do with your marriage."

Of course, after that he had assumed all was over for good and all, but in due course Barbara had been very forgiving. When he had left the law, he had joked with her that she would keep him in touch with the legal world, and she had taken this very seriously. For a while they had regular meetings, over an evening drink, at which Barbara would present him with a file of newspaper cuttings and law reports. Sometimes the feelings of discomfort would return. Barbara had a way of referring to "how things might have been" which Paddy recognised, with some embarrassment, as a phrase of his own from their "stag night" drink. At the time, it was meant as nothing more than gallantry, unfortunately overlaid with some of the nerves that most men feel when about to enter the married state. He hadn't meant to encourage her to think his words had any serious meaning. He had been very sad, however, when one day Barbara had announced her decision to move to Hong Kong.

But, as he sat holding this unlooked for an unexpected gesture of affection, he reflected that no harm had ever come of his dalliance with Barbara. Yes, at one time he had had his worries about getting in too deep with her. And so it would be with Hilary. In a year's time she would be a fond memory, and someone who brightened his life with an occasional letter from a distant place.

Paddy listened to half the tape as he drove home that day and his thoughts returned to the donor. How strange that Barbara seemed to be single still. He had been quite sure that she would return oozing proud loyalty to some self-satisfied financier, younger than Paddy but old beyond his years. So there was chance for her to get a decent man yet; and he felt only a little sorrow at the fact that it would not be him.

Paddy was very happy when he got home, and consequently was rather taken aback to find that Joss was annoyed with him. She had been, during most of the day, thinking of the forthcoming trip to Cannes, and her own aggrieved feelings. She knew that she was a good wife to Paddy, she loved him of course, but she also knew that he cared very deeply for her and relied very heavily on her support. She knew his need to stray, and could love him nonetheless, but this really had upset her. She had told him that, kept telling him. And in a little corner of her heart that she had hoped, and even believed, that he would realise how she felt. That he would not push her too far. That he would change his plans and not risk damage to their marriage which had worked so well, and pain to the wife that he loved.

He arrived home a little earlier than usual and said that he would cook supper. This was obviously intended as a significant gesture, but Joss was irritated. She was being fobbed off, and besides she had prepared a casserole already.

"Put it in the freezer," Paddy said, "I've bought some fresh salmon. You can eat the casserole while I'm away. You should invite Philippa over."

"I saw Philippa for lunch yesterday."

"Yes, but you'll want to see her next week when I'm away."

"Paddy, I think that I should be the judge of that."

Joscelyn left Paddy to his cooking. After half an hour, recovering her composure somewhat, she found a bottle of wine from the cellar and carried it purposefully back to the kitchen. She would speak clearly to Paddy about her feelings. It was too late for any arrangements to be changed now, but if they could just understand each other, this would be the best thing for the future.

Paddy had emptied his briefcase, a large bulging leather bag of almost suitcase-like proportions, on the kitchen table.

"You do have a study for all this," said Joss.

"I needed to check something. You can move it if you like."

"I think you mean 'Joss, would you mind putting all my papers in the study'," Joss said.

"Joss, would you mind putting all my papers in the study, seeing as I am so busy cooking you a delicious meal."

Joscelyn gathered up the untidy assortment of papers. Then, amongst them she saw the tape, and a letter in the irritatingly neat handwriting of Barbara Irvine, former solicitor at Slater, June and Warbeck.

"And this," she shouted, "is from bloody Barbara."

Paddy was startled. His wife's outburst of rage seemed to come from nowhere.

"What is she doing sending you tapes? You told me that you weren't in touch with her any more."

Paddy thought. Yes, he might have said something like that, months and months ago.

"Well, if I did it was a statement of fact, not any kind of promise. And I haven't been in touch with her. I had forgotten all about her. She sent me a message a couple of weeks ago. She has left Hong Kong and is taking some time out before coming home."

Joss remembered. This was the "Something" that had been winging its way when the last letter was sent. She had been so caught up in the house and the upset over Cannes, she had forgotten.

"Well, that's all I need. If it weren't bad enough that you are taking Hilary to Cannes, which you knew was what I wanted more than anything else in the world, now you are getting presents from that awful woman. And keeping it from me. How can I trust you any more?"

Paddy was upset by this accusation.

"Joss, we've been through this before. I will take you to Cannes, just not now. And I was not keeping Barbara from you. There is nothing to conceal, anyway. You saw the tape; it was there on the kitchen table with my papers. I asked you to clear it up for me. You really do get Barbara all out of proportion. Of course I'm flattered that she still thinks of me, but I never thought of her before the other day."

"Why is she sending you tapes of music?" Joscelyn held the offending object up in the air.

"I don't know. She's probably lonely. Actually I don't think she has many friends, and she must be unlucky in love because she doesn't seem to be bringing a man back with her. Strange, really, when she has so much going for her. I suppose she puts too much effort into her job, and it cuts out the social life."

"Nonsense," said Joscelyn. "I know that she is competent, but Barbara isn't a career woman. Her problem is that she hasn't yet found anyone prepared to offer her complete devotion, a total absence of criticism and all his time and money."

"I think you are a little hard on her, but you know that I wouldn't be offering her that."

"I know. But what you do offer her gives her the illusion of having it. You see her, lavish her with charm, tell her how wonderful she is, and she goes away thinking that you are just what she deserves. Can't you see how galling it is for me?"

"But she doesn't have me. You do."

"She likes to think she does. In her mind, you're all hers. The fact that various others talk to you, live with you, sleep and eat with you wouldn't stop Barbara from deluding herself that she was really your number one."

"Joscelyn, I cannot be responsible for what Barbara thinks. I don't know what Barbara thinks. You're the one who seems to be able to read people's minds."

"You encourage her."

Joscelyn sat, hunched, sad and angry, looking at the kitchen table, the mess of papers and the tape. She picked it up and looked at it. Barbara was trying to give Paddy music that he liked, but not being a fan of classical music herself, she had chosen a compilation of easy pieces. She had probably listened to the tape through herself, before sending it, or (as was more likely) she had not wanted to break the plastic seal, and had bought another one for herself. Early in her courtship with Paddy, Joss had bought him a CD of a well-known soprano singing a variety of famous arias. They had been to *Madame Butterfly* together, and Joscelyn, who had never been to an opera before, had been quite overcome. Paddy, however, had been very stern about the gift.

"These songs," he had lectured her, "are the culmination of emotional and musical high points of lots of different operas. They are not meant to be heard all together. It is quite wrong to have to listen to one after the other."

Joscelyn looked bitterly at her husband:

"These pieces seem to be 'the emotional and dramatic high points of serious pieces of music strung all together'. But you don't seem to mind when she gives them to you."

"Joss, I have no idea what you are talking about. Is this something you've got from one of your lectures?"

"No. It's what you said about that opera tape I gave you after we went to see *Madame Butterfly* that first time."

"Oh yes," he said, "I do remember. Your dreadful diva CD. It was very sweet, but I knew that you were capable of something better. Besides, I wanted to marry you."

Joscelyn sat a little longer, and then she burst into tears.

Paddy was genuinely surprised, and worried. He came and put his arms around his wife. Joss threw the Barbara tape across the room. Paddy sat with her for a moment, uncertain what to do.

Then he went and picked up the tape, and the plastic case. He walked over to the kitchen bin, and placed both inside.

"You really don't like this tape," he said.

Joscelyn looked up, and smiled wanly. Paddy looked at her, waiting for her response.

"Shall I open a bottle of wine?" she said.

They drank some wine, Paddy cooked supper, and they ate together. They both felt relieved. Disposing of Barbara's tape seemed to have done away with all the tensions between them. After supper, they moved into the garden room, lit a fire, and made love on the thick rug in front of it. They fell asleep together, and woke later when the flames had all died down; underclothed and cold, and ready for the warmth of the matrimonial bed.

Chapter 7

The next day Paddy and Joss were up early because Paddy had a morning flight to Cannes. After their late night, he had forgotten to pack a suitcase, and there was much bustling around between the two of them, making sure he had everything he needed. Joss drove him to the airport. It would have been easier for him to go by tube, but he liked to be seen off. Amazingly, they arrived in good time, and had half an hour to have a cup of coffee together, before Paddy had to go.

They sat in silence for a while, their mood much calmer than the night before.

Paddy looked across at Joscelyn.

"I do wish you were coming with me," he said.

Joss wasn't often surprised by Paddy, but this remark did make her open her eyes a little wider.

"You are going with Hilary," she said pointedly.

"Oh yes. I'd forgotten. What a shame." Paddy spoke the simple truth. He had been experiencing a rare moment of contentment, with his wife opposite him, and he felt sorry that the self-induced complexities of his life were to prevent it continuing.

"I shall miss you," he said simply. "I'll be back soon."

Joscelyn said nothing, but she looked straight at her husband. He did mean it. He would actually be happier if it were just the two of them. She could cope with all these other women coming and going from their lives. But Paddy, if he could only manage to give them up, would be happier without them.

On his own on the flight out, Paddy was thinking much the same thing. He wished he had brought Joss. She really would have liked to come, although he was sure that it would have been very boring for her. She was good at looking after herself, though, and would have taken herself round the sights, and probably met up with other holidaymakers. In some ways, he wouldn't have felt so responsible for her, as he would with Hilary. Hilary was an independent soul, bless her, but he was going to have to make something of an effort. And then there was the tension, mounting, and the fear of increasing involvement. It might all go horribly wrong. They might end up hating each other, which would be so sad. Paddy felt almost sick with an old, haunting fear of rejection and unhappiness.

"Why choose this week," he thought to himself, "which might be really useful for work? Are other men as stupid as me?"

He didn't know the answer to this. He had few men friends. In fact there was really only one, from his early childhood, who was a doctor living with his wife and two children in Dublin. He certainly didn't make the mistakes that Paddy did. He would never have the success, either, but his life was pleasant enough for that. Mike was a happy man; in the way that Paddy felt that he could never be happy. Robbed of happiness, Paddy would have success. And even if he couldn't have success, he would have Hilary.

But, thought Paddy to himself, was he foolish to try and have both?

All these thoughts faded away when he arrived in France. The sun shone, and everywhere looked so extraordinarily French. Paddy's mind became fully occupied as he struggled to revive his grasp on a language that had never been particularly good. Grey London, and the cares of the Paddy who lived there, were many miles away. He was on an adventure.

Paddy had a lunch meeting planned, and this took him to a little restaurant, where the food was good, the pace unhurried and there was a view of the palm-fringed seafront. There he had some long and intricate discussions, which were only winding down some hours later, when Hilary arrived. The hotel reception had given her the message telling her where to find Paddy, which she had duly done. She looked young, and very lovely in a long burgundy-coloured summer dress, but calm and somehow quite at home. Paddy immediately felt relieved. There was always that nagging fear that she might not turn up. She sat down with the assembled group, and merged with it. Soon, people moved on, and others arrived, and Paddy, Hilary and some others went to watch a film.

So the day continued, busy and sociable. Hilary fitted in well. She spoke French well; much better than he did. She was not outgoing, but could still be very much part of whatever group they were currently in. She had, Paddy noticed, the same ability as Joss to be patient with the bumptious, and sympathetic with the reserved. Paddy felt pleased that he'd asked her to come. It was work, after all, and this was work for Hilary every bit as much as it was for him. Joss would have hated it, she would be much happier at home.

Dinner, in their hotel, was another large and convivial affair. Several celebrities were staying there, and even Hilary turned her head to watch them come and go. Later Paddy again became involved in detailed discussions, which went on into the early hours. He was thoroughly enjoying himself. He had been in Cannes last year, and it had been fun, but much harder work. Last year, he was trying to make himself known to everyone, working hard at being sociable. This time, so it seemed, everyone wanted to meet him. It was nearly two o'clock when he realised that Hilary had gone.

"Where's Hilary?" he suddenly asked the remains of the party.

"She went to bed, about an hour ago," he was told.

This was not quite what he had planned. He and Hilary had rooms near to each other. He had planned that they would retire at the same time, and invite Hilary for a late night drink and a talk. He wouldn't be pushing too hard: just an intimate chat would have been fine. A chat that would have moved things along between them a little.

He stood outside Hilary's door for a moment. She might be furious with him if he knocked now. But he would do it anyway.

Hilary came to the door and opened it. She didn't look too friendly, but this just might have been because she had been on the verge of sleep

"I'm sorry to disturb you. I only wanted to say good night. And how much I enjoyed being with you today. You were so good with everyone we met: you really do impress people, you know. I am pleased you came. Are you?"

"Yes." The tone was non-committal. She was still standing still, in the doorway, looking, he was relieved to see, more sleepy than hostile.

"May I talk to you, or would that be keeping you awake?"

Hilary frowned. "I was asleep. We could talk tomorrow."

"Tomorrow we'll be with everyone again. This is our chance to be together. I only want to talk. In a little while I'll go to my own room and leave you in peace."

Hilary still didn't look very friendly, but she opened the door a little wider and let Paddy in. She gestured to him to sit in a chair, and she got back into her bed, sitting up with her knees under her chin, and the sheets drawn round her.

"What did you think of the film? We've been so busy; I never got the chance to ask you."

"It was good. At least it looked good. I didn't really believe that awful series of deaths, did you? It was almost comic, the mother, father, grandparents and nurse all dying one after the other. And not even a cholera epidemic to make it plausible."

"It can happen, though."

Paddy told her about himself. Not his current self, as Paddy the successful film producer, but how he came to be who he was. He told her about his childhood.

"I had quite a good start in life, if you count the first few years which I hardly remember. My parents loved me. My family are moderately well off Anglo-Irish. I only remember a very little about my parents. They died, within a year of each other, before I was four. My mother went, suddenly, of a brain tumour. My father died of heart disease, which was described to me as 'a broken heart'. I was supposed to think it was most romantic, that my father didn't want to stay on earth after my mother left it. But I just used to think what a bastard he was. That he didn't think I was worth staying for.

"I was sent successively to live with various uncles and aunts. My family were great believers in traditional values, and one of these was that there was no modern child-centred nonsense about thinking what I might like. So I was sent about in rotation. One family in term time, others for different holidays, Easter, Christmas and the summer.

"The only one who didn't agree was my Aunt May, my mother's sister. She took me on about a year after my father went, because she felt that she could provide some stability. She wasn't married, and went out to work part-time, but she decided that she could have me as well as anyone else. And she did, too, for a while. She insisted on keeping me too, through term and the holidays, and I just went to the others for visits. She lived in a sort of genteel poverty, because she had a small income of her own, and a little terraced house. She was great fun. We had walks by the sea, and picnics, and she would take me to the cinema. She would listen to me, and even in those days I could talk a great deal, but she always seemed to find it interesting."

Paddy looked so sad as he talked about his Aunt May. Hilary had never seen him look like that before. His own heart had been broken, absolutely it had. It was amazing that he was so strong, so successful, in the face of such childhood adversity. She wanted to say something, but stock phrases like "how awful" just weren't suitable, just weren't sufficient. She just stared into Paddy's sad face, and met his eyes. He smiled at her.

"At the time I didn't realise how much disapproval she faced from the others to keep me, when she didn't have what they considered to be the necessary requirements, a husband with an income, and a decent-sized house.

"And then Aunt May fell ill, too. This time it was cancer. Of course I thought it was my entire fault. All the people I had loved before had died, and now it was happening again. Logic seemed to dictate that I was the cause."

Paddy was quite affected by his own story. Hilary felt numb with shock. She would never have believed it of him; he was so robust and ebullient, so in control. And yet it was obviously the truth.

"Of course, I had some advantages. I never lacked for anything materially, and between them they paid for me to go to one of Dublin's best schools. I was desperate to get away though, and went to an English university, and have never been back since, except to visit. Joss has been very good about keeping in touch with my family. She sends all my cousins' children birthday cards, and presents. And they've all been delighted with *Terrible Beauty*. Proof that I'm true to my roots after all."

Intrigued, Hilary started to ask questions, wanted more detail about what it had all been like. Paddy was not forthcoming. He had confided as much as he wished to. He walked the few steps across the room to Hilary's bed, and put his arms around Hilary.

"It must be very late," he said. "And I have a breakfast meeting tomorrow. Americans, of course. They want to talk about Kevin MacAteer's new script."

He stroked Hilary's head. Hilary was warm and welcoming, but made no reciprocal gesture. Paddy felt tired and a little too vulnerable to attempt any further intimacy.

"I'll go back to my own room now. And leave you in peace as I promised."

"All right." Hilary really didn't want him to go now.

"See you tomorrow."

"Yes. I'll be up by half-past seven."

Paddy went, and Hilary lay awake for nearly two hours, thinking about what she had just heard.

Hilary was at the breakfast meeting, and Paddy wished that she were not. He wanted to concentrate his mind on the business in hand. Hilary wasn't being sociable, as she had been yesterday, but kept looking at him. She did care about him. This really wasn't a relationship he wanted to get wrong. It could be just the right thing for him, just what he was looking for. Not instead of Joscelyn, of course. He would have Hilary as well.

The meeting was inconclusive, and both sides were disappointed by this. The company was definitely interested in MacAteer's new script, but there were problems, and details, which couldn't be agreed. Paddy sensed that there was sufficient good will to produce a deal. On top form, he would have got much closer to getting one. He hadn't been really in there, as he should have been. But he decided not to worry about it. You can't win them all, he told himself. He would speak with them again, and when he was in better shape. At that moment, he had Hilary to think about.

After the previous night, the tables had turned somewhat, and Hilary was keen to get Paddy to herself. She was less interested in the gregarious events of the day, and sat politely, through another afternoon film, holding Paddy's hand in a proprietorial way. She had no hesitation in accepting his invitation to drink an afternoon cup of tea, on the balcony of his room, which overlooked the azure sea, and all the throngs of people walking along the seafront.

She asked Paddy lots of questions, about his childhood, which this time he agreed to answer.

"Is that why you have to chase women all the time?" she said with childlike directness.

"So various amateur psychologists have told me. I'm sure I would have been just as I am anyway. I like women. Besides I don't chase women all the time. I don't know who you've got your information from, because I know it wasn't me. I'm a romantic, women fascinate me. Yes, perhaps there's a little bit of me that's always looking for a bit of extra love. Not that I often find that. Mostly it's fun, or friendship. Joscelyn is wonderful, she understands me perfectly, and since we've been married there has been the odd one that has been a little more than flirtation. Joss hasn't minded. But in all the time I've been looking, and that's probably since I gave up on my skelextrix, when I was about fourteen, I've hardly met anyone who I felt really cared about me. Joss, of course; and maybe one or" (Paddy paused for thought) "two others."

Paddy looked so sad. Hilary leant over and kissed him. They held on to each other for a while, and then went to bed.

Some hours later, and before they had to get up, bath and meet yet more people for dinner, Paddy looked into Hilary's eyes and said,

"I think you really do care for me, don't you?"

"Yes," said Hilary, "I do."

Chapter 8

On the plane home, Paddy was thinking very different thoughts from the doubts and anxieties that had preyed on his mind on the way over. There were two women in his life now, Joscelyn and Hilary. This was just perfect, just what he needed. His senior wife, Joss, would always be a stable base, understand him perfectly and be unshakeable in her love for him. She would care for the home, and produce lots of children. Then there was Hilary, serious and talented, who would be such a practical help to his career. She was really very interested in his future. They had had lots of discussions about this. Hilary would have her own career, of course, and this would run alongside, and complement, his.

In his mind's eye he saw the kitchen in Fulham, with Joss and himself sitting at the kitchen table, and at least four little ones, eating sausages and mashed potato. Half the children would have his curly, dark hair, and the other half Joss's flaxen locks. He and Hilary would eat in restaurants, go to see films and meet actors and directors together. Hilary wouldn't want children. Except that most women did. Well, so be it. She would have two serious little girls, and Joss's children would be mostly boys, noisy and energetic. This would all be some way off, of course. He would be hugely rich by then, and they would all have the best of everything.

He would give up chasing other women. That would be one of the benefits of the whole arrangement. He would have two, stable, beneficial relationships, and between them they would give him just about all the love he needed. All that wasted time, looking for someone new to brighten his day, to make his life a few degrees warmer, that just wouldn't be necessary any more.

It was at that moment that he wished that Hilary was secure, and next to him on the plane. She was off on her own, out of his orbit. She had seemed to be very happy with him, and sad to see him go. There was no knowing, though, how she felt now. Perhaps at that very moment she was sitting on a French train, opposite a handsome young man who would charm her away completely.

These panicky thoughts reminded Paddy that his other concern that week was the fact that he hadn't quite got everything together enough on that MacAteer deal with the American film company. He was going to have to work very hard on that when he got home.

Hilary was making her way by train across southern France. She was sitting opposite two large, talkative French ladies and going to visit her father. Paddy had been quite surprised to hear about this. He knew she had a sister, in Durham, "the good one of the family" as Hilary had described her, and had in the past spoken about visits from her mother, from Newcastle-upon-Tyne. He had assumed that any father also lived up north, with her mother.

"And I thought you were a plain straightforward Northern lass, but it turns out that you have family in exotic places," he had teased her.

"Yes, even more exotic than Dublin. It's just that I don't boast about it so much."

Paddy had laughed. They had been sitting à deux in the large restaurant in the glamorous Palm Beach Casino, overlooking the sea, watching the yachts come and go. As it was their last day, had decided to forget about any more boring film showings, or parties. Each one was beginning to seem much like all the others. They had wanted to make the most of precious time. Besides, as Paddy had told Hilary, they could hardly come to Cannes without going to the Casino at least once, for a look.

Paddy was looking at his new love, all attention. Hilary,

encouraged by his interest, had gone on to tell him about her domestic self.

"Actually it was quite a shock to the whole family. One day Daddy announced his intention of moving to live in Provence. My parents had been together unhappily for years. Mother had been the vociferous one, regularly listing Daddy's inadequacies and telling Victoria and me that it was remarkable that she had put up with it for so long. I suppose we believed that they would just go on that way until one of them died."

Hilary warmed to her subject. There was a look of soft affection on her face.

"Daddy is a gentle, undemonstrative man. He spent years and years working dutifully as the chief of an inherited family business. It was a small engineering firm, which employed forty or so people. He seemed to take what comfort in life he could from his garden, and his books. Then soon after I went to Cambridge, he sold up and moved himself into our family cottage on the north Yorkshire moors."

Hilary frowned.

"I was shocked, of course. And upset, at the time. Mummy had never liked the cottage, or the moors. She felt they were bleak and unwelcoming in just about equal measure, and resented our regular family visits there 'instead of a proper holiday'. I suppose they weren't much of a holiday for her. She had to do lots of cooking and housework in a place she didn't like, and mostly it was Daddy who took us out. At first, Mummy tried to pretend that Daddy's going away was a temporary matter 'to sort out the garden'. But even she had to face a more serious rift when he announced his intention of selling the cottage and moving, all on his own, to the South of France."

Hilary's face had started to show strain, as she re-lived these events. Paddy was seeing the more vulnerable side to Hilary's normal self-possession. He reached out his hand and held hers. Hilary accepted the gesture, but only briefly, and went on with her story.

"Mummy was extremely distressed, and forced her grief

endlessly on Victoria and me. I think Victoria mostly took her side, and I had more sympathy with Daddy. But you are torn, in that situation, between your parents. It was a very difficult time. Mummy hired expensive lawyers, and then became even more agitated when she found herself paying handsomely for advice that she did not like."

Hilary laughed, remembering something.

"One day Mummy rang me up and went on for hours. She was enraged that her solicitors had told her that she couldn't go and ask the judge to order her husband to remain on British soil. She kept saying, 'I told them that someone had to knock some sense into him, but all they will say is that he is "over eighteen, Mrs Mackay". What use is that? And I suppose I'm to be destitute, too."

"Anyway Mummy didn't become destitute, because there was enough money for them both. She kept the Newcastle house and Daddy got his way and moved to France. They didn't get divorced, and I think that that was something of a comfort to Mummy. They even agreed between them to spend Christmases together with Victoria and me. It was quite sweet."

"And did that make you feel better?" Paddy was still listening very attentively. Hilary looked up at him. For a moment only, she was close to tears.

"I've been so overwhelmed by the constant outpouring of Mummy's feelings, I had hardly had any chance to consider what my own were."

There was a pause, in which Paddy kept silent, but he took Hilary's hand again, and this time she accepted his touch.

"Although I was eighteen, and grown up, I had imagined that Daddy would always be there, pottering in his greenhouse, whenever I came home. And, as Mummy kept pointing out, the South of France was a radical move. I felt more on his side, but I wasn't sure that Dad really did know what he was doing."

Paddy still said nothing, but he kept looking at Hilary. For a moment, she met his gaze and smiled, and then took up the tale with some spirit:

"But as time went on, it seemed that he did. He moved into

a converted barn with a large garden, and grew vegetables and geraniums. Remarkably, he had complete recall of his schoolboy French, which just got better and better. He gets on well with his French neighbours, as well as some of the expatriate English community. He reads a lot, which he used not to have so much time for. And then every so often he just takes off and heads East across Europe. He's bought himself a real French Citroen car."

Hilary took a photograph out of her handbag, and showed Paddy. Mr Mackay, grey-haired and upright, and looking remarkably like his daughter, stared straight out of the picture at Paddy.

"I'm never quite sure whether he misses his family," Hilary looked both fondly and wryly at the photograph. "But he writes to us, and there is no doubting his happiness with his new life."

On her train, alone, the next day, Hilary was quite relieved to be leaving all the strange emotional turmoil of her new entanglement with Paddy, and head for the more familiar emotions of her own family life. She was hoping also that this bit of extra time with her father, just the two of them, might bring them a little closer together. Her relationship with her mother was often strained, but one did always know what Mummy was thinking, and why. Dad was a little bit of a mystery. He had always been a bit distant. Hilary had always felt that his lifetime of duty, of working hard at business matters that did not really interest him, had caused his rather repressed nature. It was such a waste. Paddy, she was sure, was wasting his life too. Of course he had been brave enough to give up the law, but he was still too much of a businessman. She had watched him at Cannes. He had spent simply ages arranging to produce some film, based on a reasonably good novel; which would have been OK except that the original novel was set in Chicago, and it was to be re-set in the Far East because production costs were very cheap in the Philippines. Of course he would earn money from it, and he could continue to call himself a film producer while he was working on it, but the time spent would be a waste of his life, and his talent.

* * *

At about the time that Hilary was journeying through Provence, Joscelyn was heading across London to see her father, who was up from Wiltshire for the day. Unfortunately, she was not looking forward to it. It was going to be a strain, and one that was coming at the end of a difficult week.

She had had the decorators in, a motley crew of large cheerful men who seemed to fill every room of the house all the time, even though they were only painting two of them. She went to Paddy's office every day, to check on post and messages, and then tried to get on with the work from her new courses in History and English Literature. Until now, she had been enjoying these, but this week she had to read the poems of Alexander Pope, which did nothing to capture her imagination. Also, every time she settled to read one or other of the workmen would come in, and say cheerfully "nice to have a bit of time to read a book" and suggest that she make them all yet more cups of tea. On the second day, one of the men put a nail through a water pipe, with the result that water cascaded through the dining-room ceiling.

The men explained to her that this accident could not possibly be their fault, because "her water pipes" were in all the wrong places, but generously agreed to repaint the ceiling, once the damp had dried out. Joscelyn had to find a plumber, and with one complication and another, the house had to be virtually without water for two whole days.

It seemed very bad of Paddy to be away and avoiding all the chaos. Not that he would have done a great deal had he been there, because it was always her job to sort out such domestic crises, but at least he would have been suffering with her. She did send a fax, saying "All chaos, water pipe burst" and got a reply "Poor you. Can you stay with Philippa? I'll be back soon. Bringing lots of wine home. P.S. Please make sure none of my papers get wet."

Just when it seemed that things could hardly get worse, Joscelyn rallied her spirits. She looked at the sodden carpet, and decided to throw it away. It was an OK carpet, and they had planned to keep it, but it would never be clean again now. She fetched herself a pair of pliers, and tugged and pulled at the edges of the material, to hoist it up and away.

She would go to Fired Earth tomorrow and price for some wonderful warm terracotta tiles for the floor. They would look great. The walls could be a plain cream colour, and she could look for a predominantly red wall hanging of some kind. It would all look quite sumptuous. Expensive, of course, but Paddy could pay for it. If he had been home, she would have discussed it with him. But since he was not, he could hardly object. She would just tell him about her decisions when he got home.

Next day she came back from her reconnaissance shopping full of enthusiasm. There was a message on the answering machine from Ben, suggesting she call in for a cup of coffee when she collected the post tomorrow - which was good - and another from her father - which was not so good. He was complaining: "Why is it that whenever I telephone you I only get this machine," and telling her that he planned a trip to London on Friday, and that they could meet for lunch.

Joscelyn's father was a difficult man. He had ruled their household with aggression, and exercised a tight control, always disguised as concern, over her mother, brother and herself. The biggest practical effect of his imposition of will, as far as Joss had been concerned, was that while large sums of money had been spent on her brother's education, she had not been deemed worthy of similar expense.

"Let's not have any nonsense about this being discrimination." her father would say. "You are intelligent, but not academic. Your mother's the same. Goodness me, there is a place in this world for such people. We'll do what's best for you, and that's what matters."

Joscelyn had gone to local state schools, and done well in all her exams, including A level. This was insufficient evidence to persuade her father to change his view on her. When she suggested that she might follow her brother to university, he had made it clear that she would get no moral or financial help from him if she did. Her mother had been a little more sympathetic, but had virtually no sway on her father. Joscelyn could have defied her parents, and gone it alone, borrowing the necessary money. She would have endured the hardship; indeed the one thing that her upbringing had ideally prepared her for was endurance. But at that time what she wanted more than anything else was independence. A job as a legal secretary gave her this. A life in London on her own, and even, if she was careful, a little spare money to save for time off to study later on.

She had been saving up when she met Paddy. He was such a different man from her father. And of course with him her life had taken a new and unexpected direction.

Joscelyn and her father met at the Royal Overseas Club, near St James's Palace. Her father was a member. He wasn't a naturally clubbable man, but had at one time had visited London regularly, and needed somewhere to stay. He disliked spending the money, even though this was subsidised by way of expenses by his employers, but even more he disliked hotels of variable quality, travelling around London and unfamiliar surroundings. Membership of a club was the obvious solution, and the one adopted by many of his colleagues. He chose the Royal Overseas because the annual subscription was a little cheaper than the Oxford and Cambridge Club, but it was equally central. The oldest part of the building was a large seventeenth-century house, with a garden backing on to Green Park. Some of its public rooms were very elegant, although the overall impression of the place was of somewhere less grand, and much friendlier, than Joss would have imagined.

Her mother, who had died about a year ago, had loved the Club. This, Joss realised with intense irritation, was probably why her father had asked her there. She had no wish now, after all the twenty-seven years she had been alive, to start getting onto terms of emotional intimacy with her father, via their shared grief. It would not, in any event, be a grief shared. Her father would have to dominate, and she would be expected to fall in behind.

Besides, her mother had had to fight tooth and nail to be allowed to spend any time there. She had visited the Club, been delighted with it, and then even more delighted to discover that she could be a member too, and even stay there on her own if she wished. Her father had been appalled at the notion. "Why did she want to go to London, especially when they lived so near Bath?" he had said. He visited London too often, and he could assure her that there was no pleasure in it. "It's a noisy, overcrowded, dirty place, full of foreigners. And so expensive; we simply can't afford it."

Her mother stuck to her guns. She had inherited a little money of her own, and would pay her own subscription, and her own expenses of any visits. She wanted to go to London, to meet some of her old school friends, and one of her cousins. She wanted to go to the theatre. So she had joined the club, and had gone, twice a year to stay and have a good trip to town. Father used to be horrible to her for several weeks before she went, and sometime after she came back. But Mother didn't care. She thoroughly enjoyed herself, and it was all quite worthwhile.

Joscelyn and her father sat in the buttery. It was an attractive, friendly restaurant room, which served light meals. They had a table overlooking the garden, which was green and very pretty. Joss commented:

"The garden looks nice."

"Yes," her father replied. "Your mother loved this garden. In fact, she loved this whole place, you know."

"I do know," thought Joss, but she said nothing.

"I suppose after all the hard work she put in, bringing you and James up, and not getting about much, it was really a treat for her to come somewhere like this. It's very hard work being a mother, as I suppose you'll find out in due course."

"Yes," said Joscelyn, venturing no more.

"She was a very good woman, your mother, and I don't think any of us appreciated her enough."

"I suppose that's often the way," said Joss. It seemed best to rely on vague platitudes rather than risk expressing any of her real feelings on the subject.

"I don't think you should dismiss it so lightly. I think we should take a little time to think seriously about these matters. You may not realise it now, but the time will come when you start to regret things in your life."

Joss said nothing, relieved that a waitress had come to take their order.

Conventional wisdom, as expressed to her by the family elders, was that her father's grief should be beginning to abate, now that a year had passed since her mother's death. He had taken it very hard, and several people had told Joss that "it would take a twelvemonth" before her father would start to feel better. There was little sign of it though. At first, Joss had been relieved to see that, despite everything, her father must have loved her mother dearly. But now, sitting as they were, remembering her mother in the place that her father had done so much to prevent his wife from enjoying, she did not know whether to be sad or angry.

So much of her father's grief, it seemed, was not just sadness, not just loss. It was the bitter echoes of unresolved anger, and unexpurgated guilt.

"I must get away," she thought. "I must save myself from this."

She had stopped listening to her father, but her mind clicked back in to realise that he was asking to come and stay with Paddy and herself, now that they had a house. This would be a novel event; her parents had never stayed at either flat. It was indicative of how lonely the old man was. Angry as she was, her heart was touched.

"Of course," she said. "We're not quite shipshape yet, but it won't be long now, I hope."

She owed her Dad something after all. Paddy wouldn't be too keen, but he would do his best to be hospitable, and probably be diplomatically busy for much of the time. It was the least she could do.

She left the restaurant pleased at the thought that Paddy would be back that night. Up to the point when she had met her father, Joscelyn had still been feeling cross with Paddy, but the relief that she was married to him, rather than to someone like Dad, put Paddy in an altogether better light. He was home early, and had a bunch of pink and white roses and several bags full of bottles of French wine.

"There's a few bottles of cooking stuff, but I also bought plenty of good ones; just from the local supermarket, mostly. The savings go up, the more expensive a bottle you buy."

"Well, I can see that you have saved us a great deal of money."

Paddy noticed the irony in her tone, and smiled. "I'm wonderful, aren't I, darling? Aren't you pleased to have me home?" There was a distinct note of appeal in his voice.

"Yes, I am." Joscelyn said, slightly archly. She was still going to have to be won round. One bunch of pink and white roses, even though they were very pretty (presumably there hadn't been any red ones in the shop), was not quite compensation for a trip to Cannes. And she would cheerfully have traded a few bottles of French wine for having had Paddy around to share the discomfort of burst water pipes. But Paddy so much wanted her to love him. He needed her, and that need was almost tangible sometimes. She needed to be needed; it made her feel whole.

And life would be fun, now that he was home. They would talk, and laugh, and make love. And thank goodness, he was not sour and overbearing like her father. Thank goodness, even, that he had gone away with the basically nice Hilary instead of the awful Barbara.

Paddy felt relieved. He was forgiven. OK – so she was still being a little bit huffy, but that, he knew from experience, would soon subside.

For him, coming home was always a tremendous pleasure. He was often away, for work, for entertainment, meeting people or meeting women, and the experience of returning to base made him feel complete. In the years before he married Joss, he had often been dreadfully lonely; much lonelier than he realised at the time. In the past he had set up house with more than one girlfriend who really didn't suit him, just for that warm feeling of having someone to go home to. Joss, beautiful Joss, was always there in the house. Her very presence seemed to keep it warm. She was always there when he came home. As a secretary, she had worked shorter hours than him and had always been back to cook a meal. These days, with her University course and the work on the house, she would be out and about quite a bit, but he would always telephone her and let her know his movements; and she would invariably be home before he returned. She would be cooking, or curled by the fireside reading a book. In the days of flat ownership, she had always been almost instantly visible. Now they had a house, he had once or twice come back to what appeared to be an empty building, and on those occasions had searched the rooms in something approaching panic, calling out her name; but she had always been there, upstairs perhaps or outside in the garden.

Today she had prepared a lasagne, layered with aubergines, a large crisp green salad and a complicated pudding with apricots.

"And I'm just delighted to be here. Here with you."

Joscelyn looked at her husband, with his broad smile, and knew that he really did mean it. She could sense his appreciation of home. Poor Paddy, he had had such a terrible childhood; things as simple as a house, a wife, and an aubergine lasagne meant a huge amount to him. She softened, as Paddy knew she would, and looked at him fondly.

"We'll be home together all weekend, won't we?" As Paddy spoke, there was the same note of appeal in his voice. "We should go for a long walk one of the days. Maybe we'll get up early on Sunday and drive out to Sussex."

Joscelyn told Paddy about all her trials and tribulations while he had been away, and he listened with more patience than he normally had for long tales of woe. He promised to speak to the decorators about re-painting the dining room, and was resigned, if not delighted, at the prospect of a visit by his father-in-law.

"You'd better keep it short. That way we can both make a huge effort and make the old boy feel cared for. We're neither of us up to anything prolonged."

Paddy told Joss about all the people he had met at Cannes, his delight at the way he had been feted (something he hadn't confessed to Hilary) and the various deals he had underway.

"Did you get anywhere with Kevin MacAteer's script?" asked Joss.

Paddy frowned. "I made some progress," he replied.

Later that evening, they made a fire in the newly painted garden room, and Paddy made coffee. He had brought some very pretty-looking petits fours from France. Then he started talking about Hilary. She was really very clever, very talented. He didn't tell her the details of the relationship, but it was clear that a greater intimacy had developed while they had been away. Joscelyn mustn't worry about her; he said. She wasn't going to be any kind of threat to them.

"I think she really does care about me, though."

Joscelyn said nothing, and looked at him.

"I told her all about my childhood."

Joscelyn looked sceptical. Why did he have to keep doing this? She, Joscelyn, knew and cared about Paddy's childhood. She was the one who worked so hard to make the warm, loving home that he so much needed and appreciated because of it. Why wasn't that enough?

"Paddy, you tell all your girlfriends about your childhood. It was a very bad time you had, no-one could be unsympathetic about it."

Paddy was offended. "I certainly do not tell them all about my childhood. As you well know, it is a very sensitive subject for me. I only talk about it to people who I feel are truly concerned for me."

Joscelyn looked at Paddy.

"But you do extend the confidence, sometimes, to women with whom you become intimate?"

There was a tension between them, as Joss waited for his reply. Paddy moved closer to her on the sofa and put his arm around her.

"You are the one who really understands me. You must know that."

Neither of them had the stomach for an argument that evening. Paddy liked to talk about his girlfriends, and generally, Joss was pleased that he did. They then became "theirs" instead of just

Paddy's. And Joss would keep up with events; judge how much of a threat they seemed to pose. It was painful, of course, but she could bear the pain. She was tough. Tougher than Paddy; at least in that respect. His feelings could so easily get the better of him, whereas Joss was proud of being able to get the better of hers.

Somewhere in the very back of Joss's mind was the thought that she was perhaps (and quite unnecessarily) relieved as well as pleased when Paddy came back home. Relieved that he had come back, and not run off with Hilary, or someone else. But that wasn't going to happen. She cared for him more than anyone else could, and he knew it. She let him go, and he came back. Most women wouldn't be able to do that. They wouldn't have the strength, or the confidence. She knew that he would return, into her arms, and he always did.

There was a weekend ahead, and they were going to be together all the time, doing things that they both enjoyed, things that bound them together.

Any differences of opinion on Paddy's new girlfriend would have to wait.

Chapter 9

Paddy brought Joscelyn a cup of tea in bed.

"I'm not ready to wake up yet." Joss spoke from the depths of the duvet.

"I've got to go into work. There's going to be masses to catch up with. I can't let things slide."

Joscelyn still felt too sleepy to offer the required degree of sympathy. Then she remembered something. "I'm having lunch with Ben again today. Is that OK?"

"Of course." Paddy sounded more irritated than magnanimous. "I must go. Make sure your tea doesn't get cold."

"Ben is such a nice man," thought Joscelyn, "I wonder why he hasn't settled down with anybody yet."

She had called into the office a couple of times when Paddy was away, to check on post and messages. Ben had made her cups of coffee, and been quite solicitous. "Are you OK?" he had said one day, with his head on one side. "You look a bit fraught."

"Oh, it's just the builders." Joscelyn had explained all about the leaking roof.

"Sounds as if you could do with treating yourself," Ben had said, and they had agreed to meet for one of their lunches.

Joscelyn arrived fifteen minutes late. "The plumber promised to be with me before twelve, because I told him I would be going out, but it was twenty-five minutes past when he finally arrived."

"Well, that sounds like quite good going for a plumber. Plumbers are notorious."

"That's what the builders say."

Ben laughed.

They ordered some wine and food, and Ben said, "And how are you otherwise? Lately you haven't been looking quite your own super-calm self."

"I'm fine."

"How's the course?"

"Fine. I'm enjoying the English, but that's because I always like reading novels. I'm not quite sure how the actual work bit is going. You lose confidence, not having done any academic stuff for a while. At least all the others are mature students, with ordinary lives; so when I get to meet them I won't be making a fool myself in front of lots of eighteen-year-olds."

Ben nodded, indicating that he was listening.

"And the history tutor always sets such difficult essays. I am never quite sure what the question means. He gave me a B+ for my last one, so it must have been all right, but I still wasn't sure whether I'd actually answered the question."

"I had a tutor like that once," said Ben. "It was a bit annoying. He used to do it to try and trip us up. But in the end I got onto his wavelength and used to quite enjoy it. Once you'd worked out what the question meant it seemed relatively little trouble to answer it."

"Well, I wish I felt like that. The next one is 'Define the effective extent of the power of the late medieval kings.'"

"Well, that's easy," Ben smiled. "At least the question is easy even if the answer isn't. It's just asking you 'What could kings do?'" He spread out his hands and smiled again. "'What could they do, and what, that they might have liked or expected to do, could they not do?'"

Joscelyn looked up at Ben in admiration. On the rare occasion Paddy had been persuaded to discuss her course, he had sounded very clever, but had made everything seem terribly complicated. He bombarded her with lots of facts about Irish history, Yeats, and James Joyce, which had been ever so impressive, but hadn't helped her at all. Ben had the knack of making everything seem so simple. It really gave her confidence.

At the end of their meal, Joscelyn was preparing to leave, when Ben said:

"When is your seminar?"

"Four o'clock. Why?"

"So why don't we go and look at some late medieval kings. There are pictures of two or three of them at the top of the National Portrait Gallery. It's only ten minutes walk from here. Currently I'm dealing with some people in Miami, and they aren't awake yet. I've got an hour to spare if you have."

Joscelyn hesitated. This was a deviation from the norm. She and Ben met for lunch. She, Paddy and Ben met for dinner. She looked at Ben. He looked quite calm, as if equally prepared to accept a negative or affirmative reply.

"All right," she said, hearing the note of surprise in her own voice. "That would be nice."

Joscelyn hadn't been to the National Portrait Gallery before. Ben obviously had. When she looked a bit uncertain of the way, Ben took her gently by the arm, and directed her up to the top floor, mentioning one or two of his favourite pictures on the way up.

"There's one of Dr Johnson which makes me feel quite sorry for him. When I read about, I admire him. That's because Boswell puts me in contact with his mind. In his portrait, there's a body, a large ugly body, wrapped round a soul."

There were indeed portraits of some late medieval kings. Henry VI, Edward IV and Richard III. Two had been painted a long time after their deaths. Richard III, painted several centuries after he lived, looked like a real person: anxious and troubled, by no means the standard villain. Joscelyn looked at them doubtfully, wondering just how much she was supposed to learn from the experience.

"Well, they are real men," she said cheerfully, hoping that she didn't sound too banal.

"Of course they are. That's the first and last thing you've got to remember when you write your essays."

On her way home on the tube, Joscelyn wondered about Ben. He was probably lonely, she thought. She had been doing him a favour by spending a few hours with him. And it had been fun. Something small, but unexpected, to brighten her day.

* * *

Hilary's holiday with her father was pleasant. However, as he drove her, in his new French car, to catch her train home, she was aware that the few days of rural peace had done nothing to help her get the kind of perspective on her life that she had been hoping for.

Initially, determined to use the "quality time" with her father well, she had made a point of engaging him in conversation, asking him about the people he knew, the books he read, and his preferred methods of growing vegetables. Mr Mackay had mostly provided answers, but Hilary had not felt that any of them had helped her much towards the greater father-daughter understanding she had been hoping for. It was only on the last evening, over a bowl of home-made soup, when Hilary had given up her cross-examination that her Dad, quite unexpectedly, started to reminisce about his student days. He had studied mathematics, which was supposed to have been a good preparation for his job as managing director of an engineering firm.

"Of course it was quite the wrong subject for me," he announced. Surprised, Hilary started listening very intently. Here at last was the kind of confidence she had been hoping for. It was also hard to square with the fact that for years her mother had always attributed the majority of her father's characteristics, from his choice of clothes to his enthusiasm for the scenery of the North York Moors (which she did not share), to his being a mathematician.

"My heart was never in it, and even worse, I found I reached my mathematical ceiling in the first week I was there. Maths is like that. You can be good at one level, and I was good at school, and then just reach the point when you can't do any more. And there I was, with three years to go." Her father laughed. He looked quite relaxed now, and his eyes twinkled. It was the best thing about him. The absurdities of existence even when they were the cause of his own adversity, never failed to amuse him.

"I'd have been much better off with one of the humanities. Something like history that required me to exercise a bit of human understanding, and in the end that would have stood me in better stead."

Hilary had always known that her father might have chosen a different job than the one he inherited; but this was the first time that he had ever expressed anything like regret or disappointment aloud. He looked surprisingly untroubled, as if he had long come to terms with what, from Hilary's perspective, seemed like a cruel waste.

"I made the best of a bad job though. In those days undergraduates weren't expected to work too hard, and I had three very good years, all things considered."

Even more surprisingly, Mr Mackay told Hilary about a girlfriend, who had flame-red hair and was an enthusiastic bell-ringer. Hilary was quite taken aback at the thought that there might ever have been another woman in her father's life, besides her own mother. None had ever been mentioned before.

"I suppose that was before you met Mummy," she said.

"Oh, no, I did know your mother then. She was my home girlfriend, I suppose. But at that time Margaret was a little more to the fore, you might say."

Hilary felt quite shocked. The Mackay family party line had always been that her mother had generously, not to say foolishly, bestowed her favours on the lonely young man that her father had been in those days, despite being assiduously courted by a host of other attractive and eligible suitors. Of course it was her mother who had told everybody this, but her father had never sought to deny it. Now he was hinting that he might have had other possibilities himself. Even, perhaps, that in some ways the flame-haired Margaret might have been better suited to him?

She felt extremely curious and disorientated at the same time. She had hoped for a better understanding of her father, but it had not really occurred to her that this might require her to look at him in a different light; to understand that his life had once had complexities and choices that she had never before imagined. Choices which, had they been made differently, could have resulted in her not being born. She was just wondering whether to ask some more, when her father cleared the soup dishes away.

"I think it's going to rain tomorrow," he said, "which will be a good thing for my carrots."

Hilary knew that the conversation, fascinating and appalling as it was, was at an end.

After that little piece of self-revelation, Hilary and her father settled into a comfortable companionship, and they talked about France, and London, and a little bit about Hilary's career hopes. On the latter subject her Dad was willing to listen, but not to comment, which Hilary found a little irritating. All throughout her childhood her mother had been overbearing with her opinions, and her father unsatisfactorily distant.

One thing Hilary had not talked to her father about was Paddy. She thought a lot about him, inevitably, and in the course of her time in France made several definite decisions about the relationship, each of which felt wrong immediately afterwards. She had had a wonderful time in Cannes, and a lot of this was to do with the place, and all the people she had met, but those few precious hours spent alone with Paddy each day had made the experience very special. They talked a good deal, and she felt that increasingly Paddy respected her opinions and valued her concern for him.

It had also been nice to share a bed, and make love. Hilary's last (and first) sexual experience had been with a boyfriend whom she had met, and finished with, during her second year at Cambridge. It was dangerous, though, and she knew it. Hilary could feel the special magic that sex weaves, attaching her closer to Paddy, making her care so much more for him, miss him so much more when he was not there. It was almost palpable, as if invisible threads were beginning to bind her closer and closer to Paddy and his life. She would have physically to cut or disentangle them to get away.

This was not what she had intended to happen. Somewhere amongst her very mixed feelings was the understanding that, however much Paddy had to offer her, he was not the man she wanted to share the rest of her life with. This should not matter, of course. She was young, focussed on her career, and as far as relationships were concerned the rest of her life was a long way off. But the closer she got to Paddy, the more she began to feel as if he should be that man. Her head and her heart were telling her two very different things.

Once back in London, to the grey skies and cold bedsit, her immediate urge was to telephone Paddy, as he had asked her to do on her return, and arrange to meet as quickly as possible. But this was not wise. She knew that some decision about the future had to be made, but she resolved to delay the decision. She would not contact Paddy at all for two days, and in the meantime would give the matter some serious thought. It was still only nine o'clock, but, exhausted by travelling and inner turmoil, she declared the day over, went to bed, and took comfort in sleep.

After her early night, morning also came early. Although she was supposed to be thinking, all her instincts were to act. She would certainly have broken her resolve during the morning, if she had not had a letter calling her to a job interview. She had applied for a training post with the Royal Shakespeare Company, in London, and so long ago that she had given up all hope, but now they wanted her to go for interview. She also had a postcard from Peter in Milan.

She had been right not to contact Paddy straight away. She had her own life to lead. It might well be that Paddy would be a part of it, but she had promised herself time to think, and that was what she should have.

Paddy had a note in his diary, which said "Hilary back?" for the day she was expected to return. He was therefore very anxious when, two days later, she had not been in touch.

"It will probably be the Monday," she had said, "but I'm not exactly sure. I'll ring you when I am back."

"Promise?" he had said to her, and she had said, "Of course."

But Paddy felt uneasy. This was nothing new. He always felt uneasy when out of contact, especially at this early stage of a relationship. It never felt secure. He was busy himself, but a phone call would have made him very happy.

"Hilary hasn't been in touch," he told Joss.

This was Paddy being anxious; wanting support, even for his dalliances. Joss wondered whether the other women realised that Paddy turned to her for advice, about them.

"She's probably staying a couple of extra days with her father," she said. "She's not working just now, is she?"

Joscelyn thought of her own father. She couldn't imagine herself voluntarily extending a visit to him, but Hilary probably had a normal family background.

Paddy was talking about Hilary again. "She did genuinely seem fond of me when we were in Cannes."

Joscelyn said nothing. But Paddy wasn't going to be satisfied with his wife's silence.

"Don't you think she is?"

"I don't know." Joss allowed a flash of irritation into her voice.

"I am not asking you to know." Paddy was fierce in reply. "I am asking you to express an opinion. The fact that you are not omniscient should not allow you to avoid this question, which you know is very important to me."

Joscelyn made a big effort, and remained calm. Paddy was angry, but he was behaving like a little boy. On these occasions she was supposed to be mother, providing unconditional love.

"I expect so. I have only met her briefly, and she seems to be quite a complicated person. But I don't know what is going on her mind."

Paddy looked disappointed, and then angry, again. "You could be more supportive," he told his wife.

"I am answering your question, and I think perhaps it is her you should be asking, not me."

In fact, Joss was thinking, the truth did seem to be that Hilary wasn't as taken with Paddy as Paddy was with her. Perhaps this is something that is going to blow over very soon, she thought. Maybe she and Paddy would soon be left in peace, to be happy together. But she wasn't going to make any predictions, either to herself or to Paddy.

After a moment she said, "I care for you."

"I know you do."

She paused and looked pointedly at her spouse. "And as you're here now, I'd like us to have a nice evening."

Paddy felt quite distraught. He wanted that, too. This was the problem with these affairs. You spent so much time wanting something you hadn't, at that moment, got. It was such a waste. Here he was with Joscelyn, beautiful, kind Joscelyn, and he wanted to be happy being with her, but he couldn't.

It was all Hilary's fault. She had these great moral stances on anything and everything but lacked the capacity to be considerate to those around her. Even people who were in love with her, as he was. They do have telephones in France, he thought. Even if she were staying a few extra days, she wouldn't be putting herself out too much to lift the phone.

That was all he wanted; to be in touch. Then he could enjoy the evening with his wife.

* * *

The same day Hilary's self-imposed embargo on contact ended, her phone rang, about eight o'clock in the morning. She was hardly up, but Paddy was already in his office.

She was very pleased and relieved to hear Paddy's voice. He was suggesting lunch. Was she free?

Hilary could hardly object to lunch. Yes, she was free.

Hilary had felt nervous about meeting Paddy again, but when she saw him, smiling and confident, all her anxieties began to disappear. Paddy obviously had none. How nice for relationships to be simple, as they appeared to be for him, she thought.

She told him about her interview at the RSC, wondering if he would be disapproving about a job in the theatre, but he was not.

"Good," he had said, nodding his head. "Excellent. And I imagine you'll be just what they are looking for."

"I think there will be a lot of good competition."

"Don't even think about it," was Paddy's advice. "You're better than any of them."

A couple of glasses of wine later, though, Paddy started talking about a previous girlfriend, a travel journalist called Minerva, of whom he still seemed very fond. Hilary found herself getting very annoyed. Paddy was explaining that although Minerva had been an unpretentious person "like you" there had been an occasion when she had returned from a very gruelling trip to South America and he had taken her to the Ritz for dinner. She had eaten "what must have been her first meal for a week, because she demolished everything edible that got within a few feet of her".

Hilary felt that it was wrong of Paddy to be thinking about old girlfriends when she was sitting opposite him.

"You've never taken me to the Ritz," she said, conscious of her own unpleasant tone.

"I thought it would be too vulgar for you. But I'll be delighted to take you. Are you free tomorrow evening?"

Hilary explained that she would not be free for the rest of that week. "Besides," she said, "I shouldn't be able to afford my share."

She and Paddy often had arguments over the bill. Hilary couldn't afford to eat out as often, or as expensively, as Paddy did. Paddy often paid for their meals, which left Hilary feeling disadvantaged. She often suggested that they went somewhere cheap, where she could afford her half. Paddy sometimes agreed, but at others got quite grumpy and said that she "mustn't make such an issue over it". He could easily pay for a few meals, and didn't want his choice of eating-places to be determined by Hilary's purse.

They left each other without any definite arrangement to meet again, and Hilary could see that Paddy was disappointed. Then their bill came, and Hilary reached out for it.

"This is mine," she said. "You paid for so much in Cannes."

Somewhat to her surprise, Paddy did not demur. "Thank you very much," he said graciously.

Hilary looked at the figures in front of her. She would be hard put to afford it all, and felt rather silly. But it was too late now. She would pay. She had been saving up to buy herself a new pair of shoes: now that money would have to go on lunch.

Back home that evening, Hilary missed Paddy desperately. She had been such a fool. Why hadn't she agreed to see him that week? She didn't want to phone, so she wrote out a little note on a postcard: "Could you make dinner on Monday? I would be free then, and I would like to see you."

She took the tube over to Paddy's office, and dropped it through the letterbox. It was a long journey, and the round trip took her an hour and a half.

By the time Monday came, Hilary had had her job interview. It had gone quite well, she thought. She had spoken to all her family on the phone and told some of her friends about it. It had also given her a reason to write a long letter to Peter. But the person she most wanted to discuss the experience with, of course, was Paddy. She had always been meticulous about not contacting him too much, and especially between agreed meetings. Hilary had her own reasons for her self-denial, but she persuaded herself that they were entirely to do with her sensitivity to the fact that he was a busy, and also a married man.

By the weekend, there was practically nothing else on her mind besides Paddy and her desire to have some contact with him. She knew that he would be at home with Joscelyn. This, for the first time ever, seemed quite wrong. The whole pleasure that she had felt in being interviewed for so prestigious a job felt quite spoiled by the fact that she could not allow herself to share it with Paddy. Hilary felt hugely resentful. She was being so honourable about the whole thing, and was making herself unhappy. Other women wouldn't have cared that he was married. She wasn't like that. But it was all wrong, whatever happened, and she was, for most of the weekend, completely wretched.

Hilary knew that Paddy would probably ring on Monday, after seeing her postcard, but, unable to wait any longer, she rang his office at eight-thirty in the morning. To her huge relief, he was already in work. She wanted to tell him all about it, but he was clearly too distracted to listen.

"I'll hear all about it tonight," he said, briskly. "And I've decided on something. You must let me take you to the Ritz. Tonight."

Delighted, Hilary had agreed. But half an hour later, she thought better of it. It was suddenly very clear. She felt very sad, but not as sad as she was going to feel if the whole thing went on. She was going to get a job and if not with the RSC somewhere else. She had friends. She had, and must have, her own life. She rang back.

"It's me."

"Hello me."

"Listen, I've been thinking. Actually, Paddy, I think that it had better not be the Ritz. I've been thinking. In fact I've been thinking for some time. I need to talk to you. To have a serious talk. We should go somewhere suitable."

"And where would be suitable?" Hilary could hear the disappointment in Paddy's voice. This was going to be hard.

"I don't know." She was fighting back tears. "Just not the Ritz."

* * *

Dinner was a sombre affair. They went to an Italian restaurant, where the waiters were unrelentingly jolly. Hilary couldn't eat, although she noticed that Paddy devoured everything. She drank one glass of wine, while Paddy had the rest of the bottle. Hilary hoped that Paddy would ask her what she wanted to discuss, but disconcertingly, he did not. He asked about her interview, and then started telling her about the events of his past week, and the progress on his various work projects. He seemed impervious to her inner anguish, and not to notice her lack of appetite.

After what seemed like an eternity, Hilary took advantage of a break in the conversation.

"I did want to talk about something, something serious."

"Yes, that's what you told me," Paddy said.

There was a pause. Hilary couldn't find the words to say what she needed to say. Then, very abruptly, and without being quite sure that she was making proper sense, she explained that she couldn't go on with the affair. It was just too difficult, not what she wanted. She had had a lovely time in Cannes. She did feel very fond of him. She didn't think they were doing anything wrong, but she really wasn't cut out for a relationship with a married man.

"I think a lot of women feel the same," she said.

Paddy listened, his face impassive. Hilary had no idea what he was thinking, and this made things much worse.

Eventually, he spoke.

"I did think we cared for each other. That we had something worth pursuing, Hilary. You don't want what I have with Joscelyn. You're too young, and you have a career to forge. A good one too."

Hilary remained silent.

Then Paddy looked stern. "I am committed to Joscelyn. I'm not going to give her up."

Hilary felt angry, and suddenly this made it all much easier. "I know that. And I don't want you to."

One of the jolly waiters came to the table, seeing that Paddy had finished eating. Hilary was only half way through her pizza, but she said, very quickly "We've both finished, thank you. Can we have the bill, please?"

Paddy paid the bill, and then walked Hilary back to her tube station, down New Bond Street. They passed the Ritz. This wasn't entirely coincidence. Paddy had chosen a restaurant that wasn't too far away.

Hilary felt that she had made a real mess of things. They had ended in so bad a way. Paddy was unusually quiet as they walked along. She knew that he was unhappy too. She looked up at the Ritz.

"We never did get there for dinner," said Hilary. "I think I shall always regret that."

"We could spend the night there," said Paddy.

Hilary stood still, and looked at the opulent building, with the warm bright light inside, coming from all those huge, magnificent chandeliers. It was so sumptuous, so very much not to her taste, but so absolutely Paddy. It would always symbolise Paddy for her. It would be a shame, therefore, if she had never been there with him.

"No," she said, "I really couldn't."

She stood still, and Paddy sensed her hesitation. He took hold of her hand, and held it lightly.

"We are fond of each other, aren't we? It would be a much better way of ending things than the mess we've just made of saying goodbye."

Hilary stood on the pavement, causing an obstruction to the thick and steady flow of pedestrians out for the evening. Paddy put his arm around her.

"It would have to be for the very last time," she said, "I really do mean what I said."

"Of course," said Paddy, hoping that she would be feeling differently in an hour or two. Hilary continued to cause an obstruction on the pavement, and so Paddy began steering her up the steps, into the grand entrance.

"We really ought to end things in style."

He paused for a moment, and looked directly at her. "We are fond of each other. It would be wrong to do it any other way."

Chapter 10

Three months later, Joscelyn, Paddy and Ben were in Rome. Joscelyn was very happy. It had long been an ambition of hers to visit the Coliseum, and there she was, walking slowly round the ruins, with Ben, who was consulting the guidebook assiduously. Paddy was sitting on an ancient stone seat engaged in a heated conversation on his mobile phone. Mobile phones were new in the 1980s, and Paddy, being a businessman (as well as being keen on gadgets), had got one. They hadn't been sure it would work abroad, but remarkably it did.

Rome had been Joscelyn's idea, prompted by a feeling she had had, at one of their lunch meetings, that Ben was rather down. At first, his reaction was predictably negative:

"Very kind of you to think of me, of course. Why Rome?"

"I've never been," Joscelyn said simply,

"I've never been to Budleigh Salterton," said Ben, "but I don't consider that any argument for doing so."

"It's hardly the same thing, is it?" said Joscelyn.

"Not quite, perhaps. But Southern Italians are all peasants. No culture, horrible wine, and barely edible food."

"Surely not in Rome," Joscelyn argued. "It's the capital city."

"It is not the same situation as in Britain. London has been the major commercial and cultural centre of England for many hundreds of years. Italy hasn't even been a nation state for very long. Rome may be the seat of government, but the industrial wealth and all the intellectual traditions of the country are all in the North."

Joscelyn didn't take him seriously. Ben, like Paddy, her father and indeed most of the men she knew well was prone to these odd prejudices.

"Well, I want to see the Roman ruins," she said.

A couple of days later, Ben passed a message back, via Paddy that he would like to join them. Paddy claimed not to have known that his wife intended to invite Ben. Joscelyn was sure that she had not only mentioned it but also got Paddy's full approval to the plan. But there was no real argument. Paddy was quite happy for Ben to come along.

Joscelyn had expected to find it strange to see Ben out of London, and he had certainly surprised her, once they landed in Rome, by speaking to all the officials in fluent Italian. It turned out that his mother came from Turin.

"That's why you're prejudiced against the southern Italians," she teased him.

"That's why I know more about the subject than you do," he had observed dryly.

As she looked at the two men now, Joscelyn felt a proprietorial pleasure in them. In their own ways, they both looked happy. Strangely, they seemed much more different here in Italy. In London, they both wore a similar uniform, with smart business suits. Ben still wore a suit, lightweight and dapper, while Paddy had gone into shorts (which showed off a pair of sturdy legs), a Panama hat and obvious relaxation. Ben seemed able to stay cool, even in the hot Italian summer, while Paddy regularly mopped his brow with a large white handkerchief.

Paddy had taken the abrupt end of his brief affair with Hilary rather badly. He had told Joscelyn that it was all over, and that this had been Hilary's decision, but for a while seemed not quite to believe it. Often he talked as if he expected Hilary to be in contact again. Paddy continued to work, but for a while he was very gloomy and depressed in any kind of repose. That had been painful to endure, of course, but this phase had actually only lasted a couple of weeks. In retrospect, Joscelyn had felt pleased that she had not made too much of an issue of the trip to Cannes. If she had, the relationship would probably still be continuing now. Instead, the affair was over. After the inevitable period of disappointment Paddy was now energetic, enjoying life. Once again he looked like a man buoyed up by success.

It was a slightly odd dynamic, being the three of them. It reminded Joscelyn of a time at school when she and two other girls had all been close friends. They all got on, but more often than not there would be an alliance between two of them, and these alliances would shift and change on an almost daily basis. It was the same now; sometimes she and Paddy were together as man and wife, with Ben as a sort of friendly appendage. Other times the two men seemed more like a couple, with Joscelyn on her own, and then Paddy would opt out and she and Ben would be together.

Paddy opted out of quite a few things. He had been to Rome a couple of times before and was clear about what he was and was not prepared to revisit. He agreed to go to the Coliseum, liked the Trevi Fountain, and he wanted to go and sit in the Piazza Navona every day. He refused to see the Vatican, so Joscelyn went there with Ben.

It was one of the frustrating things about Paddy, at least from Joscelyn's point of view. Adventurous in everyday life, Paddy very easily became a creature of habit on holiday. He liked to find a cafe or restaurant that suited him, and visit it every day. Joscelyn preferred, especially on trips abroad, to see as much as she could. "I don't like to be disappointed," Paddy would argue, when Joscelyn tried to persuade him to go some new place. Fortunately Ben was an indefatigable tourist, and was happy to work through the guidebook with her.

On the evening before their penultimate day Ben had a suggestion.

"I'd like to go to Naples," he said. "It is quite a long way for a day trip, but we could do it if we're prepared to get up early."

"See Naples and die," said Joscelyn, who remembered that someone famous (although she could not remember who) had said this about the city.

"And this is the man who thinks the southern Italians are beyond the pale," said Paddy. "Aren't you into bandit country down there?"

"I believe it may be a bit run down, but Naples was a very important centre before unification," Ben replied.

"I'm not going," said Paddy decisively, "I came to visit Rome, not to go on a touring holiday. Tomorrow is our last full day, and I want to go to that place by the Trevi again for my lunch, and have a final glass of their wonderful house wine."

"Well, I am," said Ben, equally firmly.

"Honestly, Paddy," Joss tried to encourage her husband. "You might as well be in Soho, going to Gino's every day."

"I don't go to Gino's every day," said Paddy. "Besides, this is my holiday, and I am not going to be bullied into doing something I shan't enjoy."

Joscelyn felt uncomfortable. Her loyalties were divided. She would have to go with one of them. Paddy was her husband, but Ben was a guest, and had so far been a very obliging one, too. Besides, she wanted to see Naples.

She looked at the two men. They were equally resolute. Strangely, she felt that despite this, neither of them felt any ill will towards the other. They each felt that the other was mistaken in his choice, but had no intention of quarrelling over the matter. This didn't stop her from feeling awkward. She felt that she must choose between them.

"I should quite like to see Naples," she ventured.

Ben said nothing. Paddy said,

"You go with Ben then. You two are the tourists of this trip."

Joscelyn still felt very uncomfortable. "You'd be all on your own," she said to Paddy.

"I'll be all right," said Paddy. "I've got some thinking to do."

Joscelyn looked anxiously at her husband. What did he want to think about? Why did he not want her to share in his thoughts? Did he really not mind, or was he playing the martyr?

"I'm sure we could be back in time for us all to have dinner together," she said in an appeasing tone.

Paddy said nothing. Joscelyn looked at Ben.

"We could," Ben said, in a less appeasing tone.

Joscelyn hoped that Paddy would say something affirmatory, something that would set his seal of approval on the day trip. He did not.

"I'll go with Ben then, if Paddy is quite sure that he doesn't mind being left." She spoke into the air, not looking at either man.

"Fine," said Paddy.

The train journey to Naples provided time for some conversation. Until now, they had mostly been too busy looking at architecture, and absorbing new sights and sounds. Joscelyn felt even more curious about Ben, knowing that he had an Italian mother. She began to ask him about his childhood.

He seemed happy enough to talk, so long as he told her only as much as he wanted to. He had been born and brought up in England - in London, although he was not specific as to which district. His parents still lived there, although they had recently moved from the family home into an apartment. His mother was an educated woman, but she had not worked, and had sometimes felt lonely in Britain. His father had been "in business" although he did not say what. As a child, he had visited Italy at least once a year.

"Do you feel at home in Italy?" Joscelyn asked.

"I feel at home, but I don't think the Italians would see me as being one of themselves. I suppose I know the country quite well, and have a strong sentimental attachment to the place."

"Your Italian is very good," said Joscelyn.

"It is my mother's tongue. But my mother tongue is definitely English. Sometimes I struggle for a word in Italian. Of course I'm all right on a trip like this, where the only talking is about the practicalities of buying things, and booking tickets, or passing the time of day. A real conversation can lose me sometimes."

Joscelyn again fancied that Ben was a little sad. Had there

been, or was there still, some intimacy with an Italian person that had suffered from Ben's not quite perfect use of the language?

They fell silent for a while; Ben read an Italian newspaper and Joscelyn a book that she had brought with her for the holiday. In due course, a waiter came with a trolley of drinks, and Ben bought them some coffee.

Joscelyn decided to re-open the conversation. It was hard to know how best to phrase what she wanted to know. She was going to have to jump straight in.

"Have you ever been married, Ben?"

Ben took the question without any sign of emotional agitation. "No, unfortunately. I did have a girlfriend who lasted a longish time, and I did think that I was settling down with her. She seemed to feel the same way, at one point, but she changed her mind, and went back to Poland."

"Poland?" This seemed very exotic.

"Yes, Poland."

"Has there been nobody since?" Joscelyn asked.

"Nobody serious; nobody who has turned out to be serious."

Joscelyn knew that she was pushing the conversation as far as she could. Reluctantly, she returned to her novel, and swiftly, Ben picked up his newspaper.

They had a very pleasant day together. There was something very restful about Ben's company, but Naples was the most exhausting place to visit. The streets were colourful, crowded and noisy, car horns blaring, and a maze of streets so complex that they had to check their map every few hundred yards. Ben remained calm and cheerful. Joscelyn knew that he could sometimes be prey to melancholy (although today his spirits were sunny like the weather) but he lacked Paddy's restlessness. Joscelyn found herself speculating what it would be like to live with him. His reserve would be a problem, but she felt sure that the love of a good woman would overcome this in time. Life with Ben would be less exciting than life with Paddy, but only a little way underneath a slightly difficult exterior was a kind and thoughtful person. A lot of women did not want an exciting domestic life.

Joscelyn wouldn't dream of swapping Paddy for a man like Ben, but even she felt that her exciting life with Paddy could be just a bit too unstable sometimes.

While Rome, like so many famous and beautiful cities, seemed at times to be populated entirely by tourists, Naples was full of Neapolitans. They were obviously a mixed bunch, swarthy southern Italians, and immigrants from Africa in bright red and yellow clothing. It was certainly a poor place, in stark contrast to Rome, and this took some getting used to. Joscelyn always thought of herself as well-enough off but by no means rich. In Naples she felt rich, and this wasn't an altogether a comfortable experience. She said as much to Ben.

"Yes," he said, "I feel the same."

Joscelyn found herself thinking that Paddy would not have empathised with this as easily as Ben did.

Once or twice Joscelyn thought of Paddy on his own in Rome. She had worried about leaving him, but now felt no discomfort. He had made his own decision. He would probably manage a mild flirtation with a woman tourist, which might run to lunch, or at least a trip to a cafe for an exotic Italian ice cream. He might even appreciate his wife a bit more when she got back. She was normally the one waiting for him, after all.

Despite the constant struggle to find their way around, the day seemed to go very smoothly. They managed to see everything they planned to, and to find nice places for much-needed breaks for rest and drinks. It hardly seemed to matter, therefore, when their train home was fifteen or so minutes late. This was Italy, after all. Even when it was thirty minutes late, there seemed to be no real reason for concern. Joscelyn was telling Ben about a weekend course she had been on, where they had attended real lectures, and how intimidating some of her fellow students had seemed on first acquaintance.

Then Ben said, "The train is forty minutes late. I imagine that this actually counts as late, even by Neapolitan standards. I had better go and find out what is happening."

Ben went off, leaving Joscelyn sitting happily in the warm sunshine. He came back looking troubled and gloomy.

"There's been a strike. Nobody knows much. The train may come and it may not."

Joscelyn didn't feel that there should be much cause for concern. "We can wait a bit longer, can't we?"

"We have no option," said Ben.

The mood had changed. Ben seemed disproportionately upset by what had happened. They sat in silence for a short while.

"Could we get back any other way?"

"A taxi, I suppose, or an internal flight. The general view seemed to be that the trains will probably be running again tomorrow."

Joscelyn tried to be soothing. "We can wait here for a while longer. I expect the train will come. I suppose if the worst comes to the worst we could stay over and get back one way or another tomorrow. Our flight isn't until two o'clock."

"If the worst comes to the worst."

Joscelyn felt that Ben was being unnecessarily ungallant to present spending this extra time with her in Naples as the worst thing that could happen to him. She said nothing, but thought to herself how much more cheery Paddy would have been in a similar situation.

Joscelyn telephoned Paddy, who also sounded grumpy.

"I knew it wasn't a good idea."

"We had a nice day," said Joscelyn. "Did you?"

"Very nice, thanks," Paddy replied, not giving anything away.

"I'll keep you posted," said Joscelyn.

"Telephones are quicker," Paddy replied irritatingly. "I imagine that the post comes by train."

Two hours later, Joscelyn had long given up trying to make conversation. She was reading her book, and Ben his newspaper. She came to the end of her chapter, and out of the corner of her eye saw that Ben had put his paper down and was staring straight ahead.

"Do you think we should have a strategy?" she ventured. "I am quite happy waiting here, but I suppose we should decide at what point we go and look for a hotel."

"Neapolitan hotels are probably awful," Ben said gloomily.

"I expect there is at least one nice one," Joscelyn remained resolutely cheerful, "and it does seem sensible to decide at what point we give up on the train altogether and get back tomorrow."

Ben looked gloomy.

"Shall we give it another hour?" Joscelyn suggested.

"I suppose so," said Ben.

Five minutes before the hour was up, a train for Rome arrived. Ben cheered up instantly, and bought them both coffee and biscuits. Ben smiled at her across the table that separated them. "I can't deny that I am pleased to be getting back. I had plans for the last morning. A little walk on my own after an early mass."

"Are you a Roman Catholic, Ben?" Joss was surprised by this new revelation from her friend.

"Yes; although not a very devout one. You shouldn't look so surprised," he said, reading her thoughts. "My mother is Italian and like many Italians, is Roman Catholic. We are quite normal, you know. You don't have to worry about associating with me."

Joss blushed. "My parents were members of the Church of England," she said, "but very nominal ones. They went at Christmas, and for funerals and things. Actually," she went on, realising something for the first time, "I think my mother liked to go to church, but father always made a bit of a fuss if she did."

That night, in bed with Paddy, Joscelyn told him how Ben had been jilted by a Polish woman. He was not particularly interested.

"All Ben's girlfriends are foreign," he told her, "and he always seems to have trouble with them," before rolling over and going to sleep.

The next and final day, everybody's tempers were mellow again. Joscelyn was happy to join Paddy on a final tour of his favourite haunts, before catching the plane home. All were agreed that it had been a really good holiday, and they must do something similar again very soon.

Back in London, Joscelyn realised that this was the first time they had really been away since they bought the house. Already it felt like home, the place they naturally went back to.

She and Paddy sat together at the kitchen table, with a cup of their own tea, in their own bright blue home teapot, opening the post. There were bills, postcards from friends who had also been on holiday, and some for Paddy.

"Oh," Paddy said in surprise. "This one's from Hilary."

Joscelyn felt ill. This wasn't meant to happen. She didn't want Hilary back in their lives. She could see the letter as Paddy read it. It was quite short, one sheet of paper and written on only one side.

"She doesn't say much. She wants to meet up again."

"And will you?" asked Joscelyn, already knowing what the answer would be.

"Of course." said Paddy. He didn't look disturbed at all. Joscelyn had a deep sense of foreboding. Why was Hilary getting in contact? It was for no good reason, of that she was sure.

Chapter 11

Hilary was pregnant. She was a little over three months gone, and had just had confirmation, by way of a home pregnancy testing kit. She had known, of course, for some time, at least at one level of consciousness, but it had taken her all this time to have what her body had been telling her confirmed by some external evidence. Her body had been quite insistent about the fact. Not only had her periods stopped, but her breasts were swollen and sore. She felt very sick, and strangely tired. Hilary, however, had not been listening. She had at first attributed her sense of anxiety and depression to the news that she had not been given the job with the RSC. Then her tiredness to the fact that shortly afterwards she was (quite out of the blue) offered another one, as an assistant director with a large fringe theatre company. Naturally, she was working hard to impress.

If anyone had asked her what she would do if she ever became pregnant by accident, as a result of a hardly-intended affair, Hilary would have no doubt in giving her answer. She would have a termination. She had her own life, her career. She thought that children should have two parents, ideally, and if not that at least one very committed one. It wouldn't be fair on the child, never mind her.

Theoretically, this was still her position. It was therefore convenient that she did not get into a conversation with anyone about the subject. She had told no one, even her doctor, about her condition. She did not want to be asked about what she wanted to do. In order to give an answer, she would have to consider the question, and face the conflicting views taken by her head and her heart.

In the strongly emotionally-charged condition of early pregnancy, Hilary's heart wanted quite desperately to be the mother of the child she carried. Her heart had had many dealings with her head, over the years they had both inhabited Hilary's body. It knew that Hilary was a strong and, particularly, a headstrong person. The heart knew it could not win an argument, for it had lost many battles this way. It had lost the argument over Paddy. But it could win this one. For Hilary, as for many women, the love for a man could be something very compelling, very powerful. At times it might seem like the most powerful feeling in the world. But for Hilary, as for many women, it would be for her children that she would ultimately be prepared to sacrifice everything.

It was probably her heart's doing that Hilary finally began to act after about three months, when the pregnancy was well established. And having acted, and having seen her positive test result, Hilary's head took over.

She made an appointment to see her doctor; not straight away, for she had a very busy week in work, but next week, when things would be quieter. She considered who to talk to. There was her family, and of course they would have to know some time. But please not yet, she decided. It would have been so nice to speak to her father, for she had always felt a basic confidence that he would be on her side. But also, he would be upset. She really dreaded her mother knowing. It seemed likely that it was going to take more courage to deal with her mother than to look after a baby, if she had it. Her sister Victoria was another problem.

Victoria, at least in Hilary's eyes, had always been the good child, and she, Hilary, the bad one. Victoria had been outgoing and vivacious, while Hilary was reserved and self-contained. "She's more like me, and you are like your father," their mother used to say. When they were eight and ten, Victoria used to keep her room tidy, and was always able to find her PE kit, and her pencil sharpeners, which Hilary never could. As they grew older, and were affected by adolescence, Hilary had made a conscious attempt to take control of her life, and had become better organised. Victoria had relaxed and rebelled, leaving clothes, lipstick, and empty coffee cups all over the house; but somehow the roles were still fixed. Hilary was still the untidy one, no matter how much debris her sister inflicted on the Mackay household. As for Hilary, her newly-acquired capacity to look after herself went unnoticed, while any small slip was seized upon, and laughed at and regarded as proof of something that she knew was no longer true.

All this was very annoying but ultimately irrelevant to what Hilary had always felt was the key difference between her sister and herself. Her sister wanted, wholeheartedly and without resentment, to belong to the Mackay family and all that it stood for, and Hilary did not. Belonging to the Mackays was more than an accident of birth. In fact it need not be connected with birth. Hilary always felt that her mother was a much more committed Mackay than her father. There were certain core conditions, and a whole complex code of behaviour, which were required. For Victoria, as for her mother, sticking to the code was a real pleasure, rather than a duty. They could debate, between themselves, at length and in some detail, the decision of a cousin to take a holiday, or a job, or a wife, and the terms of reference were never to do with whether the choice suited their cousin's personal taste and situation, and only a little affected by how they would be regarded in the eyes of the world as a whole. It was a question of whether it was in keeping with the family tradition. Behaviour that might have been considered quite acceptable to the world at large, such as the choice of Spain as a holiday destination, could arouse great opprobrium, because one member of the clan had once (maybe thirty years before) almost married a Spaniard, only to be cruelly jilted a week before the wedding. Victoria had a detailed knowledge of numerous case histories on which the code was based. Hilary often found it hard to explain to her friends at Cambridge how her place at the university, regarded as something of an achievement in the majority of families, had caused something approaching a rift between herself and her mother.

"Why Cambridge?" Her mother had been shocked and upset when Hilary first broached the subject. "I know that you may not want to go to Durham while Victoria is there," her mother's tone of voice clearly implied that although she recognised a potential objection, she did not see it as a reasonable one, "but you would only overlap for a year. And Victoria is a very sensible girl. She wouldn't interfere with you."

"Mummy, I really don't want to go to Durham, and I wouldn't want to even if Victoria wasn't there. I want somewhere a bit further away, somewhere I don't know so well."

"But we don't know anyone there, darling." Her mother was displaying genuine distress, which upset her daughter. "You could always try Oxford. You could go to your father's college." It was clear from her tone that her father's college was a very poor second best to her sister's in Durham. "Or there's London. I could visit you there."

Hilary remembered all this and shuddered. Having a baby was going to be worse than insisting on going to Cambridge.

Putting thoughts of her family to one side, Hilary thought of Paddy. He also would need to know. He was the father after all. It would not be easy to tell Paddy, but he was at least equally responsible with her for what had happened. They had taken a risk, between them. Hilary, despite what it had landed her with, still had fond memories of that night. Sex with Paddy at Cannes had been pleasant, but he was a little more diffident than she would have imagined, and she had probably held back a little, thinking somewhere in the back of her mind that she might be making a mistake. The knowledge that she was ending the relationship had released all inhibition in her, and they had shared unrestrained passion and an unexpected tenderness.

After a short night's sleep, they had both woken early in the morning keen to make love again, but without any form of contraception, the supply that Paddy kept in his wallet having all been used up.

It was not like Hilary to take such a risk. She knew this about herself, and normally might have been annoyed with herself for behaving uncharacteristically. In fact, this very waywardness against her own nature seemed to affirm her decision. It must have been right. Hilary felt that she could not have behaved this way without good reason. Paddy was, in his business life, a risk-taker, but Hilary had a sense that in private, Paddy was different. The risk had probably not been like him either. Was this, she wondered, something they had both wanted?

Hilary's heart, determined on the baby, was prepared to have a go at getting Paddy as well.

Paddy was genuinely very busy, and when he rang Hilary on the day after his Italian trip, he explained that they could not meet, for one reason or another, for about ten days.

Hilary panicked. This was too long. Her room seemed very small, suddenly, very shabby and very lonely.

"I really do need to see you before then. There is something I want to discuss with you. It needn't take long."

"Well, I've got ten minutes now, if you want to run it past me."

Hilary felt worse and worse. Paddy sounded friendly, but pressured. She was not getting through to him.

"No, I really must see you." She was on the verge of tears.

"Come to the office tomorrow. About ten o'clock. Of course I will be delighted to see you, but I may not have long to talk."

"That's all right," said Hilary, and then, as she put down the telephone receiver, she burst into tears.

She was sitting in the office, at her new place of work. Fortunately, she was all alone. Although for the rest of the morning, long after she had dried her tears, she feared that her blotchy face would show, and that her colleagues would see that Hilary Mackay, the new assistant director, had been crying.

When Paddy went off to work the next day he was thinking about a new deal, almost but not quite done, which needed just that crucial last bit of effort. It was Joscelyn who reminded him, just before he left, that he was to see Hilary.

"Is it ten o'clock you're seeing Hilary?" she asked.

"Yes." Paddy was irritable. He must have mentioned it to Joscelyn, but why bring it up now?

"I shan't really have time," he said. "But she insisted, said it couldn't wait. She has just started a new job. She probably wants to see me about something to do with that."

Joscelyn knew for certain that Hilary did not want to talk about her new job. She hovered on the brink of saying so to Paddy, but, in the end, kept silent. Paddy had called in at home, virtually just to change his clothes and go out again. He had a business deal. He would be out late.

Joscelyn had an essay to finish, and that is what she did. It had started off quite well, but, unable to concentrate properly, she just got it done and made a much less good job of it than she was capable of. At about ten o'clock at night, having been home on her own all day, Joscelyn went to bed, not because she was tired, particularly, but because she had no more enthusiasm for staying awake. She was trying to keep thoughts of Hilary out of her mind. But there was bad news, very bad news, on the way. It seemed strange that Paddy had not recognised it himself. Men could be so obtuse, sometimes. She pulled the large, soft duvet of her and Paddy's comfortable bed nearly over her head, and firmly ignored the fact that she felt sick in the pit of her stomach.

Hilary had also been feeling sick. She had just been beginning to rally a little, after the first few months of pregnancy, but since that call from Paddy she had felt awful. Pregnancy plays some bad tricks on the body, but it has some kind magic as well. It had been very easy for Hilary, in her new hormonal state, to imagine Paddy as the good provider, kind father and worthy consort. His willingness to get her pregnant had seemed almost proof of this. His attitude on the phone, although not unkind, had caught her unawares. Here was the real Paddy, and it was disappointingly so much not what she was expecting.

By ten o'clock Hilary had steadied herself somewhat, and she walked up the stairs that led to Paddy's office carefully, and in control. Even her nausea had abated. Paddy looked very big. He held out his arms, and she noticed almost for the first time how big his hands were. He hugged her, but very briefly, and ushered her in.

The office was empty, which was a good start. Hilary had been there once or twice before, and there had sometimes been visitors, and on one occasion a secretary. Hilary suggested coffee, in an Italian cafe and sandwich bar across the road.

"I don't have time," Paddy said, "But I have some here."

He poured out a cup of filter coffee that was already made, and kept warm by a machine.

"I'm afraid I'm not drinking coffee at the moment," Hilary felt embarrassed, and to make matters worse she could feel herself going red. "I said coffee, but actually, if we had gone to Gino's I would have had tea."

Paddy looked slightly irritated, but he smiled. "I am sorry, but I don't have any tea."

Paddy was tense; he was not displeased to see her, but he did not want this to take too long. Hilary suddenly felt very vulnerable, very much at a disadvantage. Why had she not been more sensible, and either written a letter or waited until he had more time?

"Paddy," she said, feeling desperate, and hearing a wobble in her voice.

"Yes." He had sat down now, and was concentrating on her, but still not on her wavelength. How could he not see how distressed she was feeling, how important what she had to say was?

"I'm pregnant." This was not how she had meant to give him the news. Hilary was still standing, in the office, while Paddy was sitting on a chair by his desk. It was like being in the headmaster's study, called to account for something she had done. A phone rang, behind them both. Hilary gestured towards it, almost grateful to have something else to focus on.

"Do you want to answer it?"

"No."

Paddy looked as if he hadn't quite taken it in. Hilary, feeling increasingly stupid, wondered whether she should repeat her news.

Paddy drew up a chair, a little formally. "Please sit down. You shouldn't be standing."

Hilary sat, gratefully.

"I thought I ought to tell you. No-one else knows."

"Of course," Paddy nodded. "I'm sorry. What do you want to do? Do you want any help from me? You mustn't feel alone in this. I'll give you whatever help I can. Help and support."

All-encompassing as these phrases were, Hilary sensed that Paddy wasn't thinking about a child. He was assuming that she would want a termination.

"I don't know." Hilary paused, hoping that Paddy would say something to make her feel better. He looked blank; again it was impossible to see what he was thinking.

"Paddy ..." Hilary paused and then said all in a rush. "I think I might want to keep the baby." She felt quite shocked, because this was the first time she had admitted this even to herself.

"Well, you will need to be sure. Thinking that you might won't be good enough." Paddy looked severe, but at last Hilary could perceive that he was actually upset.

But upset about what? The prospect that she would go ahead and have the baby? The inconvenience to him?

Neither of them said anything for a few seconds, and then Paddy said:

"This is something that you need to think about very seriously." He still had his stern tone. Was he treating her like a naughty child?

"I haven't made up my mind yet," Hilary adopted her own serious tone, and hoped that she was sounding very firm, "but I think that it should be my decision."

"Of course." Paddy was still expressionless.

Hilary kept looking at him, trying to sense his feelings, and guess his thoughts; neither showed through his face.

The phone rang again, and then another, in Ben's office, joined in. Hilary got up.

"I think I'd better go," she said, "I need to think a bit more. I think we should talk more, too."

Paddy was still looking blank.

"I do too. I'll ring you this evening." He stretched out his hand, and held Hilary's. Hilary knew that the outstretched hand was the most physical comfort Paddy could offer her. The hug that she had received on her way in was impossible. She got up, holding herself in check, and walked away.

Chapter 12

Paddy had a busy and very difficult day. He had a lot to concentrate on, but the news he had been given would never quite go from his mind. He felt a continuing urge to be in contact with Hilary. She had left his office so suddenly, and he had felt hurt. Not that he could have allowed her to stay, of course. The few moments he had spent with her, and hearing her shocking news, had already made him late for an important meeting.

Paddy was thirty-seven, and although he had put off the prospect of having children, it was something that came into his mind from time to time. He knew plenty about children, after being brought up with lots of cousins, and something about fatherhood, but the latter second-hand. His uncles had done their best to "treat him as their own" but Paddy knew that it was never quite so. They were fair men, and never gave favours, but the young Patrick was still aware that there was a depth and intensity of feeling that they had for their own progeny which never came his way. He saw the manner of paternal love, as shown to a child, but did not feel it being bestowed on him.

He had a spare half-hour towards the end of the day, and went to a favourite cafe for a cup of tea. It was a place that normally he only went to on his own. His own refuge. Sometimes he went there when life was treating him especially well, and wanted to have a few moments of private pleasure, but also when things went wrong. It was a very ordinary cafe. He usually drank their tea, which wasn't particularly nice, and sometimes he ate a sticky, sugary jam doughnut, that was very nice indeed. The owner was an elderly Spaniard, called Marcos, who had a gentle, sympathetic nature, and the waitresses were two middle-aged women, one cheerful and the other patient. They knew Paddy liked tea, and would sometimes ask him "whether today was a doughnut day". Today was not a doughnut day; and fortunately he was served by Maria, the patient one, who just brought his tea, and left him to think his own troubled thoughts.

He had always assumed that his children would also be Joss's children. That was going to make it easier for him. Joss was such an obvious mother. She would love his children, and care for them, and this would make it possible for him to love and care for them too. He tried not to think about Joss. He had so much to think about, he could not think about Joss as well. After all, it was Hilary who was pregnant. Was she serious about keeping the child? It seemed hard to believe. He must see her again soon, must speak some more. He was off to America the next day, and would be away for over a week. It was going to be very difficult to arrange.

In fact, it was Joscelyn that he went back to, and much earlier than planned. A BBC screening, which had seemed to be a crucial part of the day's events, was suddenly quite unimportant. At about eight o'clock, and without even making his customary phone call to warn Joscelyn of his arrival, Paddy went home.

It was a great relief to him to find Joss in the kitchen, making some soup. She often made a kind of thick, red soup, with carrots, lentils and potato. The recipe came from her mother, and Paddy knew that for Joscelyn the thick, soft texture of this dish represented warmth and domestic security. He didn't hugely care for it himself, but always ate it without complaint. He sometimes called it their "symbolic soup". Joss looked so good and honest, so untroubled, that Paddy felt a sharp pang of guilt, which was softened by the enormous relief and reassurance that he felt at seeing his wife, in their home. That morning's news had been so shocking. The simple fact that he still had a house, that the furniture was still in the same place, and that his wife was stirring soup, made life bearable and possible again.

Paddy poured out two glasses of gin and tonic, and put some peanuts in a little glass bowl for them both to eat. Joscelyn was still busying herself at the stove.

"Please come and sit down with me," Paddy said. "I have poured you a glass of gin, and I don't want to sit here and drink on my own. I want you with me."

"I'll be five minutes, and then this will be ready to go into the oven." Joss indicated towards some food that she was putting into a large, rectangular brown dish.

"Please sit down with me." Paddy's tone was urgent, and Joscelyn responded.

Paddy had, on the way home, told himself that he must break the news to his wife gently.

"I saw Hilary this morning," he said.

"Yes." Joscelyn sat quite still, and absolutely terrified. There was no sign of this in her face.

"She came to the office. I didn't really have time to meet her, with my American trip and everything else, but it was obvious that she had something important to say, and so I had to see her."

Joscelyn nodded.

"She's pregnant." Paddy spoke the words slowly, looking directly at his wife.

This, Joscelyn thought, is the worst thing that could ever happen to me. It is the worst thing that could happen, and now it has happened.

She looked across the room for a moment. In the window was a bunch of flowers, irises, one of her favourites, which she had bought that morning in Fulham Broadway. They were such a beautiful colour. How sad, that her life could never again be beautiful, or happy, as it had been in the past.

"What does Hilary want to do?" Joscelyn asked, already knowing the answer. There was more pain coming. Was she going to be able to bear it?

"We only had a very brief conversation. She said she might want to keep the baby. I don't know whether she means it. It would ruin her career."

Paddy paused for a while and drank some gin, while Joscelyn watched his troubled face.

"I would have to support her," he said.

Oh, God, thought Joss. So he would. That explained her feelings, the ones she had just now, looking at the flowers. This one would go on forever and ever. It wouldn't come to an end, like the affairs and flirtations had always done, and leave them happily together. Their lives, her life with Paddy, was ruined forever.

"Of course. It would be your responsibility. Legally, and morally too."

"Yes, but I don't just mean financially." Paddy looked stern. "She might need other kinds of support as well. I would have to give them to her."

"Of course." Joscelyn felt desperate. The phrase "children come first" echoed through her mind, and she saw an image of a real live, pink baby, Paddy's baby and Hilary's and not hers. Tears welled up in her eyes, and she tried to hold them back, but some spilled out, unbidden. Paddy looked uncomfortable, and got her a tissue.

"It'll be all right," he said, stiffly. "I won't let this upset us, Joss. We'll pull through, I know we will."

They ate some soup, or rather Paddy ate, and Joscelyn sat in front of her bowl, and twirled her spoon around in it. The main course was not cooked, because Joscelyn had not put it into the oven before they began drinking their gin.

"There isn't anything else to eat; I made an egg florentine, but I didn't put it in the oven." Joss suddenly felt great distress, and she was no longer able to prevent floods of tears rolling down her cheeks.

Paddy got up from the table, and came round and hugged his wife. "We'll have a proper meal together soon. I'll cook something for us. Tonight isn't a good time."

Even as her husband hugged her, Joss felt detached, almost as if she were watching the scene from outside the window. "Tonight isn't a good time," she thought, in response to her husband's words. Well, that's an understatement! Paddy wasn't normally a man for understatement, was he? If it hadn't been so awful, it might even have been funny, except that she had no desire at all to laugh.

Paddy saw Joscelyn looking brave, but desperately sad. It was just too awful. He couldn't cope with Joss being so upset. He didn't blame her, but he just couldn't cope with it.

He felt terrible. "I'm going to America tomorrow."

Joscelyn remembered. Yes, Paddy was due to go to America tomorrow morning. He wasn't even going to be there to comfort her.

"Do you have to go?" she said, knowing the answer.

"I must. It's work, Joss. Also, I must see Hilary tonight. I'm really sorry, Joss. I couldn't be more sorry, truly, but I only saw her for fifteen minutes this morning. It would be wrong to go off without having at least a proper conversation with her. I'll try not to be late. I want to be with you tonight."

This was said in the tone of a supplicant. Paddy fixed his eyes on his wife, and waited until she nodded, almost imperceptibly. Paddy hugged and kissed her and then got up. He went away to make a telephone call. Joscelyn stayed in the kitchen.

He put his head back around the door. "I've arranged to meet her. Just for a chat. You go and see Philippa. Please don't spend the evening here on your own. And don't worry. Hilary may see sense and not go through with it. That is definitely the best thing for her, for all of us. We'll be all right, though, whatever happens. I know we will." Something of the old confidence was back in his tone.

Joss said nothing in reply to this. She remained sitting at the kitchen table, and after about ten minutes, she heard her husband leave the house.

* * *

Hilary felt momentarily confused, and then very pleased and relieved when Paddy called her. He had told her that he could not see her again before he went to America, but he had obviously made the time, and was coming over.

He stood in her doorway, large and strong-looking, and she fell into his arms. He had never been to her flat before; and it felt odd, but also very good to have him there. They sat on the tiny sofa in her room, and held on to each other. This was what she had wanted this morning, the protective father to her child.

Initially all contact between them was physical. Paddy was aware of an overpowering feeling of protectiveness, and of pleasure that he had, albeit by such an unlooked-for route, got Hilary back again. He had no idea that he was going to feel like this, no idea until he saw her. The desire to be horizontal took them down onto the floor, and they would have made love, except that Hilary, with her pregnant body, started to feel uncomfortable. Her breasts were swollen, and sore, and in the middle of it all she began to feel sick again. This reminded her that what she really wanted was to talk to Paddy; to have some reassurance and understanding.

"I'm sorry; I'm not feeling too good. It's just to do with being pregnant."

"Of course," said Paddy, feeling disappointed.

"We should talk, really."

"Yes," said Paddy.

"Would you like some tea?"

"I'd like some coffee, if you have some."

Hilary made coffee for Paddy and tea for herself. The mood had changed, but she still felt that Paddy was with her, as he had not been that morning, when things were so rushed.

"I feel that I want to keep the baby."

Paddy wrinkled his brow. He was sitting on the very small sofa in the corner of Hilary's room. It was uncomfortable, and much too small for his legs and his back.

"Yes, you said this morning." His mood had changed as well. A few minutes ago the prospect of a Hilary pregnant with his child seemed very alluring. Not so now. She was making a great mistake.

"It's your decision, certainly, and I will respect that. But is this really in your best interests? Have you thought what this will do for your career? You're doing very well, as you deserve to, but you are only just starting off. This could be a disaster for you."

"I have thought of that. I think about it quite a lot. I haven't made any final decision yet. But I do feel that I want to keep the baby. Other single mothers manage."

"Not in the theatre. Certainly not at your age, without a reputation to sustain them. I would give you financial support, of course, but you know that I'm not around much. And I have Joss."

"I'm not asking you to be around more than you can manage. Of course I'll be grateful for your support, financial or otherwise." Hilary knew that what Paddy was saying was reasonable. He spoke quite firmly, and she told herself that it was his tone and not his words that she objected to.

"Is this a point of principle? Keeping the baby?"

Paddy didn't have any moral objections to abortion himself, but he had been brought up in a community where many people had. Hilary was the kind of person who would do something on principle.

"No," Hilary felt herself beginning to waver as she was asked to justify her decision, " I just feel that I want to."

"But is that a good reason for making such a major decision? One that could ruin your life - ruin two people's lives? Supposing you feel differently when you have the baby, supposing then you feel that you don't want it, what will you do then?"

"I haven't made any final decision." Hilary didn't want to argue. She was sitting on the bed, which was the only place available, other than the floor. She really didn't want Paddy to join her. This was difficult enough with him on the other side of the room.

Paddy was annoyed. This was so unlike Hilary, to be behaving like this. She was such a rational person. Even he had recognised, much as he had disliked her decision, that when Hilary had ended the affair with him she had done so in order to take care of herself. Why was she not doing so now?

"This really isn't like you," he told her. He got up and walked towards the bed. "You are more grown-up than this. You have a good career ahead of you. A life to lead."

Hilary was angry now. She put up her hands, as if to keep Paddy away from her. There were few things she disliked more than being told that doing something that she wanted to do was "not like her". Her mother sometimes used this tactic: "Now Hilary, I know this isn't really like you."

"I can have both and a child. Plenty of women do."

Paddy had stopped moving, and was standing a few feet from the bed, with Hilary on it. "Yes, that is true, and all credit to them, but they usually plan things and get established in their careers first. They also spend time enjoying themselves. Travelling, going out and meeting people, or one of the hundreds of other things that you can't do when you have small children."

Hilary felt overwhelmed with anger, which, instead of erupting in rage, welled up in tears. She tried to hold them back, but one large drop of salt water began to run down her cheek.

"I think you'd better go," she told Paddy, trying to keep her voice calm. "We can discuss this another time."

"I'm going to America tomorrow. For ten days." Paddy felt bad, looking at Hilary's pale face and the single tear, but he felt angry too. Although his reason told him that staying and haranguing Hilary now was unlikely to change her mind, to simply walk away and let her ruin her life in this way would be just ridiculous.

"I will use that time thinking about what I want to do, and we should meet when you get back."

Hilary had rallied all her moral strength, and was looking calmer now. Paddy put his arm round her, and she accepted the gesture. He felt protective again, and again he felt that strange pleasure in the thought of her being pregnant with his child. He looked into Hilary's face. A moment ago she had been angry, and now she looked up at him, fondly.

He kissed her. A long moment passed.

"I think you should go now."

"I don't want to." Paddy was making an appeal. Hilary, however, wasn't going to submit.

"I'll get your coat."

"Don't you worry," Paddy said. "I'll get it."

On his way home, Paddy went to his office, and listened to some Mozart on CD. His office was equipped for all-night negotiations with foreign lands, and he even had a camp bed there. He would have liked to stay, on his own, but he knew that this would upset Joss.

Even so, it was nearly one o'clock in the morning when he reached the marital bed. He woke Joss, who had been asleep, but only for about half an hour. Before slipping into unconsciousness, she had been thinking of various people in her life, and what they would say if they knew that a girlfriend of Paddy's was pregnant. Her brother James might be supportive, but her father would castigate her endlessly for her foolishness in marrying Paddy in the first place. Her relationship with her father, already strained, would become impossible.

She was reluctant to tell Philippa. Paddy would urge her to go to Philippa for support, but she didn't even want to do that. This was such a difficult subject; it made her feel so vulnerable. She didn't want to open up that vulnerability, even to Philippa.

As she thought about it, Joscelyn realised that, at the moment, the only person she wanted to talk this through with was Paddy. He was the one who had caused this problem, and he was her husband, the closest and most important person in her life. It was from him that she wanted comfort. It was with him that she would need to find some way forward, in this dreadful new world they were now in.

Eventually, though, other people would have to know. Bit by bit, she hoped, not all at once. And then an awful thought struck her mind; supposing Barbara got to know? Thank goodness she was so far away, and thank goodness Paddy wasn't in contact with her just now. How pleased Barbara would be to hear of Joscelyn's troubles.

This thought, in all its full horror, finally stirred Joss into feeling a little courage, a little defiance. Never mind what people thought, even if those people were as malicious and horrible as Barbara. She and Paddy would survive this. Anyone who thought that what she and Paddy had together would be destroyed by the first serious difficulty of their marriage didn't reckon on how tough Joss was. She was no quitter.

Even so, when Paddy finally got under the duvet, next to her, Joscelyn kept her eyes firmly closed, and said nothing.

Chapter 13

Paddy went to America, and Joscelyn missed him terribly. She found herself waiting, and hoping, every day for a phone call from him, feeling a great sense of relief when one came and pain and disappointment if there was nothing. Sometimes she would call his hotel and leave a message. Of course this didn't make her feel any better, but she couldn't help doing it.

Paddy sent several messages, which repeatedly urged her to spend time with some of the new friends that she had been making via the Open University, or contact Philippa. This really annoyed her. Paddy had caused her present unhappiness, but his only solution to it seemed to be to palm her off onto the care of others. Responding like a rebellious child, she remained resolutely alone for the ten days her husband was away. Some days she managed to be busy, and to clear her mind sufficiently to do her course work. On others she felt low, did little, and the time passed slowly and painfully.

It was on one of these days that her father called, wanting to arrange a visit. She had promised this, at their last meeting, but the prospect of her father, in their already unhappy house, was just more than she could bear.

"I could do with a break myself," she found herself saying, "and some country air and walks. Paddy's away a good deal at the moment. Why don't I come down for a weekend?"

"You know that I'm not well enough to go on any walks with you," was her father's response.

"I'll be happy to go on my own. Or maybe Mary will want to come with me." Mary was an old school friend, who still lived in the village where they had both been brought up.

"I imagine Mary will be far too busy." Her father's tone implied that his daughter's suggestion was one of pure selfishness. There could be no possibility that her old friend might actually welcome any contact, "Her husband is not away all the time, and she is kept very much occupied with her mother, who is not at all well."

"I'll go on my own then," Joscelyn kept her tone resolutely cheerful. "And I can cook us some nice meals. If you like I'll take you into Bath on Saturday."

Father often complained that he didn't get into Bath much these days.

"Bath is impossible on a Saturday. Full to the brim of shoppers and tourists. And my digestion is poor these days. I have to be very careful what I eat."

"I'm sorry," Joscelyn found herself apologising, "I could come mid-week, though, some time."

"Oh, I don't want you to put yourself out," replied her Dad, sourly.

This was the familiar point which Joscelyn reached in so many of her telephone conversations with her father when she wanted simply to put the phone down, and leave the cantankerous old man alone. But, as usual she persisted, and arranged a date for her trip.

Seeing her father, difficult as it would be, would at least be an old familiar difficulty, and might relieve some of the tension of her present situation.

Paddy had managed to put Hilary, Joscelyn and his child out of his mind, at least to a certain extent, while he was away. The distance, the different landscape, and people all helped. He knew that Hilary would not be in contact, and that helped, too. It was best, he realised, that he didn't pressurise her, but this was difficult to resist when they were together. She was basically a sensible person, and that ought to count for a good deal.

On the plane home, it was of course the first thought to come into his mind. He didn't really understand when she spoke about having the child "feeling like" the right thing to do. Women did sometimes talk this way. Paddy reckoned that he understood women fairly well - at least he ought to - and he liked and sympathised with their tendency to follow their emotional instinct in everyday matters. But in something so important, so potentially disastrous as this, that would be just plain stupid.

He wondered again whether behind it all was some moral sense. Hilary was a principled sort of person. She might feel morally obliged to keep a child, although this conflicted with the liberal gloss she put on life. Paddy would be able to understand that. He could respect it. He had always admired people who did things on a point of principle. And if it was a moral stand, it was something you did regardless of the hardship involved. Had Hilary and Paddy ever been any sort of couple, she would have been the one who took stands on a point of principle, and he would have felt strength through association with her.

Thinking this way made him feel very fond of Hilary again. He imagined her keeping the baby (would it be a boy or girl?) and being very brave and strong. She would be a very conscientious mother. Joss would be a natural, but Hilary a very committed parent. It would be his duty to help care for her and the child.

As he allowed his imagination a little freedom, Paddy started to see himself living with Hilary and their child. He wouldn't lose Joscelyn, of course; that would be unthinkable. And she would have to stay in the new house; it meant so much to her. But she had her course, which she fortunately seemed to be enjoying. This might be a good time for her to start her teacher training. Actually, now he came to think about it, that would really be good for her. She still suffered from her father's tyrannical refusal to support her education. Joss still felt (although he was quite sure that no-one else did) a little inferior from only having been a secretary, when his women friends, and even hers, were usually university graduates with good careers. It would be a big boost to her confidence.

Wandering a little more into fantasy, Paddy thought how much he would like to put these two women into one. In his dreams, it didn't seem so unreasonable a desire. Hilary's challenging mind, her talent, her capacity for commitment, with Joscelyn's devotion, calm and even wisdom. Between them they would make the perfect wife, and of course the perfect mother.

The plane touched down, and he was in London, where Hilary and Joscelyn were still two, not quite perfect, people.

Joscelyn heard the message on the answer machine, which told her that Paddy was back on British soil. Normally, this would have pleased and comforted her, but today she felt annoyed. Paddy was vague about his return time. This was not unusual, but she still felt that this time he could have done better. They had had virtually no time together since the terrible news. Paddy had spent most of his last night before he went away with Hilary. She, Joscelyn, had been helpful, supportive, as she always was. Surely, the promise of an evening at home with her was not too much to ask?

Joscelyn also realised that he had not rung her as soon as he landed. From the time of the return flight, she deduced that his call had not come from the airport, but somewhere else later on. Normally, Joscelyn left Paddy to his own devices, feeling confident that she would not be forgotten. That confidence was beginning to waver, and she felt the unpleasant churning of suspicion inside her stomach.

She was booked that day to have lunch with Ben, and during the morning she thought about her lunch date, not because of the prospect of spending time with Ben, but because she was to meet him at the office, and Paddy might be there. If he were, then she would have a chance to judge his attitude to her, and a natural opportunity to ask him when he would be coming home.

When she arrived, however, Paddy was not there. Where was he then? Had he gone straight to Hilary?

Ben was very pleased to see her. Joscelyn felt grateful, and just a little guilty that she had virtually forgotten that the reason for coming to Wardour Street was to see him.

"And here you are, fresh from your studies." Ben smiled warmly. "I thought we'd try somewhere new. It's about ten minutes walk. Is that OK?"

That was fine. It had just started to rain, but Ben had a large umbrella and there was plenty of space for both of them to shelter. Ben was cheerful. One of his recent business ventures had just prospered, and he was touchingly proud of himself.

"What does he do with his money?" Joscelyn wondered. She had never been to his flat. She knew he went abroad a lot, but she wasn't quite sure how much for work and how much for pleasure. At the moment at least, there didn't seem to be a woman in his life.

"And what will you spend the money on?" she said boldly, but attempting a jovial tone.

"This and that. I may buy a picture. And as I'm such a sensible person, I daresay some of it will end up being invested."

Joscelyn considered asking him what kind of pictures he liked, but feared betraying her ignorance of art when he gave his reply.

They ate French onion soup, delicious, in a quite unaccountable way, when it was just onion in a brown stock, with bread and melted cheese.

"I've tried making this myself, but it just tasted like onion in flavoured water." Joscelyn smiled wryly.

"I've never even tried." Ben smiled back.

There was a pause in the conversation, and Joscelyn's thoughts went back to Paddy.

"What's troubling you?" said Ben.

Despite being difficult to pin down himself, Ben could be disconcertingly direct in asking about other people's emotions.

"Oh, nothing much," Joscelyn felt flustered, and thought she must be going red. But she felt that she should offer some sort of explanation.

"My father is getting very difficult these days. He wants to come and stay with Paddy and me, even though he doesn't seem to enjoy his visits and he and Paddy don't get on. I've arranged to go and stay with him instead, but he seems very grumpy about it. So of course I'm not really looking forward to going."

"Why go, if it's not what either of you wants?"

"He does want to see me. He gets lonely. He's just extremely cantankerous these days. In fact he was always difficult. And I shan't mind having a bit of time away."

"So Paddy gets home, and you go away. Perhaps this is a recipe for happy married life."

"Well," Joscelyn recognised that Ben was on to something. She struggled for words, and was unable to resist the desperate wave of sadness rising inside her, "I suppose that Paddy and I aren't having a particularly good time at the moment."

She put down her knife and fork, and avoided Ben's eye, in an attempt to recover her calm, and think about what she should say.

"A girlfriend of Paddy's is pregnant. We knew about it just before he went to America. She hasn't decided whether or not she's going to keep the baby."

A tear formed in her eye, and started to roll down her cheek.

"I haven't talked about it to anyone," Joscelyn felt a bit foolish saying this. As if it mattered to Ben whether he was the first or fortieth to receive the news.

Ben was looking straight at her.

"I'm so sorry," he said.

Joscelyn had recovered her calm, mostly through the shock of realising what she had just done. She had never before confided in Ben about her relationship with Paddy. She wasn't even sure how much Ben knew about Paddy's other women.

"I suppose this was always a risk, but you must be feeling awful about it," said Ben.

Evidently he knew quite enough not to be surprised.

"I'm fine," said Joscelyn resolutely. She'd been coping well. She really didn't want Ben to think she wasn't coping.

"I shouldn't have bothered you about it. I meant to go and have a good chat to my friend Philippa, but I haven't seen her since the news."

"You are too independent sometimes. Your friends are there to help you."

"That's what Paddy says," said Joscelyn, with a wry smile.

"Well, it's right. I can see that it might be annoying if Paddy says it, if you think that he's the one who should be helping you. But we are here for you. I think that you should try and forget whether or not it suits Paddy, and think only about whether or not it suits you."

How does Ben manage to be so perceptive? thought Joscelyn.

And so she talked, and talked, and Ben listened. She told him about Minerva, and the awful Barbara, as well as one or two others, as if in order to explain her current predicament and feelings she had to tell her whole story. In fact she was only just getting onto Hilary when they had both finished their coffees and lunch was indisputably over.

"You need to get back to the office now," Joscelyn told Ben, a little shamefacedly.

"I'm afraid I do."

"I'm sorry to have bothered you with all of this," said Joscelyn.

"It's OK," said Ben. "We must do this again soon."

Joscelyn felt uncomfortable. "I shall have to tell Paddy I've told you."

"Of course." Ben was getting into business-like mode. "I shall be very discreet. Not a word to a soul."

Ben paid the bill, and before they left he said, "Joscelyn, you are such a strong person. All the ups and downs you have had. Paddy panics and gets into a state and you are so calm, and so brave. But you don't always need to be. Paddy can look after you sometimes. Your friends can look after you. And one day you may have a problem that you just don't want to take onto your own shoulders and then you can say you just won't deal with it. You really can."

"Does Paddy panic, do you think?" Joscelyn was secretly pleased that Ben had spotted this. Paddy did panic. She was his steadying force. But most of the outside world seemed to think that he was the strong, dominant one, not her.

"Of course he does. Remember I've known him longer than you have, if not quite so intimately. Long enough to notice these things. But I have also noticed something about you, and that is that you do a number of things that don't really seem to be in your own best interests. I don't doubt your courage, but I do question your wisdom, sometimes."

As she walked back to the tube station, Joscelyn thought about this advice. It seemed rather inappropriate. She could hardly say that Hilary having a baby was something she wasn't prepared to deal with, could she? After all it was out of her hands. If Hilary decided to keep the baby, there would be nothing Joss could do about it.

Hilary spent the weekend when Paddy was away with old friends of the Mackay family, who lived in the country. In the cosy atmosphere of their home, she wished she could talk to them about her situation, but she didn't really know them well enough. In fact, Hilary realised, she had chosen them partly because they were not on sufficiently intimate terms with her to tempt her into a confession. She had, rather like Joscelyn, been avoiding her close friends for a while. Their presence, their concern for her might induce her to let out her secret. There would be so much she would have to tell, and she wasn't ready for that yet. So far, she hadn't really told any of them anything about Paddy. And now there wasn't just Paddy to tell them about. It was all just too much.

Sometimes she thought about her mother, and how she would react. It was bound to be horrible. Hilary even tried to plan how she could get away without telling her family at all, but reason had to dictate that this simply wouldn't be possible. Reason also told her that she had to make a decision about the baby. She had more or less told Paddy that he would hear that decision on his return from America, and this gave her a deadline.

The day before Paddy's return, she wrote him another letter. It was quite simple really. There was no agonising to do. It was simply a question of finally being open about what she had known all along. She would keep the baby. She would appreciate Paddy's support, she told him, but would not expect it. If necessary, this was something that she would do alone.

* * *

Paddy did return to Joss early that evening, and his customary phone call came from the car just five minutes beforehand. He looked tired and was easily irritated. Joscelyn poured him a glass of gin and tonic.

"I'll have a glass of whiskey, thank you," he said.

Joscelyn felt rejected. Paddy always had a glass of gin after a hard day. He only drank whiskey for colds, or sometimes after dinner, if they had a formal dinner party.

Paddy sat in silence with his whiskey, with Joscelyn and two glasses of gin and tonic opposite him. After a short while, Joscelyn could wait in silence no longer.

"Have you heard from Hilary?"

"Yes, there was a message at the office." Paddy sat for a few more long seconds, in silence.

"She's going to keep the baby."

"I thought she might." Joscelyn felt unbearably sad, and part of that sadness was resignation. She was not surprised.

Paddy still said nothing, and for a few agonising seconds Joscelyn was left alone with her own grief. Then she said,

"Oh Paddy, what have you done to me?"

She looked at him, waiting for his anger. He always responded to reproach with anger. In his way of operating, attack was the best means of defence. But it didn't come. Instead he came and put his arms around her.

"I know. This is all my fault. I have done something dreadful and I couldn't be more sorry. I don't know how I am ever going to make it up to you."

This was disarming. Joscelyn had never heard him talk like this before, and she felt confused. She looked up at him, and kissed him.

Then he said,

"I will need to give Hilary some support." He spoke resolutely. "She says that she is prepared to have the baby on her own, but I don't think that she should have to. I am responsible."

"Of course," Joscelyn said bravely. Here, in all the awfulness of the situation, was something she could be proud of Paddy for. He was not a bad man. But surely Paddy only meant providing financial support? Of course he would have to do that.

"What kind of support do you think you will give?"

"I don't know yet. She and I will have to discuss it."

"And you and I will have to discuss it. It will be my concern as well."

"Of course I will talk to you. You are my wife."

Joscelyn didn't feel much reassured by this answer. The problem was such a large and practical one. Was he talking about contact with the child? That would certainly involve her, but it was all so far off and she didn't feel ready to think about that yet.

Again she had that feeling of being outside the room, looking at the two of them. She watched herself say, "Shall we lay the table? I have made supper."

"Of course." Paddy looked tenderly at her. She watched his tender expression. She was supposed to be comforted, reassured by it, but she wasn't. She was feeling too numb for either the bad feelings or any of the good ones to get through.

Paddy got up to make the coffee, but before doing so he hugged her.

"I know that this isn't easy for you. Have your friends been looking after you while I have been away?"

Joscelyn hesitated for a few moments.

"I know that you will need some support." Paddy's tone was measured and reasonable. "I presume that you have spoken to Philippa. But I don't think we should be telling everyone about this, at least not at the moment. Will you be sure to let me know who you've told?"

Joscelyn felt herself going red. "I hadn't told anyone; until today. I had lunch with Ben, and it just slipped out."

"You told Ben?" Paddy was shocked. "Why didn't you tell Philippa? Did you see her while I was away?" He was angry now, and shouting.

"No," said Joscelyn, taking a deep breath.

"Why not? I told you to!"

Joscelyn felt her hands sweating. Paddy was behaving just like her father. He wasn't normally like this. She forced herself to remain calm. He responded better if she could remain calm

"I don't think that you should be ordering me to see my friends."

"No, but - " Paddy looked exasperated " - It would have been all right to tell Philippa. You would have felt better; she would have supported you. But Ben! I work next to him, for heaven's sake."

"He's a friend of us both."

"Listen, if I want to tell any of my friends then I will. I don't need you to do it for me."

"He said he would be totally discreet." Joscelyn's eyes started to water. This was just like it had been when she was six, and dealing with her father. Now she was going to cry. "I didn't mean to tell him, it just happened."

Paddy looked at her sternly.

"Well, it mustn't happen again. You must not mention it again to Ben. In fact I think that it would be better if you didn't see him for lunch again. You may tell Philippa, but no one else without my express permission. Is that all right?"

Joscelyn shook her head. Paddy wasn't her father. He didn't normally behave like this, and anyway, she wasn't going to let him.

Paddy was still looking stern. "It's not just for me. It's for Hilary. I think she deserves some privacy."

Joscelyn looked at Paddy, and said,

"I understand how you feel. I feel the same way myself, in fact. I don't want all and sundry knowing about our private unhappiness, at least until we have found a way of coming to terms with it a bit better. Hilary has got herself into this situation and her privacy has to be her own lookout. But I will look out for yours and mine."

Paddy was glaring at her. The angry words would be coming soon. Joss braced herself.

"I will consider your request not to see Ben for a while."

Paddy got up. "I hope you will."

Then he went upstairs, to his study, saying that he had work to do.

Chapter 14

For Hilary, the moment when she had finally told Paddy that she was resolved to keep her child was such a momentous one that she expected her whole life to change after it. But it did not. She spoke with her doctor, who had been kindly and professional and arranged for her to have the appropriate antenatal care. She told her manager at work, who again had been concerned and professional, and had told her that she might have a short period of maternity leave, and then finish her year's contract.

After a few weeks, she spoke also to just one of her girl-friends, who was shocked and very obviously worried about her, and to such an extent that Hilary became cautious about imparting her news any further. She avoided quite a few normal social invitations, using work as an excuse. As a result her life became smaller and more contained. In fact, outside work it became confined virtually to the four walls of her own room. She continued writing to Peter in Milan, but made no mention of her pregnancy.

Three months after she had told Paddy, and six months into her pregnancy, she was feeling well, and a little stout; but she could still (if she chose her clothes carefully) pass for a simply more substantial version of her normal self.

Contact with Paddy had been problematic. The time they spent together veered disconcertingly between the almost blissfully happy and the downright unpleasant. On the former occasions

Hilary's heart would plan a happy ever after, and even her head would be persuaded to some arrangement where Paddy was an involved father and offered her "support" in ill-defined terms. On the others, she looked at the increasingly disturbing prospect of going it all alone.

The last occasion had been one of the bad times. They had been to the theatre, and Paddy had arrived late. Neither of them had enjoyed the play, and Hilary had been very irritated by the fact that Paddy had wanted to spend a good long part of supper afterwards dissecting the weaknesses of plot and performance. Hilary really would have appreciated a break from this kind of discussion, after a long day at work with a production that was not going well in rehearsal. She had less patience in her pregnant state, and became easily tetchy.

She also found that being a couple of hours late for a meal could make her feel quite weak with hunger. Although she had explained this to Paddy, he had refused to do what she would have liked, which was to dive into the first restaurant they saw which had space and the prospect of prompt service. Instead he insisted on walking to his favourite Chinese and then waiting what, to Hilary, seemed an endless fifteen minutes for a table. At the end of the meal, he had become serious and explained to her (for what seemed to be the hundredth time) that he had no intention of leaving Joscelyn, even if he offered her "support".

In her rosy-edged moments Hilary had imagined Paddy leaving Joscelyn for her. She had only a vague notion of Joscelyn as a real person, and in fact could only just remember what she looked like. When she had first met Paddy, she had been clear in her mind that she must not do anything to disturb his marriage; but now, as the mother of his child, she really did have a special claim. She did not plan to ask Paddy to leave Joscelyn, but sometimes felt that at some point he would be bound to see sense and do so.

So this time, when Paddy said, "You realise that my first loyalty is to Joscelyn. I won't be leaving her," Hilary had replied rather testily, "I know. You have told me lots of times. I am quite clear about that. But you do talk in rather vague terms about offering me support. And, I presume, you will feel that you owe some kind of loyalty to your child, when it is born. I'd like you to think about exactly what you will be able to offer me."

"All right," Paddy had said, "I will."

Hilary heard nothing from Paddy for nearly two weeks, and then one dark December evening he rang, asking if he could call round. He did this sometimes, and had even stayed the night once or twice. It was nine o'clock. Hilary had had a long day, and a hard week, and was just planning to go to bed, to re-read a section of a well-thumbed copy of *Middlemarch*. It was so good to hear from him, indeed from anyone, in her current state of self-imposed loneliness, that she agreed at once. Paddy arrived within twenty minutes and it was a huge relief to see his large body, familiar face and warm smile in her doorway.

Paddy made more tea for her and some coffee for himself. He explained that Joscelyn had decided to go away for the weekend. Hilary noted that Joscelyn going away on her own was something that seemed to be happening rather a lot recently, and wondered what significance this had. Paddy had told her that Joss was being "wonderful and supportive" about the baby, but she found herself wondering what that meant, in practice.

They chatted for a while. Paddy settled himself a little uncomfortably on the very small sofa that was somehow not even big enough for one person of normal size, and Hilary lay on the floor, a position she found increasingly comfortable these days. Hilary was pleased that Paddy was there. He would stay the night now, and she already felt a sense of warm anticipation. It would be very good to have his comforting body in her bed. There would be no harm in it. It would be just a nice thing to do.

"I have given some thought to your questions," Paddy said.

Hilary couldn't remember asking any questions. She looked up at Paddy. He was calm, but a little serious, with some furrows in his brow.

"About what support I shall offer you, in practical terms, once the baby is born."

Hilary remembered her words. It was a surprise to see that

Paddy had obviously taken them so seriously. She felt rather embarrassed.

Paddy started to talk about money, in a calm, lawyer-like way. He explained that his legal responsibility was only to help maintain the child, but that he wanted to give her some financial support as well. They had had that conversation before, and Hilary's embarrassment turned quickly to irritation.

"Yes, you have told me. And I am grateful. But I do intend to work and earn my own living. I shall be happy to accept help from you as an interim measure, but I don't expect to need it forever. Not for myself, that is."

She heard herself talking rather formally, as befitted the subject matter.

Paddy was still looking grave.

"It may be some little time before you earn at all well, especially with your chosen career. I think you may find that supporting yourself is all very well, but even providing suitable accommodation for a child won't be so easy."

Hilary looked at him sulkily.

"We have had this conversation before," she said.

"And we have also spoken about support in terms of time, as well as money." Paddy was still using his lawyer-like voice. "You raised the point, by asking exactly what support I would offer. I have been thinking about it. You were right to ask. I can see that me coming and going as I do now isn't going to work in the future."

Hilary looked straight at Paddy. He had an unusual calm in his face.

"I think that we ought to think about some more structured arrangement."

"Structured?" Hilary was completely taken off guard. Whatever could he mean?

"To give you some stability and security. And for everybody's sake, so that we all know where we stand."

Hilary just looked at Paddy, waiting for his words.

"I thought that I should stay with you at least two nights a week.

As far as possible they should be the same nights." Paddy's face started to look a little agitated, but his voice remained measured.

"I have been thinking that I ought to help you find a place to live. Somewhere that suits us both. You will need some help with all the practicalities, as well. It's not fair to leave you to sort out all that yourself. And there are the weekends, of course."

Paddy took a breath, and then continued, with Hilary's eyes on his face. "I would have to share those out."

Hilary looked at him, feeling almost dispassionate about the man. She could see dark circles under his eyes, and his voice was losing the professional calm.

"Joscelyn has taken to going away on her own quite often at weekends, which is a good thing. So I shall be free some weekends anyway. I am still thinking it through. I would like you to think about it too."

Hilary was stunned. Before any coherent thoughts found their way into her head, she found herself saying,

"What does Joscelyn think about all this?"

"I haven't spoken to her about it yet. It was you who asked me to consider arrangements, and so I am broaching it with you first. She is a sensible and compassionate person."

Some feeling got through to Hilary, at last, and it was anger. Unexpected anger, on Joscelyn's behalf. Why should Paddy be relying on his wife's good sense and compassion? It was truly awful. If she were Joscelyn she would be very angry. And then her own feelings flooded in, disappointment, outrage, all intermixed with shame that she had so completely failed to face the facts of her situation, of the practical implication of the "support" that she and Paddy had talked about.

Paddy's proposal simply would not work. Not for her. He would pay for a flat, but it would not be her flat. He would have a share in it, in the same way as he would have a share in her. She would be a part-time partner. She had contemplated this certainly, but never on so calculated a basis. Paddy would have a time-share in her, and as a result she would lose her independence and gain – well, she would gain some security, it was true, but not the kind of relationship she wanted.

She got up from Paddy's feet, and walked a few feet across the room. Then she sat down again. She looked at Paddy, hating him. Hating herself, for refusing until now to face the consequences of her own expectations.

Strong as her emotions were, she did not feel capable of expressing them. "I shall have to think about this. I think it might be quite problematic. I need to think."

"Of course." Paddy seemed quite relieved not to have a definite response straight away. "Look, we could both do with a break. Why don't we get out of London tomorrow? There's a new West-End try-out in Oldchester I want to see. We could have a gentle walk in the countryside, a pub lunch and a night away."

"Oldchester?" Hilary reacted in outrage, all her inner turmoil beginning to erupt out of her.

"Yes," Paddy looked quite hurt, but she did not notice.

"I do not want to go to Oldchester. And most particularly I don't want to go to the theatre there. It's not a real theatre, a place where real theatre actually happens. It's for people with more money than sense and no artistic taste whatsoever."

"If you say so," said Paddy.

They were both silent for a moment.

"Well, I'm going anyway," said Paddy. "I'm sorry that you're not coming with me."

"I'm not." Hilary heard the petulance in her voice, and disliked herself for it.

There was another pause.

"I think I'll go home." Paddy got up. "We obviously aren't getting on well at the moment. I'll call you in a few days, and we can have another talk."

Just before he opened the door, he said, "Do think about my offer of support. I think it's the best way forward."

Paddy was very hurt by Hilary's reaction. He had spent a lot of time thinking about his proposals, and they had caused him a lot of heartache. It had been right for Hilary to put him on the spot. He had felt good about himself that he had taken his future responsibilities seriously, and tried to come up with something that might suit everybody.

It wasn't going to be easy for him. He felt that Hilary's open challenges, and the rather passive, sad way in which Joss often looked at him these days, all presupposed that they suffered and that he, because he was in the wrong, did not. He did feel hugely guilty almost all the time, and although there was a sense in which he seemed to have got what he wanted - both Hilary and Joscelyn in his life - it was going to be very hard keeping everybody happy. And keeping everybody happy seemed to be his job. There were other aspects as well. He was being generous in offering to pay for a flat for Hilary. Financial generosity normally came easily to him, but this was going to be an appreciable sum on a monthly basis. His turnover was reasonable, but finances in his new line of work were always uncertain. Economy, except on a very small scale, was impossible. He was just going to have to work harder and be more successful.

He was hurt as well that she'd refused the trip to Oldchester. He knew that what she'd said was all hyperbole, as she'd been upset, and the theatre there wasn't going to be to her taste, because the productions weren't exactly cutting edge, but it was a decent place, and she shouldn't be so bloody politically correct about everything. Some things could be just an experience.

Also, although Hilary did not know it, he loved Oldchester because his beloved Aunt May used to take him there every summer, to stay with the Webb family. The father, Tom Webb, was large and genial, his wife Emily gentle and kind. They had a large, comfortable untidy house that was always full of dogs, cats and goldfish; and children, indigenous and otherwise. There was always space to spare, food to spare and love to spare. The young Paddy had felt comfortable, cosseted and cared for in that home as never before, and only since with Joss. He had lost touch for some years after Aunty May died, but had found the family again, and visited when he was at university. Tom and Emily were older of course, but endlessly welcoming to the sophisticated but inwardly tortured adolescent that Paddy had become. They were not there now, having retired to the Lake District, which had been Tom Webb's boyhood home.

Even without them, the small cathedral city still seemed warm and welcoming, whenever he went. Paddy had had it in mind to take Hilary and show her the suburban house, with its cherry tree, and let her into that part of his past life. It had been foolish, of course. It was just not her kind of place.

When he got home the house was cold. It was always cold when Joss wasn't there. Sometimes this was because he forgot to programme the central heating properly, but even when he did the lack of Joscelyn busying herself about, or curling on the sofa like a cat, with a book, seemed to lower the temperature by a few critical degrees. She was away with Philippa, in the country cottage that Alistair paid for but never visited. The two of them would be drinking a late-night cup of hot chocolate by the embers of an open fire and complaining about their husbands. Women always complained about their men when they got together.

Hell, he thought. What was so very awful about him and Alistair? They were both well-intentioned. Both cared for their wives in their own ways, as best they could. Joscelyn seemed not to care about him these days. He still cared for her; never mind Hilary and the baby. In the past, he had never doubted her concern for him; but these days she often looked at him in a distant, distracted way. He looked at the answer machine. Its small red eye refused to flash at him. She hadn't phoned, and Paddy felt quite bereft without her.

The next day he did go to Oldchester, but on his own. This was an uncharacteristic thing for him to do. Paddy was used to travelling on his own for business, and could be content enough with his own company for days and even weeks if there was a career objective in sight. The trip to the theatre was only really peripheral to his work; there was certainly no need for him to make a day and a night of it. He went, however, as a defiant gesture against Hilary, and also against Joscelyn. The two women in his life, both of whom, in their different ways, had refused to come with him.

Left to himself, without an objective or a companion, Paddy was conscious of just how much time there was in a day. By mid-afternoon he had done all those things that he had planned to do with Hilary, and was back in his hotel. He had been to see the Webbs' old house, which had new paintwork in an alarming bright blue colour, to the Cathedral, which was in an elegant Queen Anne square in the centre of the town. His hotel was cold, or rather cool; so that sitting in his room was just not quite comfortable enough. He made himself some tea, which tasted awful. It would have been better to go downstairs and order tea in the hotel lounge, where the armchairs were more comfortable and the room warmer, but he was not inclined to do so.

Paddy, who spent a good deal of his life happily and confidently alone, was left with an emptiness that was unpleasant to the point of actually being scary.

He thought of Hilary, and their very unsatisfactory meeting the day before. His suggestion hadn't gone down well. He had a suspicion that Joscelyn wouldn't be delighted with the idea either. He tried to imagine what it would be like to be a father. He couldn't. He thought of his own childhood, with his distant uncles, and Tom Webb, the one and only affectionate father figure he had actually known. His eyes filled with tears, and he felt sorry for his own past self.

Perhaps the child should come first. People always talked about children coming first. In his current predicament, thinking that way certainly made things easier; rather than trying to balance the concern he felt for his two women. This would mean living with Hilary, and while still caring for Joscelyn, asking her to take an important but less present place in his life.

He imagined himself telling Joss this, trying to think of the right words. "Responsibility" and "having no real choice" seemed to be the phrases he would have to use. At first, he felt a glint of pleasure; both at imagining himself being so selfless, and also at separating himself from Joss, who had been so cold towards him of late.

Then he thought of Hilary, who was so high-minded in such a

juvenile way. Who knew he was married, and who nevertheless made the decision to keep his child. She challenged him to define what support he could offer, and then was so sniffy and difficult when he made an honest attempt to do what she asked. Why should she be taking him away from the woman he loved? How dare she?

Anger, disappointment, sadness all culminated in something very like despair. Paddy sat in the small, anonymous room that seemed to be getting colder every minute and felt a real sense of panic. He was trapped. There were routes he could take, a bewildering choice of routes, but they all led to an uncertain and unhappy end.

Paddy sat quite still, for what must have been two whole minutes. Then, quite desperate for human contact, he went over to the telephone by the bed, and dialled a number that he knew off by heart.

It was a number in Dublin, Paddy's home town. It was not the first time that Paddy had considered contacting his friend Mike. His one male friend who had been at school with him, gone on a grand tour of Europe with him one summer holiday when they were both students, and who had become a lawyer in Dublin. Mike had the gift of being happy. Mike had been happy at school, for at least fifty per cent of the time, he'd been happy on long train journeys between Berlin and Budapest. He had met a girl in his first year at university, and married after graduation and the two of them loved and cared for each other and their two daughters. Mike could be irritable, he could be indignant, he could be worried. But life rewarded him with a basic pleasure in simply being alive, a pleasure that Paddy knew he never had. It gave Mike a happy marriage, and, quite effortlessly so it seemed, all the right skills to be a good parent. He was good to those people who came within the cloak of his concern, and miraculously Paddy had always been one of them. Mike had been a great support to him over the years. True, the two men had never discussed their problems or their emotions, except in the most general way; but then there was no need. Mike was on his side, and Paddy was grateful for it.

Mike, of course, was also a man. Paddy normally only spoke about his emotional life to women, and normally he wouldn't have had a problem for very long without finding a sympathetic female to share it with. But this time he wanted the support of his own sex, for it was only another man who might possibly understand the dreadful mistake that he had made, and the awful dilemma that he now faced.

But it was not easy. One reason why Paddy had not spoken to Mike already - apart from the simple fact that he simply wouldn't know where to start - was a fear that Mike was not the sort of man who would understand, because it was inconceivable that he would have made such a mistake himself. Michael Bradshaw was a decent man. He was tolerant of others, in a general way, but he himself would always have been a faithful husband and a reliable father. He might take the view that Paddy had done wrong, or at the very least been extremely foolish, and what's more he might say so.

Even as he lifted the receiver, Paddy contemplated the conversation taking this particular turn. He would admit to being foolish, but not to being wrong.

Of course it was not Mike who answered the phone, but one of his young daughters, who after a lot of persuasion managed to produce their mother. Paddy was about to give up on the call by now.

"I'd been hoping to have a word with Mike. But I imagine he's busy."

He had a picture of what was the Bradshaw family would be doing at four o'clock on a Saturday afternoon. Tea in front of a roaring fire, Paddy thought, conjuring up an image from the Webbs and his own childhood. Mike would be helping with Lego, or some other game, and his wife Anne would toast teacakes on the open fire with the aid of a long-handled toasting fork.

"No, I'm sure he'd like a word with you." Anne had a very tranquil voice, which somehow only served to demonstrate to Paddy how very nervous he felt himself.

Mike was cheerful, and asked after Joss, and business. It was

all very painful, especially talking about Joss. Then they reached the point in the conversation when Paddy would have explained his reason for ringing; a planned trip to Dublin perhaps, or some advice to be asked. Paddy hesitated, and Mike gave him the lead,
"So when are we going to see you in Dublin next?"
"I don't know. Life is rather difficult at the moment."
"Aha?" There was a gentle note of interrogation in his friend's tone.

So Paddy started to talk, at first awkwardly, but then all in a rush as the whole story came out. Just the story, though. Paddy longed to tell Mike how awful he felt, how torn, and how guilty, and how worried, but somehow he just did not.

Mike remained calm. He didn't seem at all surprised, which was a relief. He said that it was a great shame, and a very difficult situation. He asked where Paddy was, and Paddy felt strangely very embarrassed to admit that he was on his own.

"Joss is away. She has taken to going away on her own now and again. Her father isn't well, and sometimes she keeps her friend Philippa company on a trip away."

"Perhaps you should have a trip away. You'd be welcome here. We could play a game of squash, and go out for a Guinness."

It was a kind offer. Paddy realised that the Bradshaws were probably the only people he knew who would be offering him hospitality out of simple friendship. This made him feel bad, and somehow he didn't want to go. He didn't want to feel the difference between his situation and theirs.

"Yes, when I can find the time. Work is busy just now, which is a good thing in the circumstances."

As the conversation ended Mike said, "I'm here if you want to talk again." And then he said:

"This may not be for you, Paddy, but I'd recommend you talking to God about it. He cares, you know, whatever fix you're in."

Paddy and Mike had discussed theology before, on long train journeys across Europe. They had been young men then, and it had not been so personal.

"The trouble with God," said Paddy, "is that he has such an awful way of showing it."

On Sunday morning Paddy woke early, and he was home in Fulham by ten o'clock. The play had been OK, and he had managed a drink with the director and a couple of actors afterwards, which had made him able to justify the trip to himself a little more. Back in his London house, he was hit by that dreadful sense of emptiness again, an emptiness that stretched forward into an indefinite future. He sat in the kitchen after breakfast, with the Sunday papers in front of him. If Joss had been there, he would have made more coffee, and they would have argued in a friendly way over who read the interesting sections first. Without Joss there, none of it seemed appealing at all. There was no real news that week, only silly stories about ridiculously self-important people. Paddy considered phoning Joss, but decided against. Clearly, he couldn't speak to Mike again so soon and anyway he didn't know whether he wanted to.

It was then that he remembered Barbara and also that her Australian phone number was sitting in his address book.

He dialled it. Amazingly, she answered.

"Barbara. It's Paddy."

"Paddy!"

Now here was someone who really was pleased to speak to him. At last! For months, now, so Paddy realised, he had been battling against other people's unhappiness, dislike or disapproval, actual or imagined. But there was only the positive, the warm and the affectionate from Barbara.

"Just a moment, I'm just seeing someone out."

Barbara had to make a point of the fact that her life was busy, that she was in demand. She was always like that. But her voice told him that this other person was no competition.

Paddy hadn't meant to, but after an exchange of greetings, and learning from Barbara that "Australia was absolutely fabulous" and that she might be tempted to stay, if there were not "so much to bring me back home," he found himself telling Barbara about Hilary and the baby. He wasn't quite sure how, but Barbara homed in on his unhappiness (which in truth he didn't wish to conceal) and kept asking questions. It was easier the second time; he could even re-use certain phrases which set out the story in an efficient way. Even so, he wondered as he did so whether taking Barbara into his confidence might be a big mistake. She might take it personally and suddenly, he even imagined Barbara getting annoyed with him in the way Joscelyn hadn't, but other wives probably would have. So it was a relief when, before he had even quite finished, she interjected.

"Poor, poor you. Oh Paddy, what a terrible hard time you've been having. I do wish you'd told me before. I may be a long way away, but I can still listen, wherever I am. I can even write, you know!"

Barbara's jocularity could sometimes be a little heavy, but Paddy didn't even notice this now. Paddy started to say what he had not told Mike, about how bad he felt, how worried he was for the future.

"Of course," Barbara spoke with full feeling, "Of course you will feel bad. You are a nice man, Paddy. And of course you want to do your best for everyone, and the child. You would. You are the type of person that takes his responsibilities seriously. I don't think that everyone realises that about you, Paddy. You are a nice man ..." Barbara emphasised each word of the phrase, "and you mustn't forget yourself in all this. Hilary has made her own decision, and she obviously hasn't taken your situation into account at all, so you certainly mustn't be worrying about her. And as to your own domestic life, you know, this may be a bit of a signal. It *could* be that this has happened because you haven't been entirely happy in your home life. I think you need to think about yourself a bit more."

Encouraged by her tone, and not listening particularly carefully to her words, Paddy spoke some more. He found himself talking about Joscelyn, how she had been very half-hearted about her plans for the future. He had tried to encourage her to apply for teacher training, to give her something to focus on for the future, but she was being slow to make any decisions.

"Well, I think that it would be a very good thing for her." Barbara spoke even more emphatically than before. Paddy was a little surprised. Barbara had never expressed an opinion on what would be good for Joscelyn before. He wouldn't have thought that she had a view on the subject. "I think that in a situation like this she needs to be thinking about her own future. She shouldn't just be expecting you to be providing everything for her all the time."

"I had wondered whether she might want to have a baby herself. To make it seem better for her."

Paddy surprised himself by saying this. It was something that he had thought, sometimes, but he had not raised the subject even with Joscelyn herself, before.

"Would that really be wise, Paddy?" Barbara's voice went very quiet and serious.

"It might reconcile Joss to the situation. And we had always planned to have a family at some point."

"That's exactly what I mean, Paddy. You are not thinking about yourself enough. Could you really cope with being a father to two new babies?"

Paddy felt that he was losing Barbara's approval. "Maybe not," he said, a little vaguely.

Barbara brightened up, and was again telling him that he was a good man and that she felt sorry for him.

"Look at all the options in front of you," she said, bracingly, "and have a long, hard think about what's best. And remember that the choices in front of you may not just be the obvious ones. Sometimes, in a situation such as you are in, you need to think out of the box."

When Paddy finally put the phone down, he felt better than he had done in three whole months.

The conversation with Barbara must have lasted quite a long time, given that it was a daytime call to Australia, and Hilary, who had made three attempts to telephone him, had heard the engaged tone each time.

* * *

Hilary had spent a solitary weekend, and more than once had wished herself with Paddy in Oldchester. She'd thought a lot about his proposals, and was at a loss, a complete loss. They wouldn't suit her, but she didn't know what would. She wanted her independence, and central to that was that any flat (even if Paddy paid for it) must be hers, and not his and hers. Not unless they were to become a full-time committed couple, and that simply wasn't going to happen. For the first time in her relatively short life, she saw the value of money as a real source of independence.

The telephone call to Paddy was not to discuss any of these big issues, but just to be in contact again, and on good terms. She wrestled with her conscience a little, because although she had the number, she had never before rung Paddy at his home in Fulham. But she knew that Joscelyn was away.

The fact that the telephone was engaged when she rang first told her that he was probably at home; the fact that it was again the second time confirmed her belief.

The third attempt, which produced another engaged tone, just made everything clear. Paddy was one of those people who would always be on the phone. Anyone could have a long conversation to someone else. Anyone could have other commitments. But Paddy would never be available enough. He was married. Even if he were not, a relationship with him would always mean settling for too little. He was not the man for her.

But she did need to speak to someone. Without consciously making a choice, she dialled home.

"Hello darling." Her mother sounded apprehensive.

Preliminaries quickly over, Hilary said simply:

"I'm pregnant."

She explained, very briefly, that it had been a mistake. She had decided to keep the baby. She had liked the man who was to be the father, and had even wondered (she said for the baby's sake) if they could make a go of a relationship. But that wasn't going to be possible.

Her mother sounded almost relieved. "Oh, darling. I knew something wasn't right. You're so brave." There was a pause. "Darling, we'll help you all we can. All of us. Even your father, I'm sure he'll do whatever he can." Her mother's tone made it clear that her father's maximum efforts might not amount to very much.

"Hilary, you must come home. Promise me you'll come home next weekend."

"Yes," said Hilary gratefully. "I will."

Chapter 15

Joscelyn was away with Philippa and her three children. She was fond of all three little ones. Despite being well disciplined, well turned out and following the fashion of middle class families in having traditional names, James and Tom, for the boys and one unusual one, Tara, for the girl, they were bright and lively, energetic, quarrelsome and distinctively themselves. Joscelyn was pleased to be of help to her friend on these country weekends, a second adult to provide entertainment for the children in the day and companionship over a glass of wine in the evening.

Philippa, being Philippa, had country weekends organised to be right in every detail. She had bought the cottage in a somewhat derelict state, and had organised a small army of architects, builders, decorators and garden designers to transform it into a little haven that would have graced any glossy magazine. Interior design was just becoming fashionable in 1980s Britain. She had to apply to the local council to re-route a public footpath, which ran through the garden. (This was not covered in the glossy magazines and had been the main subject of several long telephone conversations between the two women.) Then, the garden behind the property was on a slope. Undaunted, Philippa had arranged for walls and terraces to be built, with steps and pathways between the various levels. There was a wood-burning stove in the kitchen, an open fire in the living room, and the garden even had a little summerhouse and a pond like the ones in the TV programmes. Although one could not feel exactly sorry for someone as energetic and competent as her friend, Joscelyn had in the past reflected that Philippa had everything except the love of her husband; at least love in any kind of present and active sense. She, Joscelyn, might live through uncertainty and domestic upheaval but could always bask in Paddy's warm affectionate need for her.

She watched the way Philippa made porridge for everybody at breakfast, while the children, wrapped in thick anoraks and hand-knitted scarves, played hide and seek in the garden. They looked like a living cliché of happy childhood; and later when they went for a walk even the weather seemed to be just right, with crisp white frost beautifully arranged on the local Hampshire hedgerows. These things seemed to serve as a tribute to the way in which Philippa, glowing with enthusiasm for life, went right out and took all that it had to offer her. Life did not offer her everything, of course, but Philippa really could make it seem as though it did. She made her own happiness; Joscelyn was dependent for so much of hers on Paddy.

Joscelyn still loved Paddy very much, but the act of loving was becoming more effort, more pain, more giving and less and less return. And of course Philippa had children. Three lovely, thriving children, all born of a faithful husband.

It was an action-packed weekend: a walk, a trip to the local town, a noisy game of Monopoly, children's supper, baths and stories. The first opportunity for real adult conversation came on the Saturday evening, when the children were upstairs.

It was Philippa who brought up the inevitable subject. "You seem low," she said.

"I have really been enjoying myself," Joscelyn replied. "It's just been a perfect weekend."

"Yes, you've been enjoying yourself, but underneath you are still low. It's not surprising exactly. You are entitled to feel unhappy."

Philippa had made a fire at tea-time, and during the early

evening, whilst the children had been having their baths and stories, it had died down to a few embers with just one good-sized lump of wood. Joscelyn rebuilt it, and now she puffed the still-glowing remnants with some bellows, energetically, to show that she was still capable of putting effort into life. Then, still looking at the fire rather than her friend, she said,

"I should have had Paddy's baby. What has happened is just wrong. I still don't believe it." Tears formed in Joscelyn's eyes. Philippa moved off the sofa, took her hand, and held it in both of hers. She could do that; there was something simple and direct about her.

"Of course you should." Philippa made statements that went with her simple, definite personality.

"There's no point in telling Paddy."

"Why not?"

"Well, he can hardly do anything about it now, can he?"

"Yes, but you needn't be asking him to do anything about it. You'd simply be telling him how you feel."

"It would only make him feel more guilty. He does feel very guilty." Joscelyn's tone was becoming more defensive of her husband.

"I expect he does. And it is quite appropriate guilt. I think that you could still tell him. He will live through it."

"I expect so."

"You should though; you should take the bull by the horns."

"I don't see why I should." Joscelyn spoke sharply. "You talk as if you believe that I would like to behave like you would, but just don't have the courage. I thought you knew me better than that. I admire you, Philippa, but I don't always want to be like you. I have a different way of doing things."

Philippa was silent for a moment. Joscelyn looked at her friend's impassive face. This was a real difference of opinion. Were they going to fall out over this?

"I know that you have plenty of courage. I've watched you over the years. You've been a great support to me, too and always when I've most needed it. But I think that you misdirect your strength, sometimes. And as your friend I do feel sorry about that. If you put half the effort you put into looking after Paddy into - well almost anything else, you'd be a real achiever. You already are a real achiever. You were just tremendously good at your old job and now you've got your course, and all those qualities we love about you: your sense of humour, your perceptiveness, and your optimism. There is so much more you could do. Paddy is capable of looking after himself. If you let him, it would free up so much of your time."

The fire was burning quite brightly now, and giving off a very comforting heat. Joscelyn put another log on the blaze, pleased that her efforts had been rewarded. It was good to have Philippa's concern, but she did not really agree.

"I don't spend time looking after Paddy. No more than most wives, anyway. He's very busy, and very capable."

"He is certainly both those things. Especially capable. Look, it's not just time I'm talking about, but energy; emotional energy. Joss, I just want to see you look after yourself a bit better. Now I know that that might shift the balance of your relationship with Paddy, and that would have consequences. Maybe consequences you don't want."

"But I should care for Paddy," Joss felt herself getting angry. "I'm his wife. And you needn't worry about me because I don't worry about myself."

"Yes, you should care for him, at least up to a point, and he should care for you."

This one hit home. Since the news about Hilary's baby, Paddy hadn't been doing a very good job of looking after her. Joss felt angry with her friend. Philippa couldn't have the moral high ground on this one. How much time did Alistair spend looking after her? Or the three children? But she said nothing.

"You are very stubborn, Joss. Did anyone ever tell you that before?" The two women looked at each other. Then Philippa shook her head.

"We could do with a cup of tea. Let me make it."

Their argument, Joss knew, would not spoil their friendship.

But on one point, Joscelyn was determined to be stubborn. She had spent years focussing on Paddy, rather than herself, feeling his pain, rather than her own. This was not the moment to change, to stop worrying about Paddy and begin worrying about herself. After all, now, she had so much to worry about. Perhaps more than she believed she could deal with, if she actually started dealing with it. Paddy's feelings, and his dramas, provided much too big a distraction to be abandoned now.

Paddy's guilt, in Joss's eyes, was going to be like Paddy's pain, more than he could bear. And it was Joscelyn's self-appointed task to save him from that suffering. She would do it for him.

* * *

The next day Paddy went into his office. It was Sunday afternoon before his wife's return. Waiting for him, dangling from the fax machine, were two pages of a hand-written letter from Barbara.

He tore the long strip of paper off the machine, and read. Barbara had very neat handwriting, slightly ornate, evenly spaced, and set in straight lines. She began by explaining that she was coming home from Australia in a few days' time, but that she had booked a long trip back by cruiser, which would take several weeks to reach Southampton.

"I am so sorry that I shan't be with you in person, all this long time," she said, but gave him, in great detail, instructions about how he could contact her on board ship. The rest of the letter reverberated with sympathy and concern.

"I am so very sorry about your current situation," she wrote, *"I could tell how sad, how worried, how responsible you felt. You are a nice man, Paddy. A concerned and responsible man ..."*

Paddy read, feeling warm and comforted, affirmed. Yes, he was a nice man. His guilt and the way that Hilary and Joscelyn had been treating him over the last months had robbed him of his self-esteem.

"You must remember yourself in all this, Paddy," she wrote. *"You talked to me about Hilary, the baby and Joscelyn, but you are important too. It was entirely Hilary's choice to have the baby, and you really must not take that onto your shoulders in a wholly inappropriate way. And you are important for your own, dear sake, and as the baby's father, but think less about your responsibility to others (which anyway they have taken upon themselves) and more about that to yourself. You and your feelings are important too."*

Paddy looked at these words. Yes, he was the father. This did make him important. He felt filled with pride, with confusion, and with fear.

"I am your friend," wrote Barbara, *"and as your friend I will help you all I can."*

These few lines having made such an impact on him, Paddy's eyes filled with tears of pleasure and relief. He read the rest with a little less care. Barbara wrote quite a full paragraph about Joscelyn. She expressed her view, very strongly. This would be a most unwise moment for Joscelyn to have a baby as well:

"She also has to find her own way out of this difficult time, and developing her own career would undoubtedly be the best thing for her. But Paddy, back to you. Sometimes a problem like this tells us something. You really do need to think what this problem tells you about your own happiness, and whether your own domestic life is as you want it to be."

Paddy didn't take this last advice too seriously. A career woman like Barbara was bound to urge professional success as a route to happiness. Besides, all couples had their difficulties. He and Joss managed pretty damn well, considering. But overall, he was delighted with the letter. He straight away typed and then faxed a few lines in response.

> "To the Good Ship Barbara. Avast and Ahoy and all that stuff. May your timbers never be shivered. Dear Ba, How good to have your fax. There really is no one quite like you. I always knew you were a fierce pirate when it came to sailing the legal sea, but in the last few days, through our phone call, and your fax, I have seen quite a different side to you. A more caring and compassionate side. You are the ship's doctor, the kindest port in a storm a man could wish for. It would be so good to see you again, instead of just squinting at you down the wrong end of a telescope. Enjoy yourself, but tell the captain full steam ahead. And tell him to keep his mainbrace to himself. Over and out, Paddy."

And then, wholehearted as he had not been for months, spent the afternoon working, with total concentration.

Joscelyn arrived back from the country in the early evening, and Paddy, as if psychic, appeared fifteen minutes after her. He was smiling, and carried a large bunch of red roses. Joscelyn was caught unawares. Paddy hadn't been like this for ages, warm, happy, all ready to engulf her with affection. She hugged him.

"I missed you," she said.

"And I missed you," Paddy replied.

Joss put the roses in water, and Paddy made them both a cup of tea. He put it on a tray, and took it into the garden room. They sat together on their large comfy sofa, and Joss told Paddy about her weekend away.

Just as she was describing the way in which the youngest, Tom, kept bringing her storybooks and sitting on her lap, Paddy interrupted:

"Don't you think you should have a baby?"

Joscelyn was startled.

Paddy was looking very earnest. Joscelyn was alarmed at this new turn of events, but this was a proposition that she could hardly reject out of hand.

"We have always meant to have children. And of course I still want us to."

"Then I think we should." Paddy spoke softly and deliberately as if talking to a small child.

"What, now?" Joss tried to make her tone humorous.

"As soon as practicable. I'd like you to have a baby. You'd be a wonderful mother. I think that it would be the right thing for you."

Joscelyn's head swam with confusion. Did she want a baby now? And why did Paddy want one?

"And what about you? Would it be the best thing for you?"

"Yes, I think so." He stroked her head, in a gesture that was meant to be comforting, but felt oddly patronising. "Then I can get into fatherhood in a big way."

"But perhaps that's not such a good idea. Perhaps one child at a time is quite enough."

Joscelyn put her cup of tea on the floor. This was such a serious conversation; she couldn't be holding teacups at the same time. She felt very aware of Paddy's large presence on the sofa beside her and she wished him further away, so that she had the space to think her own thoughts. Instead, she took his hand, and saw him look gratefully at her. Was Paddy offering her this as parity with Hilary? And how much of a father would her child have, sharing him not just with his work, but with Hilary and another baby as well?

"I'll have to think about it. I really don't know."

Later that evening, when they were both in bed, Joscelyn said to Paddy:

"I would like a child, of course, but not yet. I think that times are difficult enough. Maybe next year. Once Hilary's baby is born, and we know how things are working out."

And then she said, "Let's wait until we feel strong enough. You have been asking a lot of me lately. To be honest, I feel really stretched, emotionally. I'd love a baby. You know I would, but I'd like our baby to be an event in itself, one we can both really concentrate on. Not something that is crowded in with a lot of other very stressful things."

It was dark, but she could still see the outline of Paddy's face, looking rejected.

"I'm hurt that you don't think we're strong enough now. Maybe you're actually telling me something else. That you have some doubts. Doubts that I don't think I've given you cause to have, about us and our relationship."

"Maybe I do have some doubts. I hope that we're going to be just fine together, but we have enough challenges, to face at the moment."

After Paddy had gone to sleep, Joscelyn kept thinking about what Paddy had just said. Despite her clear rejection of the offer, Joscelyn was very, very tempted by it. She wanted a baby more than anything else in the world. But she had always hoped and believed that her baby would be born to two happy parents, who loved each other, in the way her parents sadly never had.

Not so long ago, she would have had no doubt that she and Paddy would be just right for parenthood. Now she was not so sure. Paddy seemed to be thinking of a baby as a distraction, or a compensation for her, like the bunch of red roses, which even now were beautifully displayed in their garden room.

Even so, she hadn't given up hope that one day her and Paddy's relationship would feel good and strong again. Strong enough to be sure of being parents, together.

It was while she was in this emotional state that Joscelyn saw the fax that Barbara had sent Paddy in the office.

Joscelyn did, from time to time, see such missives from various women, or notes that Paddy had sent to such women. In theory, Paddy kept them out of Joscelyn's sight, to be discreet, for the sake of all concerned. In the case of certain women, of which Barbara was one, Paddy would have told anyone who asked that he was extremely careful to keep them away from Joss. Joscelyn didn't like Barbara, and Barbara was very keen on her own privacy. But in fact, the odd one or two would, somehow or other, end up in places where it was very easy for Joss to see then. Places like the top of his desk in the study in the Fulham house, where Joscelyn sometimes put post for him to deal with. Or maybe they would be lying somewhere in view in his office in Wardour Street on days when (and always with Paddy's full knowledge) Joscelyn visited.

Joscelyn always did notice these documents. She had special antennae for them. She found that sometimes she could walk into a room and the piece of paper in question would seem to flash a little light at her. "Look at me," it would say. Usually she did look at them, and if she did not it was because she made a conscious decision not to. Sometimes she read them, sometimes she glanced and read a few lines, others she would identify, but not read. It all depended on what she chose to do. Once or twice, in the past she had told Paddy that she had seen such and such a letter; and he would always express a rather lordly surprise.

"Did I really leave it there? How extraordinary. I must make sure not to do it again."

This particular Barbara fax was in the office in Wardour Street. It was pinned up on a clip by the side of a word-processor, face outwards. Paddy would have sworn that it had been filed carefully away. But in fact, on the day after it had arrived, Paddy, had been called away at short notice, and being without any secretarial help, phoned his wife asking her to go and check post. She found it there; dangling and shouting, as soon as she walked into the room, "Look at me, look at me!"

It never occurred to Paddy that he was not, in fact, as averse to his wife seeing these things as he would have insisted. That he actually wanted Joscelyn to know about his emotional life, and that in particular there would be times that he wanted her to be aware of another woman's interest. This knowledge, after all, would provoke some reaction from Joscelyn, and some reaction from his wife was always better than none. When things were basically good between them, Joscelyn's reaction could be favourable. A little more attention, perhaps, a few more questions, about what he was doing, might be all the response he got, but it was still worth having. Of course Paddy's unconscious knew what Joss thought about Barbara. But still, Barbara cared for him. She was thinking about him and what was best for him; and for the moment Joscelyn was not. And this was something that Paddy was not at all averse to Joscelyn knowing.

So Joscelyn did see, and she read every word, several times. Every infuriating, insulting word.

And although every word hurt, there was one passage in it that took her quite unawares. It was the paragraph about her, and the wisdom of her conceiving Paddy's child. It really had never occurred to her that Paddy would be so disloyal as to discuss her in this way with Barbara. To raise with Barbara of all people the very intimate subject of whether or not they would have a child. In fact, had it not just actually happened, she would have thought it unthinkable.

Suddenly, the absent Paddy no longer felt like the man she loved: the talented, energetic, enthusiastic, generous affectionate man that she cared for. He was weak and feeble, cruel and deceitful, endlessly demanding, and completely unable to offer her in return the one and only thing she currently asked of him; which was that he kept out of contact with this particular hateful woman.

Why had she married Paddy? Joscelyn sat at the desk, in front of the word processor, shocked and numb, looking at the letter, with its aggravatingly neat handwriting. Why had she married such an inadequate man? A man who had all her love, and yes probably Hilary's as well, but who in the face of difficulties in his life had to turn to someone as poisonous as Barbara. Someone whom he knew she hated, just because she was an ever-ready source of adoration. Surely he must know that?

Barbara, whatever soft, sweet exterior she presented to her men, was unhappy, manipulative and heartless.

Of course Paddy would always keep Barbara at a safe distance. Safe enough for him, to avoid too much of the control that she would dearly love to exert, but not safe enough for Joscelyn. She would be the one to suffer. And why should she suffer her husband with Barbara? Had she not suffered enough? Had she not done her utmost to support him over Hilary and the baby?

She had been low and depressed lately, and yes, Paddy saw that as a withdrawal of her love. But had she not always loved him from the very bottom of her heart? Could he not allow her a little sadness, without turning to the woman that she probably disliked most in the world?

Joscelyn sat for a moment, feeling neither angry nor sad, but strangely detached.

"If I packed up all my bags and left home," she thought, "I could get work as a secretary again. We could sell the house, and I would get somewhere of my own." This last thought came to her as a complete surprise, for her mind had simply never wandered along these paths before. "It would see me through my studies. I could live a life that was free from all this pain."

She thought about all the demands that Paddy placed on her, demands that she willingly met when she had the warmth of his love, and had been confident of a base level of loyalty. Suddenly, those demands felt like a real weight on her shoulders, and in front of her she could almost see, stretching out before her, years of bearing their burden. There would always be other women, of course. Some would be basically nice, like Minerva, the travel journalist, but others nasty like Barbara. At that moment, in a flash of clarity, Joscelyn divined that in the good times, when his career and their marriage went well, there would be the nice women. The ones who were prepared to take Paddy for what he was, and wouldn't make too many demands. In the bad times, when he was low and unhappy, he would fall prey to the Barbaras, women who would lavish affection and attention on their man in order to get their "prize" and attempt to fill the gap in their own emotional lives.

The price of any kind of problem, whether preventable or not, would be a Barbara to share it with.

On her way out, she saw Ben, who was in the office next door. She hadn't been in contact with Ben for a while, after Paddy had forbidden their lunches.

"Hello," she said.

"Hello." Ben was obviously pleased to see her.

"How are you?"

"Not too bad." Joscelyn was unable to describe her well being with any more enthusiasm.

"We must have lunch together soon."

"Yes," said Joscelyn. She hesitated, and then said, "I haven't got my diary with me. Can I ring you later?"

"Certainly," said Ben. "I shall look forward to it."

* * *

Joscelyn's next contact with her husband was when he telephoned home and asked if she would come into town for dinner.

"I've got MacAteer coming, and someone from the film company who is in London, just now, and one or two others."

Joscelyn had expected Paddy home that evening, and had been planning to face him with her discovery. Now she was going to have to go into town, make an effort with people, and see Paddy, towards whom she currently had such unhappy feelings, across the distance of a restaurant table. She thought of refusing to go, but that would require some explanation. She would hold fire, for a few more hours.

The arrangement was to meet at Paddy's office. Much to her relief, Joscelyn arrived to find one of the dinner guests was already there. She was an American woman, extremely tall, and statuesque, with dark hair and striking green eyes. Joscelyn felt that she knew her, but she wasn't sure where from.

"Eugenie Pendlebury," the woman said, in a surprisingly soft, but still definite voice.

"Oh yes," Joss remembered. "I met you a while ago. We had dinner at a Chinese restaurant." That was the dinner when she had met Hilary, which now felt so long ago.

"It's wonderful to see you again." Eugenie actually did look delighted, as if Joscelyn was the person that she had come all the way across the Atlantic to see. Impossible as this obviously was, Joss still felt flattered, and a little disoriented at the same time.

"Eugenie is from First Word," said Paddy. "The people who may be producing Kevin MacAteer's new film script. She's in London for three months." Paddy was always very good at providing his wife with these detailed introductions; Joscelyn was aware of Paddy as the strong, supportive man, who helped her help him.

"And I'm loving every minute of it," said Eugenie, smiling broadly.

Joscelyn tried to organise her mind to think of a few polite questions, but was beaten to it by Eugenie. Eugenie had soon established where the Gregories lived, that they had just recently moved there, that Joscelyn was a student ("How wonderful," she said, as if she really meant it) and the extent of the refurbishment in the new house. By this time, several others had appeared, and they moved on to a restaurant.

Joscelyn sat next to a large, placid-looking man in late middle age, who turned out to have a cheerful sense of humour, and a capacity to draw all those around him into conversation. Paddy, at the other end of the table near to Eugenie and MacAteer, was clearly working hard. Joscelyn thought of his struggles in his new career, the risks he had taken. She also watched Eugenie. She was more animated than the first time Joss had seen her, presumably because she had a professional interest in MacAteer's script. At a distance, when she was concentrating the charm on other people, you could see how calculated it was. She smiled, and her brilliant white teeth flashed, but her eyes didn't smile with her mouth. She told everyone how wonderful they were, in a clever way – she seemed to be able to spot people's individual vanities, and play on them. She was a clever woman, but not a nice one.

She looked at Paddy too, and wondered if he was taken in. Unfortunately, it looked as though he was.

"Honestly," she thought, wearily. "All that experience of women. And he still can't spot the difference between real and feigned admiration. Or perhaps he doesn't want to. Perhaps in his book, any admiration will do."

It was late when everyone went home. Joscelyn, who normally

started to wilt around midnight, had completely exhausted the little store of benevolence Eugenie had built up with her at the beginning of the meal, when she took a very long time to go. And Paddy, still basking in the fake admiration, had showed not the slightest sign of impatience about being detained. So in the end it was she who said,

"I'm afraid we both have an early start tomorrow, Eugenie. We're going to have to get home."

Eugenie, all smiles, took her leave. Joscelyn half-expected Paddy to be annoyed at her intervention, but he said nothing, except:

"I just need to get a few papers from the office, so we'll call by there before going back."

"Why didn't you get them before we came here?" Joscelyn's irritation was automatic and immediate.

"I was busy looking after my guests. Besides, something came up in conversation with Eugenie, and now I want to look at that script again. MacAteer goes right off the rails at the end of the second act."

Joscelyn said nothing.

"It won't take long." Paddy's tone was only on the verge of being conciliatory.

They walked back through the still-busy London streets, and then up the dark stairway to the office, Joscelyn behind Paddy. Paddy went over to his desk, preoccupied, and started sorting through papers. Joscelyn sat in the comfy chair that was provided for guests, and looked at them suspiciously. Her tiredness was gone now, and her eyes followed every piece of paper her husband handled. They were, as she could see, scripts, business letters, and invoices but within each, there might, by some chance, be something from Barbara.

"I saw Barbara's fax." Joscelyn spoke without thinking beforehand.

"Where?" Paddy spoke sharply; straight on the offensive although Joscelyn could see from his face that she had caught him quite unawares.

"Here, in this office."

"And what were you doing, in my office, reading my private papers?"

"I was here because you asked me to come. I missed all my free time coming over here this afternoon to pick up those faxes you wanted."

"Well, Barbara's wasn't amongst those I asked you to come and collect, so you must have been snooping around."

"I was not snooping. It was pinned up for all the world to see, there by the word processor."

"It was for me to see; and not for you to read."

"It was there!" Joscelyn gesticulated to the now-empty space by the side of the machine on Paddy's desk, where in her mind's eye the neatly written bit of paper still hung.

Paddy said nothing for a moment, but he looked angry and unrepentant.

"You told me that you weren't in contact with Barbara!" Joss was shouting now.

"I haven't been for ages. Not for months. She is just about to leave Australia. We had one phone call, and she sent me a fax."

"A fax telling you how bloody wonderful you are. And all about whether we should have a baby. How dare you!"

"It was not all about whether we should have a baby. And I clearly didn't take a shred of notice of what she said because I had that fax on Sunday afternoon, and the very same evening I told you that I thought you should have a baby. It was mostly about me, expressing concern for me and my problems. She, unlike you and Hilary, actually likes me. She sees some good in me."

"I see good in you, Paddy," Joscelyn was in tears now. "But it is very hard when you do things like this to me."

Paddy looked less angry, and more uncomfortable. But his words, when they came, were not conciliatory.

"I normally think good things about you, but it's not so easy when I find that you have been reading my private mail."

"Paddy, it was out for me to see. And she was saying that you had gone off with Hilary because I am a bad wife."

Paddy, in his big impressive swivel chair, looked exasperated.

"For goodness sake, Joss, you really are becoming hysterical over this. She said no such thing. And if she did I wouldn't take the slightest bit of notice."

And then, with an attempt at a conciliatory tone, he went on, "Joss, do you really think that I am going to run off with Barbara, just because she sends me a friendly letter?"

Joscelyn got out of her seat. Normally this would be the prelude to her saying something affectionate, which Paddy would acknowledge, and would sooner or later bring the matter to a close. But this time she said:

"Will you promise me not to be in touch with Barbara again?"

"Why?"

"Because I hate her. And because I love you. It's all I ask: that you keep right away from her, and have no contact with her. None at all."

"And why should there be one person in the world that I am not allowed to be in contact with?"

"Because I hate her. And because I am asking you to do this for me."

"I'll think about it," said Paddy.

Joscelyn looked at him. It wasn't what she wanted. She hadn't won this one yet. But inside, she felt strong. She was going to insist. She really was going to insist. This time, she didn't care about the consequences.

When they got home, Joscelyn went straight to bed. Paddy followed an hour or so later. The next morning, he brought his wife a cup of tea in bed.

"I will think about what you said about Barbara. I can see that it means a lot to you."

It wasn't quite what she had asked for, but Joscelyn was prepared to give him a day to think.

"OK," she said. "Let me know when you have thought."

The fine balance of their relationship, so often upset these days, was, for the moment, almost restored.

Had the day after his argument with Joss been a good day

for business, which it was not, Paddy might have responded to the second message from Barbara in so many days in a way that would have satisfied his wife. In fact, the second, long note had confirmed all Barbara's travel details. She expressed some regret that she was committed to a long sea voyage - "I shall do my best to enjoy myself as planned, but I shall be thinking of you and your troubles, and offer what friendship and support I can from the middle of the ocean" - and had provided proof that not everything and everyone was against him.

He knew that the issue of Barbara was a tricky one and it was probably just as well that she was not actually in London. But there could be no harm in dashing off a quick reply: cheery, non-committal and friendly, and with a little drawing of Barbara on board ship, and batting it right back.

It was therefore guilt that struck him that evening, when Joscelyn again raised the subject. He did not want to be reminded that, having promised to at least give the matter consideration, his renewed relationship with Barbara was just an iota more involved than the day before.

"Have you thought about Barbara?" his wife said.

Joscelyn stood at the other end of the kitchen, and spoke to her husband's back, as he looked in the cupboard for some peanuts to go with their evening drink. He felt ambushed.

"Joscelyn, I can never promise you not to think about certain women." Paddy didn't turn round to look at his wife. There was a thinly veiled tone of antagonism beneath the humour.

"Well, actually," said his wife archly, "you did promise me that you would think about her. I made it clear that I don't want you to be in touch."

"So you think that I should contact Barbara and say that you don't want us to be in touch?" Paddy's tone was ironic, and a little more hostile than before.

"Of course I don't." Joscelyn was getting angry now. "I want you to stop contact with her, for my sake. And to tell her so."

"Joscelyn, as it happens, I do like having the occasional supportive note from her. I don't see that it does a lot of harm.

I did say that I would consider putting a stop to this entirely harmless activity, and I am still considering. There isn't any great hurry that I can see. I presume that you will also object to me meeting her, but she is coming home by boat and the journey will take several weeks."

The two of them stared at each other. But Joscelyn's patience had gone, gone completely. She said,

"Paddy, if you don't, now, this minute, get in touch and tell her that you can't be in contact with her at all, anyhow, in person or otherwise, I will leave you. I really will."

Paddy was shocked, but so was his wife. It was something that he had never expected to hear, but equally it was something she had never expected to say. And more than this, they both realised, again at about the same time, that Joscelyn was in complete earnest.

They stared at each other for a while longer. Joscelyn again felt quite calm. Not forced calm, when she controlled her own feelings, but a sense that she could just let things happen. It was a win-win situation, she thought. Either Paddy gave up Barbara absolutely, in which case she won, or else he would just go away and she would start divorce proceedings and the rest of her life. That would be a gain, too. And at that moment, the second option felt slightly preferable.

Then Paddy got up.

"Since this means so much to you, then I will. I will go and do it now; in my office. You will not see the letter."

He walked to the door, turned round and said, "And I shan't be back tonight. I'll be staying in my office."

And he was gone.

Chapter 16

Hilary was met at the station in Newcastle-upon-Tyne by her brother-in-law, Glyn.

She was a little surprised to see him, having expected her mother. The prospect of her wider family, and old friends and acquaintances, being apprised of her plight was something that she knew she couldn't put off any longer. So it was a relief that Glyn, whom she hardly knew (even though he was her sister's husband), looked normal and affable.

Once settled into the car, Hilary felt that she ought to make some conversation. Glyn was a tall, thin, serious man, whose only real interest in life was his work. He was a lecturer in astrophysics at the University. Unfortunately, this made conversation difficult; because not only was Hilary unsure what astrophysics actually was, but she was aware that any mis-targeted question could be the cause of great offence. The very first time she had met him she had quite cheerfully confessed her ignorance about his work and he had told her,

"You are not alone. Quite recently, two people, on being told that I am an astrophysicist, have challenged me to guess their star sign."

Hilary had begun to laugh, but on seeing the look of real pain in her future brother-in-law's eyes at the way society undervalued him, had been forced to suppress her amusement.

So she attempted a very general question on the progress of his research, and was rewarded with a very detailed reply about how his teaching commitment made it virtually impossible for him to devote sufficient time to his studies. It was Glyn's first year in post, as well as his first year of marriage to Victoria, and Hilary couldn't help feeling that he ought to be more willing, especially at this early stage in his career, to make a full contribution to the University who employed him, by teaching its undergraduates.

"When you go to university, you think that they are places for students to learn," said Hilary robustly, "but then it turns out that they are places for lecturers to do their research, and that the students are a bit of a nuisance."

"I wouldn't call my students a nuisance," said Glyn gravely, and with a tone of deliberate charity, "but they do take up more of my time than they should."

Glyn was a good man, or so it seemed, but communication between them would be so much easier if they shared a sense of humour.

When they arrived at 14 Witch Hazel Gardens, Glyn announced, "Victoria is here. I know she is looking forward to seeing you."

So there was a family reception to welcome her. This was a surprise, but also a clear indication that the Mackay family was demonstrating its wholehearted support to her in her difficulties. It was a bit daunting. Hilary had become so used to coping alone. How would she fare in the face of all this sympathy?

"How are you, darling? You look quite tired. Would you like a cup of coffee?" Her mother looked pleased and relieved to see her, and Victoria, who was standing behind mother in the hallway, had a positive look on her face. Glyn was despatched upstairs with Hilary's suitcase and Victoria to the kitchen to put the kettle on. The familiar smell of chicken casserole wafted through the hallway as the kitchen door opened: there would be a large lunch ready, with baked potatoes and a choice of vegetables and probably two puddings as well.

Victoria brought coffee for herself and their mother, and tea for Hilary, into the drawing room. Hilary was getting visitor treatment, and in fact she sank rather thankfully into a large comfy sofa that she had been forbidden to bounce on as a small child.

"I'm afraid that Glyn has to go to a conference, even though it's Saturday," said Mrs Mackay, "so he won't be able to stay for lunch."

Glyn looked relieved; and this gave him his cue to get up. "Very nice to see you, Hilary," he said, "I hope you have a good stay. I think that Victoria is hoping that you will accompany her to a concert this evening. I'm afraid that I have to entertain a visiting speaker, and will be busy all evening."

Glyn looked enormously proud of himself, and Victoria explained that Glyn had been given the honour of looking after a visiting Hungarian academic for the evening.

"András wants to drink some Newcastle Brown ale," Victoria said, with loyal pride, "and so Glyn has been finding out the best pubs to visit. Glyn doesn't normally drink much, so he's had to do quite a bit of research."

"But only theoretical research," her husband replied gravely. "I have my list of suitable places, and my street map, but most of them will be a new experience for me as well as for my guest."

Glyn really was the most unlikely man to take anyone, especially a hard-drinking Hungarian, on a pub crawl.

Hilary looked at her sister gazing devotedly at her husband. Glyn obviously put a great deal of energy and time into anything connected with his work. Victoria, a history teacher in a local school, must have more free time. She could see that she would be doing Victoria a favour by spending the Saturday evening with her.

Lunch was served, with a lot of thought about Hilary's wellbeing. She was given a chair nearest the radiator so that she should be warm enough, and Victoria and her mother had a long discussion between them as to whether or not it would be wise for Hilary to accept a glass of wine.

"I really don't think one glass would hurt," said her mother. "It is relaxing after all."

"It probably wouldn't hurt, but there is always a risk." Victoria looked severely at Mrs Mackay. "I don't think pregnant women should drink at all."

"I don't really want a glass of wine, thank you," Hilary said, "I'm very thirsty and would prefer water."

This answer, which was designed to satisfy both her relatives, actually pleased neither of them.

"Well, darling, you could always have both." Mrs Mackay began to look hurt at the rejection of her hospitality.

"I don't think you should," reiterated Victoria, turning a piercing gaze onto Hilary, obviously concerned that her sister was showing insufficient understanding of the theoretical danger in which she was placing her unborn child.

The telephone rang, and Mrs Mackay left the room, grumbling about what an inconvenient hour this was to phone anyone. Her daughters had sometimes tried to persuade her to buy an answerphone, to avoid such inconveniences, but she steadfastly refused. She came back almost immediately, and looked at Hilary.

"It's for you, darling," she said. "Someone called Paddy."

The two telephones in the house were in the hall and in her mother's bedroom. Even by the standards of the 1980s, this was an old-fashioned arrangement, her mother being an old-fashioned woman. She would have to answer the one in the hall. There was a chair, but it was hard and awkwardly placed.

Angry and surprised, she launched an attack straight away. "How did you get this number?" she barked into the mouthpiece.

"From directory inquiries," Paddy's voice sounded cheerful.

Of course. Hilary had not thought of anything so obvious.

"I'm in Newcastle," Paddy's voice said, still cheerful.

"In Newcastle!" This was extraordinary. Did he plan to come round? The idea was, frankly, too awful to contemplate.

"It was a spur-of-the-moment decision. I wanted to talk to you. I thought we could meet up, see something of where you come from. I don't need to be introduced to the family, unless that's what you want. I thought we could have a walk and chat."

There was a brief pause, in which Hilary said nothing.

"It was a lovely journey here on the train," said Paddy

cheerfully. "Absolutely fantastic view of Durham Cathedral on the way up. And really this is a great city."

"I am here with my family." Hilary found herself adopting a Victoria-like tone, which the occasion really did seem to demand. "It is not going to be a particularly easy weekend, and I shall need to concentrate on the people I am with. Besides, all my time will be taken up. I shan't be able to get away."

She took a deep breath and continued, "We obviously do need to talk. Get some things clear. But not here; next week, in London."

"But I am here now." Paddy sounded hurt. "I came up here to see you. And we can get things as clear as you like."

"No," said Hilary, trying not to raise her voice and attract attention to herself. "Please don't ring me again while I am here."

"Listen," said Paddy. "You must be going home by train. So am I. Why don't we travel together?"

For a moment, this suggestion was actually quite tempting. Paddy would fuss over her a little, buying her cups of tea from the buffet, and carrying her luggage. He would probably insist on upgrading her ticket to first class, so that she could sit next to him.

"I'm not sure exactly when I'm going back. Really, I needed more notice of this, Paddy." Hilary heard her voice sounding agitated, and not at all like Victoria. "Besides, we do need to sort a few things out; practical arrangements about the future. And a train full of people isn't the best place for this."

"All right." Paddy sounded hurt again. "You ring me when you are back in London,"

"Yes," said Hilary.

"Hilary?" Paddy caught her attention just before she put down the receiver.

"Yes?"

"I didn't want to upset you. I just wanted to spend a little time with you here, in your home town."

"Yes," said Hilary, and put down the phone. What else, she thought, can I say to that?

Hilary explained to her family that it had been a work colleague on the phone, a story that her mother seemed quite happy to accept, although Victoria looked at her rather keenly. Hilary felt guilty. The Mackay family didn't normally tell lies. But how could she tell the truth?

Lunch went smoothly, with Mrs Mackay and Victoria talking to each other, sometimes about, but rarely to Hilary, whilst Hilary ate a great deal and nodded from time to time.

Her sister left shortly after lunch, and Hilary was alone with her mother. This moment, which had been the cause of so much apprehension, was disturbingly unlike anything she had imagined, and therefore prepared herself for. Sitting in the comfy chair in the drawing room, sleepy and full of food, being fussed over by her mother, Hilary wondered whether the Prodigal Son had felt the same sense of grateful pleasure, mixed with unease.

She had expected a lot of questions; and indeed they came, but none of the ones she feared. When the baby was due, whether she was taking iron tablets, which hospital she was booked into, her arrangements for maternity leave.

She explained that she planned to have time off, and then finish the last few months of her contract.

"I can understand you wanting to work more or less up to the last minute," her mother said, "but you won't want to stay in London after the baby is born, will you?"

Her mother had always had a habit of telling her daughters what they would, or would not, want to do.

"I've been asking around, and Mrs Mitchell would be very happy for you to have her flat. It will be empty at the end of the month, because the present tenant is leaving."

Mrs Mitchell was a vague friend of her mother's, who let out the basement of her house.

"It would be very convenient for getting prams in and out. And you would have use of that little courtyard at the back to hang your washing out. I know that it is a bit of a walk from here, but I could collect you and bring you over here in the car, when you wanted. Mr Monk would do a bit of decorating for you, and make the place look more cheerful."

Mr Monk was a decorator and handyman who had done a lot of work for Mrs Mackay over the years.

Hilary looked at her mother, in a way that was meant to be grateful, but non-committal.

So it was all arranged, at least as far as her mother was concerned. Hilary was to move back to Newcastle, and re-enter the bosom of the Mackay family. It was not what she wanted, but at that moment, and from the depths of that chair, the proposition was not entirely unwelcome.

It would even deal with Paddy. Her family cared so little about him that they didn't even ask who he was. She would just tell him that she'd moved back home. He would fade from her life. He wouldn't be coming up on the train from London every weekend.

"This is all rather a lot to think about," Hilary told her mother. And then she said, "Mummy, I'm so tired, would you mind if I had a little sleep?"

"Of course, darling. It would do you the world of good."

And so Hilary slept, leaving the question of her future life still unresolved.

Paddy tried not to be downhearted by Hilary's reaction to his phone call. He told himself that he had played things wrong. Perhaps she would spend some time thinking about him, and then ring him on his mobile.

But the buoyant mood he had been in only half an hour before had been well and truly pierced. Sending that message to the cruise ship had cost Paddy a lot of emotional effort. He didn't want to lose Barbara, and he still felt that Joscelyn was making a fundamentally unreasonable request. Somewhere inside him was the rather begrudging notion that he was being a good husband by giving his wife what she wanted, and certainly one part of Paddy did want to be a good husband. But, after spending a night on the camp bed he kept in his office for times when it was necessary to keep a late-night vigil over transatlantic deals, he was still not ready to return home. Entirely on impulse, he had decided, the next morning, to take a train to Newcastle-upon-Tyne.

Paddy enjoyed train journeys, and had done ever since he was a boy. These days they were a rarer event in his life than a trip on a plane. He always took plenty of reading material, and since he had owned one his lap-top computer; but he also liked being able to look out of the window at leisure, and watch his journey progress. He hoped to see Hilary, certainly, but Newcastle was somewhere new. Somewhere he hadn't planned to go and didn't even need to visit. He was on an adventure.

Once arrived, he rang home, and left a message on the answer machine. This was a good thing. He hadn't wanted to speak to Joss.

"It's me. I've been called away. I'm in the North of England. I'll let you have hotel details later. It's a lovely bright day here. Have a good day."

He found a hotel, left his luggage, such as it was, and went for a walk, through the centre of the town. Newcastle, he found, was a grand, eighteenth-century city, a little down-at heel but alive and busy on a Saturday morning. Bits of it reminded him of Dublin, and he reflected that perhaps he and Hilary had more in common than he often imagined.

After that, he tried not to think too much about Hilary.

Paddy had lunch in a wine bar, and flirted with a spirited Geordie waitress, and went to a film in the afternoon. It was a good film. He felt a little better.

In the evening he went to the theatre, and, although they neither of them knew it, was at one time just a couple of streets away from Hilary and her sister Victoria. It wasn't a great play, or a great production, but the actors were all people he hadn't seen before, and the author was a local writer who clearly had some talent. I ought to get out of London more, Paddy thought. I go to Rome, and the States, but I should get to other parts of Britain more often.

Hilary still hadn't been in contact, but he was beginning to regain a little hope that she would be. She had told him that her mother was a great organiser. Besides, Hilary had her pride, and wasn't going to backtrack on her firm stance so quickly. Tomorrow was more likely.

It was after the theatre that he got a call from America; it was bad news on the MacAteer deal. He was being blocked again. It was difficult, and Paddy didn't quite have the edge. He knew it. It happened sometimes, although latterly it was happening just a bit too often.

The call ended, and Paddy knew that he hadn't handled it quite right. Suddenly he felt angry, really angry.

"All these bloody women," he thought. "Playing silly games with me. Being upset and expecting me to make things right for them." He had Hilary, he reflected, who wouldn't accept help, and seemed to distrust him even when he was doing his best, and Joss, whom he just couldn't help because the one thing she wanted was for the past to be undone.

"I'm not bloody God!" he said, to the walls of his hotel room. And all he seemed to get in reply was an image of Joscelyn, looking at him helplessly as she did these days with big sad eyes. Sad Joscelyn, who made him feel helpless. Angry Joscelyn who made him give up on the one little bit of harmless pleasure that currently made him feel valued and appreciated.

Paddy picked up his phone, and made another call to America. He was trying to win back some of the ground he had lost. Again, it wasn't quite working. "You should speak about this with Eugenie Pendlebury," the distant voice was saying. "She's our person on the ground, in London."

He was being fobbed off. But after the call ended, he did ring Eugenie.

"Sorry it's so late," he said. "I've just come off the phone to one of your colleagues. It's still the working day over there."

"It's still the working day for me here," said Eugenie. "And I'm delighted to hear from you."

Chapter 17

Hilary returned to London, a little anxious in case she met Paddy on the train, but otherwise refreshed in body and spirit. It had been simply wonderful to relax, to be taken care of, and to be with people who, whatever their faults, cared so much about her. There was a price to be paid, of course, for all the offers of help. She would be expected to join the clan, wholeheartedly, and the only way that she could see herself doing this was by remaining in that state of child-like dependence that had been so nurturing for a weekend's rest but could become slow torture over the years to come. On Newcastle Central station, that price had almost seemed worth paying, but by the time of her arrival at King's Cross she had no wish to return anywhere but her own flat.

There was still Paddy to face. With him, she was going to have to strike a delicate balance between accepting the help that her budget absolutely required and maintaining the freedom she needed.

Joscelyn meanwhile was numb, still only half-aware of her life in crisis. This was not the first time Paddy had made a sudden disappearance. She remembered the time they had had an argument over some saucepans. Joss had given them away to a friend who had unexpectedly become homeless after leaving her husband, taking two small children, one suitcase and nothing else. Paddy claimed they were his favourite saucepans, and that Joss had no right to them because they had been his before they were married. Joss said they were old and almost never used, and how could she not help a friend in such desperate straits. The disagreement would not have been serious, except that it had turned into one about husbands in general, and then Paddy in particular. Barbara Irvine, Joss remembered, had featured in that quarrel as well, and Paddy had left, at seven in the evening, to return, equally unexpectedly at seven the next morning, having spent the night in his office.

Joscelyn could still remember the sense of relief and freedom she had felt, as he slammed the door. How she had stayed up late spring-cleaning the kitchen, and re-arranging all the contents of the cupboards; as if Paddy had gone for good and she was starting life again on her own terms. And then, on his return, he had been so pleased to see her and she him.

On that occasion, it had all seemed so simple. She had been relieved when he had gone, and pleased when he came back. Now she felt anguished and confused. For a while, she resisted a strong temptation to try calling him; a temptation that she gave into after only an hour, to get an answer phone. She didn't leave a message.

At ten o'clock, she sought refuge in bed, but was unable to sleep. Half of her missed Paddy, desperately and physically, as if there were a large Paddy-shaped hole in the bed where he was not. The other half, weary with the agony of recent months, told her that she could only rest and be happy if he would be gone from her life for good.

On Saturday morning, fortified a little by several cups of tea, she went into the office in Wardour Street. Again, she knew that this was probably not a wise move. If Paddy were there, he would be unlikely to be ready to see her again, and would feel pursued. If he were not she would be thwarted, anxious, and unhappy.

Paddy was not there. She cast her eyes across his desk, and filing cabinets, looking for letters to or from Barbara. There were none, at least none on the surfaces, waiting to be read. There was a fax dangling from the machine, but it was a piece of junk mail, advertising cheap air fares to Guernsey.

Joscelyn stood in the middle of the room, her mind temporarily disengaged.

"Hello," said a voice.

Joscelyn jumped.

"Are you OK?" said the voice from the door; "you look terrible."

It was Ben.

"What are you doing here, so early on a Saturday morning?" Joscelyn heard her own voice, sounding quite unnecessarily accusing.

"I could ask you the same question." Ben was smiling at her. She saw that he was holding the morning's post in his hand. "You've just missed Paddy. He left about half an hour ago, just after I arrived."

"Oh."

"How are you?" Ben asked. "You look as if you could do with a cup of coffee. Shall we go to Gino's?"

How nice it would be, to sit in a cafe, drink coffee, and be soothed by Ben's company. To tell him all, or at least some of her troubles. He was so nice, Ben. She'd been avoiding him ever so slightly recently. In fact she had promised, just the other day to ring him and arrange lunch, and forgotten to do so. But he hadn't taken it amiss.

There was nothing for it but to tell him the truth.

"Ben, Paddy was very angry that I told you all about Hilary and the baby. He didn't want you to know. He doesn't really want anyone to know. He told me not to have lunch with you. I'm sorry I didn't tell you. You must think I've been avoiding you."

Ben looked blank for a moment. Joscelyn realised that she might, in fact, have upset him.

"It's not what I want, Ben. I've missed seeing you. I've been having such a bad time recently; I really value the support of my friends. And you've been a good friend to me. You really have."

She saw the expression on Ben's face; still unsatisfied with the explanation he had been given.

"So we've been banned from seeing each other?"

"Well, not for ever, I'm sure. Paddy's very sensitive about that particular subject. He doesn't want us discussing it."

"That seems to be quite a burden for you to carry."

It was a burden. For a moment, she hesitated. Paddy was really being quite unreasonable banning her from spending time with Ben. But just now, just as she had insisted on Paddy cutting off contact with Barbara, it would be a bad time to ignore his request about Ben.

"I talk to Philippa, to some of my women friends. Paddy doesn't mind that."

"Good." Ben looked at her. "We could have a cup of coffee and talk about other things. How Les is getting on with your decorating and I will tell you about my latest outrageous client, and answer your question about why I am here so early on a Saturday morning."

Joscelyn hadn't expected Ben to be so persistent. He clearly thought that Paddy's ban was unreasonable, and wasn't inclined to be bound by it.

It was tempting. But she said, "I'd better not. But I will talk to Paddy and say I'd like to see you for lunch again and that we won't talk about Hilary."

"Get the ban lifted; or partially lifted." Ben was looking sceptical again.

"He is my husband, Ben."

"Yes," said Ben, impassively.

"Goodbye."

"Goodbye, Joscelyn."

Ben opened the office door for her, and watched her walk down the stairs. As she went, slowly, step by step, Joscelyn found herself thinking that Ben, who had never met Les the decorator, could remember his name; whilst Paddy, who had fallen over him in the house several times, could not.

She also thought how much she would have liked to spend the morning with Ben.

* * *

As soon as she was home, the telephone rang. That must be Paddy, Joss thought. But it was her father. He never rang just for a chat; or rather when he did, there was always a pretext. This time it was an article he had seen in the paper about the Open University. Did Joscelyn want to see it?

"Yes," she said politely, she would like to see it.

Would she like him to send it in the post, or should he keep it until her next visit?

These questions were always ostensibly put with great concern for her opinion, which always annoyed her. Beneath the show of concern was really a demand for recognition of the trouble he was taking.

"I really don't mind, Daddy. Whichever is easier for you."

This was the wrong answer. "Well, if I post it, I shall have to make a special trip to the post office, to buy a stamp. I don't have any stamps in the house. I think I may also be out of envelopes. But of course if I keep it I will have to put it away in a place where I shall be guaranteed to remember it. My memory isn't as good as it was. And I shall have to make sure that Mrs Hogan doesn't throw it away."

Mrs Hogan was the cleaning lady who came once a week. She did have a tendency to throw things away.

"Besides, I don't know how long it will be before you come here again."

So Joscelyn asked her father to post the article. He seemed reasonably satisfied, and explained that it might be two or three days before he got to the post office, and he might or might not manage a letter to go with it.

Joscelyn went out in the afternoon, and she bought some olives, and freshly baked bread, thinking that Paddy would probably be home for supper and that they should have something nice to eat. And if he wasn't, she told herself, she should have something nice anyway.

She had half hoped to be out when he returned, and even delayed her shopping trip a little beyond the time she was actually enjoying the experience, to facilitate this. It was disappointing, therefore, to come back again to an empty house, at about five o'clock in the afternoon. Paddy had been away a long time, and for the first time she began to wonder whether he actually did plan to return. That seemed ridiculous. Of course he would be back at some point. But he seemed to be deliberately staying away beyond the point when he could easily be forgiven.

Then he phoned.

"Where on earth are you?" she said.

"I'm in Newcastle," he told her, managing to sound as if this was quite normal, and he was just letting her know. "I decided to take a local theatre company up on their offer of a free ticket. It was a lovely journey up here, on the train. I ought to get out of London more often."

Joscelyn was relieved to hear from Paddy; relieved also that he was safe and well. But he shouldn't go off like this and then pretend everything was fine. But why Newcastle? Was he meeting Hilary's family?

"Are you seeing Hilary?" she said, sounding aggrieved.

"No." Paddy was terse and defensive. There was a pause.

"When are you coming home?"

"Tomorrow. I don't know when. Don't expect me any particular time. Why don't you ring Philippa, and arrange something with her?"

"No," she shouted. "I don't want to see Philippa!"

"I'm only thinking of you."

There was a silence, in which Joss found herself fighting back tears.

"I'll see you tomorrow, then," she heard Paddy say.

"Yes."

Joscelyn put the phone down, and the flood of hot, angry tears coursed down her face.

Paddy came home first thing on Sunday, and went to his office. There was a message from Barbara.

"Of course I will stay out of contact for a while if that is really what you want," she said, "and all that I will say is what I said before that you shouldn't forget yourself in all this. Fondest thoughts, which I will now just have to keep to myself. Barbara."

It seemed churlish not to reply. Paddy replied, "Great to hear from you. I'll miss those sweet notes. Safe journey. Paddy."

His phone rang. It was Eugenie, confirming a time and place for lunch, that very day, to discuss the MacAteer project.

Chapter 18

Lunch with Eugenie had been disappointingly short, for she had another engagement that afternoon. She arrived at the restaurant a few minutes before him, and he was treated to the big welcoming smile, and a flash of those large green eyes. They talked relatively little about the MacAteer project. Paddy wasn't really in a work frame of mind, and Eugenie behaved as if the meeting was entirely social. She asked him lots of questions about himself, and looked hugely admiring as he talked. Then, just as Paddy was feeling really relaxed and contented, Eugenie had announced that she had to be going. Paddy was surprised and more than a little upset to be losing her. He then broached the question of the project that had been the intended subject of the meeting. Eugenie responded by saying that there was just so much to discuss that they really should stake out a good couple of hours to go through it all.

This seemed like a good idea, and Paddy was happy to concur.

"It's been good to get to know you a little better," Eugenie said. Paddy had agreed that he felt just the same way.

When he got home, Joscelyn was sitting in the garden room, which was cold in the winter months because of all the glass in the French windows, wrapped in a blanket and with a book on her lap. She wasn't reading it.

Paddy offered to make tea, and Joscelyn came into the kitchen with him. He made Lapsang Souchong, which he didn't care for much himself, because this was a blend that his wife liked. She was annoyed with him that he served it in a mug, instead of a cup.

"You know that I like to drink Lapsang out of a cup," she said, accusingly.

"No, I don't know. I know that you like this type of tea, and that's why I made it for you."

"I have told you I don't know how many times."

Paddy really had wanted to make a gesture that Joscelyn would appreciate. He said nothing.

"Why were you in Newcastle?"

"I told you. I saw a play at the Playhouse. It was very good. You would have liked it."

"You didn't invite me."

"That's because we were not on good terms on Friday evening."

This was Joscelyn's opportunity to make peace; but she was not inclined to do so.

"So you didn't see Hilary?"

"I did contact her; she was staying with her family. But she didn't have time to see me. I hadn't arranged to go and see her."

Joscelyn understood the fuller truth from this. That Paddy had gone in the hope of meeting Hilary, a hope that had not materialised.

"Have you met her family?"

"No." Again, Paddy was terse. "But I may have to meet them. They will be closely related to my child."

The awful truth of this hit Joscelyn right in the heart. "Please will you tell me when you do."

"All right." Paddy looked at her, surprised and defensive.

"In fact, I think I should be there when you do."

Joscelyn had not thought this through before, but she felt that her request was reasonable.

"Perhaps; I'll have to think about that." Paddy looked distant - many emotional miles from her, and her pain. He felt cornered. This was something he'd not thought about. He wanted time to react. Joscelyn, usually so measured in her dealings with him, was pushing too hard.

"Did you write to Barbara?"

"I did write to Barbara."

"Did you make it quite clear?"

"Yes."

Joscelyn looked at her husband. He wasn't giving her the reassurance she wanted. The kind of reassurance that, in the past, had been the key to the success of their marriage.

Paddy looked at his wife. She didn't trust him any more. She had always trusted him.

Joscelyn thought for a moment. "Did you get a response?"

"A response?"

"From Barbara."

Paddy said, with deliberate calm: "She did reply, yes, to let me know that she had received my message."

"And I hope you didn't reply?"

Paddy became angry. "What the hell does it matter whether I replied or not! I did what you asked. We are not in touch anymore."

Joscelyn looked at her husband. He had replied to Barbara, of course. He hadn't been able to resist. Again, for the second time in so many months, the man that she loved so much appeared a weak, miserable creature in her eyes.

"I'm going out this evening," she said. "Some people from my course. We're going to the theatre."

"Very well," said Paddy formally, "and I have a great deal of work to do. I'm going to go and do it."

Joscelyn watched her husband get up and go to his study. She had so much wanted the end to his contact with Barbara. So much that she had been prepared to stake her marriage on it. And now that it had happened, she felt not the happiness and warm reassurance that she had wanted, and expected to feel, but a cold, sad disappointment.

* * *

Hilary, six months pregnant, at last had come to terms with the increasingly imminent arrival of her baby. Now that her family, even her dour brother-in-law, had seen and accepted her as a pregnant woman, it seemed possible for her to do the same. She began looking in shops that sold cots, prams and baby clothes. None of her ordinary clothes fitted any more, and in the last few weeks she had been making do with one loose pinafore-type dress from Monsoon, which she wore every day, changing the polo-neck tops that went underneath, and washing the dress at weekends. Her mother had given her a cheque, and gratefully she went out and bought two more outfits - this time of real maternity clothes in bright, positive colours. She looked nice in them, and when she looked in the mirror - which again she had not been doing for a while - she saw herself looking surprisingly well, with pink cheeks and a rounder-than-usual face.

 She even summoned the courage to write to her father. This was really very difficult indeed; but he would know soon anyway, courtesy of her mother or Victoria. Several drafts and as many restless nights produced a very short letter: setting out the simple facts of the situation, explaining that although at one point she had had "some - rather unrealistic" hope of a continuing relationship, with the father, this was not to be. Mother and Victoria, she told him, were being very supportive.

 At one point the letter, in its draft form, contained a phrase which said something like "I'm sorry to have disappointed you, which I believe I shall have done," but on reflection, she deleted these words. They did reflect her feelings, but she never discussed her feelings with her father. This did not seem to be the time to start.

 Her letter was rewarded with a brief, but very swift reply. He had already heard the news, he said, but was pleased that she had written herself. "These things do happen," he said, "and sometimes they happen not just to other people but to us and our own loved ones. No one lives into adulthood without making mistakes and suffering setbacks. I am sorry that you are facing such a major challenge so soon in your life, but you appear to be facing it with great courage."

 Her father said that he would, of course, offer what help he could. In a final sentence, he told his daughter that he believed that she would make an "excellent mother".

This last assurance, so unexpected, caught Hilary quite unawares. She sat, and looked at her letter for a long time, and then wept unrestrainedly for several minutes.

Soon it would be Christmas. She was to spend two weeks in Newcastle, and before then, she had to get herself organised, which meant that she had to sort something out with Paddy.

She had put in a call to Paddy on the Monday after the weekend in Newcastle, and had been both relieved and annoyed to find that he seemed more than happy to wait a few days before seeing her.

"There is a lot we have to discuss; practical things."

"Yes," he had agreed, but without giving anything away.

With her new mood, she became a little more able to confide, and had spoken to two friends about her situation. One was Jane, from her old school, who'd remained loyal despite the divergence of their paths to different universities, and the other Miranda, an ex-Cambridge girl whom she had been avoiding recently as her pregnant state became increasingly obvious. The response from both was so affectionate that Hilary felt surprised that she had denied herself their support before. Jane rang up, almost straight away after receiving her letter, and offered to visit, or be visited the very next weekend. And Miranda was obviously relieved.

"We did wonder what was wrong," she said. This surprised Hilary, who believed that she had done a good job of keeping her troubles to herself.

"Candace thought you might be pregnant. You don't drink these days, and you've been putting on a bit of weight. Why didn't you tell us?"

Hilary explained her current dilemma to her friends: how to accept Paddy's financial support (which she really was going to need) and maintain her own independence.

To her friends, it was simple. Of course she should accept whatever money Paddy offered. It was not for her; it was for the baby. They thought she should simply tell Paddy this, and explain that she no longer wanted a relationship with him. Jane thought that she should see a solicitor, and get a formal agreement. Miranda thought that if Paddy was offering more than he legally need, Hilary should have no conscience about taking it.

Overwhelmed by the prospect of discussing all this face to face with Paddy, Hilary took what she deemed to be the coward's way out. She wrote him a note.

> *"I have given the matter a lot of thought,"* she wrote, formally, *"and I realise that I don't want a continued relationship with you. This, of course, is only the same decision as I had made before I became pregnant. Unfortunately, the situation has become a little confused recently."*

She went on to say that she would be happy for him to see the child, on a regular basis.

Once a week, she suggested.

The question of money was more difficult. Hilary stated, again rather formally, as befitted the subject matter, that he "had a legal duty to maintain the child" and that "she knew that he regarded this as a moral duty as well". Finally, feeling more than a little embarrassed, she reminded him that he had offered to pay for a flat "to tide her over" when she took her maternity leave. She explained, with as much dignity as she could muster, that she didn't want him to share the flat at all, but she would still like him to pay for it.

Finally, she explained that she was shortly to go home for Christmas, and would be away for two weeks. Please would he not contact her, they should meet and talk in the New Year.

Paddy took this letter, and the inevitable sense of defeat that followed it, with a fair degree of resignation. He responded, quickly so as to give himself no time for hesitation, with what he hoped was a mixture of generosity tempered with fairness.

He agreed that he had a legal liability to maintain the child, and suggested that he paid whatever sum a Court would order, and more if he had the means. As to rent, he had already spoken to a business acquaintance, and arranged to take a six months lease on a flat in Putney. It was a small, ground floor flat, but bigger than the room she had at the moment and he hoped that it would provide reasonable accommodation. Hilary could move in after Christmas. She would be there for the last month of her pregnancy and the first months with the new baby. He would pay any moving costs.

"After these six months," he went on, "I don't feel that I should have any more financial responsibility other than to maintain the child. I hope that you don't mind me reminding you that having this baby was your decision, and that you have also decided that you do not want any continuing relationship with me."

He added that he hoped that they would remain friends, and that they would be keeping in contact via the baby. He posted the letter to her in Newcastle. He didn't think that she could really object to this. He now wanted, as far as was possible, to put her out of his mind.

Christmas is one of those times that celebrates the happiness of happy people, and emphasises the unhappiness of unhappy ones. Hilary was surprised to find herself having a remarkably good time over the festive period. Her father was home for a few days, and she watched her parents slipping back into their old roles, as if her Dad had never gone away. Victoria commented on this:

"I could imagine Daddy coming back one day, with his suitcase, and it would be as if nothing had ever happened between them."

Hilary nodded, although she added, "I don't think that it's very likely."

Surprisingly, also, she actually got on well with Victoria. It was as if her sister liked her better for being pregnant, somehow. One day she had even had a letter from Peter in Milan. He had heard about her pregnancy from Miranda, their mutual friend, who had also passed on her Newcastle address. In a typically masculine way, he explained briefly the fact that he knew the information, and who had told him, but said little else on the subject. He was going to be in London over Christmas. Was it possible they might meet?

It would have been nice to see him. And Hilary was relieved and delighted that he still wanted to see her; you were never sure whether to expect support from men, but she was equally relieved that she would not be back in London until the day of his return to Milan. It wasn't so much that she minded discussing her situation with him; that might have been comforting: but she didn't want to show herself to him pregnant. In a flight of fancy she imagined herself meeting him again in a few months time. The baby would be sleeping in its cot, or maybe they would be going for a walk and pushing it in a pram, and she would be back to her old thin, energetic self.

* * *

Paddy and Joscelyn had Christmas at home. In the weeks beforehand, things had become much more settled between them. Paddy had explained to Joss the package of support he was giving Hilary, and that all contact between Hilary and him would be on a strictly business footing in future. Joss watched both the office and the study at home for communication from Barbara, but there was no sign of any. Paddy must have said something fairly clear to stop communication, Joss thought; although in her fantasies she imagined a freak wave sweeping on board ship, carrying Barbara off beyond reach of rescue. In these fantasies, Barbara was the only passenger to be swept off in this way, although some of the others were a bit shocked, and wet.

Paddy was home a good deal in the evenings. He was worried about the new MacAteer deal, and often talked about this. If he could secure a second MacAteer deal, with himself as producer, his career as a film producer would be firmly established.

For her part, Joss gained a distinction in one of her Open University exams. Paddy had been delighted for her, and had taken her to the Bear to celebrate.

After a huge "at home" all day in Fulham on Christmas Eve, they were left together, just the two of them. Joscelyn's father had gone to her brother, and was to stay with them for New Year.

Joscelyn woke up late on Christmas Day, to find that Paddy was already awake, and had been doing the last bits of clearing up from the day before. He brought her a cup of tea.

"Darling, you didn't need to have done all that work."

"I quite enjoyed myself. I've been listening to Mozart. And you worked so hard yesterday, you needed some sleep."

It was ages since Paddy had made her tea in bed. Paddy got back into bed with his tea, and put his arm around his wife. For the first time for ages and ages, Joscelyn really felt relaxed. She and Paddy were all alone together. They had the ingredients for a slightly exotic but still traditional lunch that they would prepare together and eat in the afternoon. At some point they would go out for a walk, through London streets that were almost devoid of traffic. They would see families out and about after Christmas lunch, with small children trying out new bicycles. That bit would be difficult. But things were so much better now, between Paddy and her. She could even imagine that by next Christmas she and Paddy would have a baby of their own.

And today, just today, nobody would get to them. She looked at Paddy, and said, "Isn't this nice." He smiled. A relaxed smile, such as she really hadn't seen for months and months.

"Yes," he said. "It is."

And at the end of the day, when the two of them were settled on the sofa together, drinking coffee, listening to the Bruch violin concerto, one of Joscelyn's favourites, the telephone rang.

Paddy answered. It was Joscelyn's brother, James. It was odd for him to ring. Joscelyn had spoken to him that morning, and to her father, who was with them.

"I'm afraid I've got some bad news," he said. "We've had to take Dad to hospital. He seems to have had some kind of stroke. He can't talk, or move very much. The doctors seem to think that it will be a few days before they will know how well he is likely to recover."

"I'll come down now." This was Joss's immediate response. After all, she had to do something, and what else would she do?

"We will have to start thinking about the future," her brother went on. "Dad may need more looking after when he comes home."

Chapter 19

Joscelyn's father was in his seventies, and he had for years suffered from high blood pressure. Almost every time he and Joss spoke on the phone, he found an opportunity to remind her that his health was not good. But that was just Dad. He had complained about his own health, loudly and tactlessly, even through the months when her mother was dying of cancer. Joscelyn found him a trial, but had expected him to remain a healthy trial for twenty years to come.

Suddenly, and quite unexpectedly, she was overcome with sadness and remorse. She thought of the old and unhappy man who had the misfortune to be in hospital on Christmas Day. Who needed, above all, control and was now in an environment where control had to be surrendered: that would terrify him. He was her father, when all was said and done.

She gave the news to Paddy.

"Trust your Dad," he said. "To ruin our Christmas, just as we were having a really good day. I wouldn't be surprised if the old bugger hadn't done it deliberately."

Joss looked at Paddy, surprised at the vehemence of his reaction, and with tears beginning to fill her eyes.

"He is my father," she said.

"Yes. The only parent we have between us. Who remarkably has managed to be nothing but a source of unhappiness to both of us all through our marriage."

Paddy had never liked his father-in-law, and the feeling had been mutual. Paddy's own annoyance with Joss's father, as a tetchy and selfish individual with whom he had been forced to spend too many precious days of his life, had been exacerbated by the fact that the old man always seemed to make Joscelyn unhappy too.

"He is my father, Paddy, whatever his faults. I have to go to Wiltshire tomorrow. I shall have to. James is coping now but he needs my help."

Paddy had planned a couple of days off. Some time with his wife. "Can't James manage? He is a bit nearer. And I never get to see you these days."

Joss thought: "Whose fault is that?" But she said, "I want to see Dad. He will hate being in hospital. I need at least to go and see him."

"Your father hates being anywhere. He may dislike hospital a bit more than most places, because he'll have to fit in with them and their routine, and not they with his."

Joss glared at Paddy, who realised that he had gone a bit too far. "Look, of course you should go and see him. But why not wait one more day?"

"No. I can't. It wouldn't be fair to James. And Dad will be so unhappy. I ought to see him. I really ought."

Joscelyn went back into the kitchen and phoned her brother. Then, as a peace offering, she made more coffee and brought the whiskey in on a tray. Paddy declined the coffee.

"I've had too much today, thank you." He poured some whiskey, and drank morosely.

The evening had somehow come to an end. Paddy did some washing up, while Joscelyn watched a programme on the television. At night, they lay each on their own side of the bed, deliberately not touching, and Joscelyn woke in the early hours, suffering from indigestion, and a sense that her husband had, yet again, let her down.

She got up early in the morning, while Paddy slept. She packed a bag with a few clothes, and in a reversal of their normal roles, made some tea for them both.

Paddy looked at her fondly. "I'm sorry you are going." His voice had none of the resentment of the day before.

Joscelyn held his hand. "We had a nice Christmas together, didn't we?" she said.

"Yes. Although I wish it could be a bit longer."

"He is my father, and he is very ill."

"Yes, I know. I know you have to go."

The telephone rang. Paddy answered. "Yes," he said, "she's here."

It was James. Unexpectedly, her father had had another stroke in the early hours of the morning. He was dead. Joscelyn told her brother that she was on her way.

She relayed this to Paddy. He was silent for a moment. Then he said, "You are very upset. That's quite natural of course. But I don't think that you should go to Wiltshire now. You may not be well enough to drive. You can stay with me, and have a quiet day, like the one we planned."

He paused, and seeing the look of amazement on Joscelyn's face, and said, like a patient teacher explaining to a slow-witted child, "You can't do anything now. You were going to see your father. You can't do that now."

Joscelyn could not believe how little Paddy understood her feelings, although it was an incredulity with which she was beginning to feel familiar. Instead of saying so, she answered his argument with one of her own.

"There is still a lot to do, arrangements to make; people to telephone."

"Yes, but most of that you can do from here. It's just a question of speaking to James, deciding who you should each be responsible for speaking to. You may need to go down in a few days. But not today, you can stay here."

"But Paddy," Joss said. "I am already late as it is. Too late; I should have liked to see my father before he died."

The telephone rang again. Joscelyn answered this time. It was James, with more information, and more requests.

When she came off the phone, she told Paddy, "That was

James. I've definitely arranged to go. James is expecting me. He sounds very upset. I don't think he'd cope very well on his own. I told him I was coming."

Paddy nodded, morosely.

The two of them had breakfast, quietly, and afterwards Joscelyn packed the car. When it was time to go, she looked for Paddy, who was in the study.

"I'm off, now."

"OK."

Paddy made no move toward her, and looked sad. Joscelyn hugged him, to provide him with some reassurance, but she felt little affection. Paddy came with her to the car, and waved her off looking forlorn.

As she left London, Joscelyn's thoughts were with Paddy. She reminded herself that Paddy did not, and could not, understand the loyalty one felt to even the most defective parent. "It's not his fault," she thought, "it's just outside his experience." But even so, she was pleased to be away from him.

Over the ensuing days she made funeral arrangements, faced the sympathy of the people in her home village, the sad, empty house where her parents once lived, and the intense and completely unexpected distress of her brother, who in life had hated his father. Through all this she longed for comfort, and for that comfort to come from Paddy. She spoke to him on the phone once or twice, but he always seemed distracted. She told him, at length, of all her troubles, and how difficult everything was being. He agreed that her life was not easy but kept insisting that the solution was for her to return home, and as quickly as possible. The funeral was arranged and she stayed, on the basis that Paddy would join her in her parents' house the night before.

"I will just about last out until he comes," Joscelyn thought. Paddy was always slightly business-like on the phone. He had been shocked at the news, and had reacted badly and selfishly. But once the shock was over, and once they were together, she was sure he must be kind and supportive. When he actually came, and wrapped his arms around her, she would at last feel better.

* * *

Paddy, back in London, was very angry with his dead father-in-law, and more than a little angry with his wife. Joscelyn's father had been a controlling man who had contrived to make Joscelyn's mother, for whom Paddy had felt affection, and Joscelyn herself unhappy, and his son insecure and demoralised. Additionally, he had never liked Paddy, and had shown it. His choice of time to die, just as he and Joscelyn seemed to be on the verge of peace and reconciliation (and just as Paddy had planned a few days holiday to share with his wife) seemed wilful and was entirely typical of the man. And Joscelyn, who had allowed her herself (despite her own good sense and Paddy's constant good advice) to be endlessly wound up by this awful man in his lifetime, was responding to the demands of his death just as she had to those he had made in life.

Paddy didn't remember his own parents, but he did realise that Joscelyn owed some sort of duty to her father, however dreadful the man had been. He had tried to be patient and understanding about this. But he had not liked sharing Joss with her father. There had been times when it had been very hard to see Joss pulling away from him and towards the old man. Now the old man was dead and still pulling Joss away.

Paddy knew that it was his duty to go to the funeral, and had agreed to join Joscelyn in Wiltshire. He dreaded the prospect. Paddy hated funerals. He didn't remember those of his own parents, but each one he attended reminded him of their untimely deaths. He did remember the funeral of his beloved Aunt May, with lots of family, lots of fuss (none of which seemed to be directed towards him), and he himself had been deemed too young to go. They had all gone off, leaving him with a neighbour and the sense of resentment that he, as the only one (at least in his view) who really loved Aunt May, should not be able to say goodbye.

So it was something of a relief when he was offered a meeting about the MacAteer deal, in London, but with a conference call link-up to America, on the day his father-in-law was to be buried.

He did, rather half-heartedly, suggest that he had other plans for the day, but was not sorry to be told that this was the only time convenient for all involved.

It was, in fact, a genuine surprise to him when Joscelyn was seriously distressed to hear that he would not be there. "But Paddy, I need you to be there," she had said.

"Joss, I'm no good at these occasions. I know the old man was your father, but he and I didn't get on. It's no disrespect to the dead. I would feel that my presence was somewhat inappropriate."

"But what about me? Don't I matter?"

"Of course you do. We had a wonderful Christmas together, didn't we? I'm just looking forward to us being together again. I'll arrange something really nice for when you come back. Look, I did try to re-arrange this meeting but it just wasn't possible. It's about the MacAteer project, and you know how important that is to me. I would have come if I could."

Joscelyn did not answer. She could not, because the tears, pouring down her face, made speech impossible.

Joscelyn stood alone at the funeral, next to her brother and sister-in-law. It was bitterly cold, and the day before it had snowed, although it had been a fine powdery snow that had all melted or turned to ice. A little group of people from the village were there, including her old school friend Mary who had come to provide support.

The small group, after a brief service, trudged outside to the burial. There was space in the village churchyard, and therefore no need to go to one of the large cemeteries in the area. This had been, in her father's view, one of the big advantages in living in the village. Joscelyn could only think of Paddy, and his absence. I may as well be separated, or widowed, she thought, to be here without him.

At the same time Paddy was in his meeting. He'd spent a few lonely days on his own. This made him reflect on Hilary, which made him sad, as well as guilty, and a little on Joscelyn, which had chiefly made him angry. He had been quite churned up to hear how upset she was. But what could he do?

The Americans were offering to buy out the MacAteer script from Paddy. Paddy owned the copyright, having bought it from MacAteer. They had offered this before, and he had refused. He wanted to stay on board, as he had done before. He risked getting nothing from his investment, but stood to gain far more, professionally and financially.

Paddy was aware that Eugenie Pendlebury was not helping him much. She was supposed to be on his side (at least that was what she had always told him) but she was definitely not helping.

As the meeting progressed, Paddy suddenly lost heart. I'll sell the bloody thing, he thought. I'll get the best price I can, but I'll sell it. I've got other work on. And the money will come in useful. And so he did, and for a good price, which made him, at the end of the day, a little bit happier.

Joscelyn was supposed to come home to Paddy straight after the funeral. But by then it was snowing heavily, and road conditions were bad. Her friend Mary invited her to supper, and she was glad to accept. She didn't much want to go home, anyway. She would stay one more night in her parents' old home. It would be sold soon; there might not be another chance.

She told Paddy over the phone. He said little. He didn't tell her about the MacAteer deal, and how he had sold out. He said that he would be out that evening.

Paddy then caught Eugenie, who was, as usual, taking a long time to go. And then Paddy spent the evening with her; and as Joscelyn spent the night in her old home, Paddy spent his with Eugenie.

Chapter 20

In the six weeks before she gave birth, Hilary saw nothing of Paddy. He telephoned now and again, and she did the same. Even this was against the rules she had set herself. She had decided that she needed time away from him, independent time, so that when he started to come and see the baby she would feel free of his influence, suitably unconnected to him.

Occasionally, though, she would still feel the urge to be in contact, and call. He was always willing to speak to her, and there were never any arguments, but the communication never helped. Sometimes he would suggest a meeting, but was never disappointed when she declined. Each time, she would vow not to do it again.

Otherwise she was well, mentally and physically: better than she had been for many months. The flat that Paddy had organised was small, and a bit dingy (it was in a basement), but quite comfortable. It was a real flat: she had her own kitchen and bathroom, which seemed like total luxury. She had even begun to enjoy being pregnant. Large as she was, now, she felt less tired, and less anxious. She took maternity leave; began to enjoy the antenatal classes at the hospital where she met other first-time mothers-to-be. Hilary found that the class fell broadly into two groups, the older middle-class mums and the young working-class ones. She straddled the two, making friends, and meeting some of them for coffee in the daytime. She also made more effort with her university friends, and found that once she was happy to see them, they were pleased to see her. The days went by quickly, she read a little, and went for a short walk each day. Somehow just the process of cooking and caring for herself managed to take up all her time.

In fact, her pregnancy, which for the first seven months she had tried to ignore, had now become an end in itself.

It was therefore, a complete shock when she awoke in the early hours of a cold March morning, with the fuzzy sensation that something was very different from the way it had been the evening before. She got up, and went to the lavatory, and sat as a mixture of blood and water drained out of her.

"My waters have broken." Hilary knew all the drill, from the antenatal class. If your waters broke, you had to go into hospital straight away. It was not quite so easy to do, somehow, when the situation actually arose. Hilary knew that she had to ring the hospital, find her reference number from a card, and tell them her name and number. But the card was in the kitchen, at the other end of the flat, and she was draining clear liquid. And not only was the card in the kitchen, but the phone was in the living room.

It was possible, though. She wrapped herself in towels, found the card, and found the phone. The receptionist sounded very calm, as did the nurse on the maternity ward.

"I don't have a car or anyone to drive me," Hilary could hear the panic in her own voice, "and I can't take a taxi, I'm in such a mess!"

"We'll send an ambulance then, love," said the calm voice. "Where are you?"

As she sat in the ambulance, holding her overnight bag, with a large avuncular-looking ambulance man who had said, "Don't look so worried, love, we'll get you there in time," Hilary's first thought was, "Thank God for the National Health Service" and then, as the realisation dawned, "I'm going to have a baby. Tomorrow, probably. By tomorrow evening, I am actually going to have a baby."

It was in fact, about eleven o'clock the next morning when, shocked and exhausted, Hilary gave birth. The baby was a little girl. She weighed exactly 7lb.

"What a lovely little girl," the midwife said.

Hilary didn't much care for this midwife. They had kept changing shifts, and this was her third, who'd been with her just for the last hour, and the birth itself. Hilary had been very comfortable with the one before, and had felt quite outraged when she had finished her shift and gone home. Consequently, of course, she hadn't taken to the next one at all.

Hilary looked at her daughter, who was definitely a real baby, pink-looking and sweet. She felt exhausted, and quite unequal to the task of caring for her. This was no joke, this baby. It was all hers. She was going to have to look after it, day and night, for years; forever.

"My life," Hilary thought, "is ruined. I am tied to this small creature forever, and there is nothing I can do about it."

Hilary rang Paddy's office number and left a message. She rang her mother, who seemed very excited ("what has she got to be excited about?" thought Hilary) and said she would be down as soon as she could.

The day was very long. The baby fed a little, although neither the baby nor Hilary had quite worked out what to do. The baby seemed to be awake for ages, when Hilary was desperate to sleep, and then in the late afternoon slept for so long that Hilary thought that perhaps her daughter had died. All that time Hilary lay, still exhausted, but too tense to rest, watching her breathe.

She watched the other mothers, with their visitors. Husbands, partners, older children, parents, uncles and aunts; a whole stream of them came through the wards with chocolates, and bunches of flowers, noise, irritation and jollity. And she had no one. The nurses were kind, but rushed off their feet. One stopped her work for a little while, noticing that Hilary had been on her own all day, and chatted. Hilary explained that her mother was coming, but all the way from Newcastle. She said nothing about Paddy.

Paddy did come, in fact, as soon as he heard Hilary's message, but that was not until after five o'clock that day. He hadn't been in the office before then.

This, of course made him feel guilty, but also angry. "Why didn't she try my mobile?" he thought, although he knew that it had been switched off most of the time.

The maternity ward was very busy. All the beds were occupied, and Paddy was discomforted to find that his first sight of Hilary as a mother, and of his own child, was in a very busy, bustling atmosphere. Hilary was looking pale, and all alone. Most of the other mothers and babies appeared to be surrounded with visitors, or at least an array of cards and flowers. Paddy realised that he should have brought something - a large bunch of flowers at least. Feeling badly wrong-footed, and for the second time that day, he felt a simmering, ill-directed anger at the world.

"How are you both?" he said, trying to sound as up-beat as possible.

"Fine. We are both fine." Hilary spoke in a quiet, rather hoarse voice.

"Has she got a name?" Paddy glanced in the direction of his tiny daughter, actually too frightened to look too closely.

"No." Hilary still sounded very quiet. "I had thought of some names, but none of them seem quite right, now."

It was something they had never discussed. Paddy had not realised this before. Had it been Joss's baby, they would have had long discussions, arguments probably, lists and finally an agreement. He would have brought a bottle of champagne. Why had he not brought a bottle of champagne?

Angrily, Paddy decided that it must be Hilary's fault. She had been so discouraging of even friendly contact of late. And she was such a puritan. Champagne wasn't really her style.

The night at the Ritz, the fateful night that had led to all this, when they had shared a very un-puritan twelve hours, was long forgotten.

"Well, please let me know as soon as you decide."

Paddy felt angry again. It was his daughter. He ought to have been involved in the choice of name. But he wasn't going to risk Hilary's cold reaction by suggesting it.

What else was he supposed to say? Should he ask about the birth?

"Did everything go OK?"

"Yes, fine. It all seemed to take a long time. I still feel tired."

"Of course. Perhaps I should come back tomorrow?"

"Yes."

There was a pause, with Paddy itching to leave, but not quite liking to. Hilary, of course, sensed this. "You haven't had a proper look at the baby." She sounded resentful. Hilary wasn't normally resentful. She was direct. This was one of her virtues.

Paddy went round and stood by the cot. His daughter was tiny, wrinkled, and asleep. He felt nothing. Absolutely nothing.

"She's nice. I hope she looks like you when she gets a bit older, and then she'll be even nicer."

After he left, to go home, Hilary, already low, started to feel seriously depressed. Paddy, still slightly numb, was only ashamed.

* * *

Paddy related these events to his wife.

"Hilary had her baby this morning," he told her. "She left a message on my machine at work. Of course I didn't get it until about five o'clock because I didn't go in until after lunch."

Joscelyn's stomach tightened. Although Paddy had poured them both a drink, she didn't sit down with him, but carried on with the washing up she was doing, turning her head to look at Paddy when she spoke.

"Was it a girl or a boy?"

"A girl. She hasn't given it a name yet. Do you know, we never discussed names? Can you believe it? It's extraordinary."

Paddy spread his hands out in a wide, expansive gesture. Then he looked at his wife. "Do you know what I felt, when I looked at the baby? I felt nothing. Absolutely nothing."

His eyes filled with tears, and Joscelyn, still standing at the kitchen sink, followed suit. Joss was grateful that she had Paddy's feelings to concentrate on. In a situation like this, practised as she was, it was very hard to shut out her own.

"I'm sorry." She watched Paddy. After a few moments, she said,

"How was Hilary?"

"Fine. A bit tired, but fine. Hilary will be all right. She's a toughie. And she doesn't really want me involved in her life.

"But you will still see the baby?"

"If she wants me to, but I don't think that's very likely."

He sounded bitter, but Joss was relieved. If she worked really hard at shutting out thoughts of Hilary's baby, and if Paddy didn't see it or talk about it, she might just manage to get through.

* * *

After Paddy had gone, Hilary lay still. She felt dreadful. She hated Paddy. He was a complete bastard, she thought. He clearly couldn't wait to get out of the hospital. And he hadn't even brought her a bunch of flowers. All day, there had been a stream of men coming through the ward bearing these brightly-coloured tokens of love and respect for the mothers of their children. Some managed the grand gesture, but plenty more arrived shuffling slightly and embarrassed, handing over their bouquet with noticeable relief.

"I hope these are the ones you like, love," the husband of the woman in the next bed had said, with an anxious look "I know there is a kind you like, but when I got to the shop I couldn't remember what it was."

Yes, there had been men in that ward that day, Hilary thought to herself, who looked as if they wouldn't be able to say what a florist was, if they had been stopped on the way to work and asked the question by a passing TV crew. But they had all managed to get themselves into one, at least today. All except Paddy. Paddy, the one for the big gesture, the man who could normally conjure a bunch of carnations from his back pocket anywhere, at any time. And she was the one mother with nothing.

About half an hour after Paddy had gone, her mother arrived. She brought, not flowers, but packets of biscuits, soap, tissues, and some brand new towels and flannels. She was flustered, because the trains from Newcastle had been running late, after an accident on the line, and then there was a tube strike in London.

"So I decided I had to go straight to my hotel, darling. It does mean that I am even later getting here than planned, but I had such a hell of a journey."

Mrs Mackay didn't normally use words like "hell", and it was said with great emphasis.

"You've done wonderfully, Mummy. And I can't tell you how pleased I am to see you."

The baby woke, and needed feeding. Mrs Mackay fussed a great deal, giving lots of advice about sore nipples and diet. She then decided that Hilary must have a cup of tea, and went off to speak to the nurses.

"Oh, mother, you shouldn't have," Hilary said, as her mother returned, triumphantly, with a cup and saucer. "Honestly, there are set times when we get given drinks and food. You'll make me ever so unpopular, demanding special treatment like this."

"Nonsense, darling, they were perfectly happy about it. I explained that you were on your own, and that while I was here you had the chance of a nice cup of tea while I held the baby. Sister said that was just what you needed."

It was something of a relief when her mother had gone. Hilary again hoped for sleep, which did not come. The hospital supper, of a rather nice fish pie, carrots and green beans, followed by jam tart and custard, had come at half past five. It was now half past eight, and there was a whole evening ahead. Hilary had a book, a novel about a middle-aged female accountant who left her husband and family to live in the Outer Hebrides. It had seemed reasonably entertaining even the day before, but today she had no patience with it. The heroine seemed to have very little to complain about in her life with her family in Leytonstone. She was simply a selfish cow who chose to abandon those who relied on her and do something romantic.

"It's just as well," Hilary thought to herself, "that self-centred people like her usually only dream, or at most write novels about that kind of thing, instead of doing it. Otherwise nice places like the Outer Hebrides would be packed full of a lot of very unpleasant people."

This uncharitable thought was just making her feel a little sleepy, when the baby woke up and started to cry. Hilary fed her, but she still cried. At a loss for what to do, she got out of bed, put on her best dressing-gown (bought specially for the hospital), and tried walking around with the baby on her shoulder.

It was then that she met Peter Saville. He was carrying a huge bunch of flowers.

"Hello," he said.

"Hello," replied Hilary, feeling herself going bright red. "Why aren't you in Milan?"

"Actually, I'm here on business for a couple of days."

"How did you know where I was?"

"Telepathy." Peter paused for a moment, but when he saw the confused look on Hilary's face, said, "I rang you and there was no answer, so I tried your mother's. Your sister answered the phone. She was there to feed the cat, and explained where you were."

Hilary, in her dressing-gown, was conscious all at once of her still-pregnant tummy, her crying baby, and the large bunch of flowers that she should be graciously accepting if she had had an arm to spare.

The baby wailed. The bunch of flowers was still in Peter's hands.

At that moment, one of the nurses appeared.

"Let me have her for a moment," she said. The nurse took the baby, and walked up and down the ward, and within five minutes it was asleep on her shoulder.

Hilary, sensing that she had found someone who would care for her in her hour of need, said, "My friend has brought me some flowers. Is there a vase to put them in, please?"

"Yes, I'll get you a vase." The nurse was about twenty-five, small and very pretty. She put the baby back in the cot, and went off and fetched a vase full of water.

"There you are. What lovely flowers!" She smiled and went away.

"That nurse is an angel," thought Hilary, in a state of helpless gratitude.

Peter smiled at her. "You both look very well," he said. "What are you going to call her?"

He was one of several people to ask that question that day, but this time Hilary had a definite answer.

"Sophie," she said. "I'd like to call her Sophie."

"That's a very nice name," said her friend.

Chapter 21

The birth of baby Sophie made little outward difference to Paddy, or to Joscelyn. Paddy became even more elusive than usual, and Joscelyn planned life more and more on her own. She saw a lot of Philippa, but also began to spend more time with new friends from the Open University. She and Paddy met up now and again, sometimes amicably and sometimes not.

They had not argued, though, since some time before the baby had been born. Since, in fact Paddy's decision to sell the rights in the MacAteer script. He did not tell Joscelyn about this until one day, several weeks after the event, she said to him,

"You don't seem to be getting much progress with the MacAteer project?" and Paddy had replied, "I sold out."

Joscelyn had been completely taken aback. "Sold out?"

"That's right. I sold the rights in the script to the Americans; for a good sum too. We can pay a chunk off the mortgage, and have a nice holiday."

"Paddy!" Joscelyn was shocked.

Paddy looked defensive, but said nothing.

"You were going to insist on staying on board, like you did last time. See it through to another film. It was your best chance to stay in films; in the big time."

Paddy stayed deliberately calm. "I didn't think so. It was my decision. I'm not opting out of the big time or out of films. It's quite likely that this one won't even get made, and I shall do very nicely out of it."

"But Paddy," Joscelyn still couldn't quite believe it, "after you worked so hard to stay with the last one, against all the odds. How could you give up now?"

"I did not give up." Paddy was angry now. "I made a decision. A business decision, and, as it happens, a personal one." He got up and walked to the other side of the room

"I have a wife who doesn't work, and who may or may not want a child, and I have Hilary who has presented me with a child that I did not want but shall have to pay for. This all costs money. And as a self-employed businessman I have to be thinking about my bank balance." He got up and walked out of the room and up the stairs to his study.

Joscelyn watched him go. So it was all her fault. All hers and Hilary's - at least in Paddy's eyes. She followed him, as far as the bottom of the stairs, and shouted:

"The last time you wanted to stay on board a film project I went out to work to support us both. Do you remember that? Why didn't you talk to me, before selling out? Last time, you talked to me, and we agreed on a plan of action, together. You may not have noticed, but I see the two of us as a partnership, even if you don't."

Paddy appeared at the top of the stairs, and shouted down, "We didn't have a mortgage then. Not on this house, that you set so much store by. You couldn't pay for this on a secretary's wages. And I shouldn't ask you to pay for Hilary's baby. I know that you have a pretty low opinion of me, but I don't suppose even you suspect that of me."

That evening, Joscelyn had a crisis meeting with Philippa. Philippa was good at crises. Once her children were in bed she was usually pleased to have a companion for the evening, and Alistair was invariably out. Even when he did come home, from a late night in the office, or some meeting or other, he would normally just put his head round the door, nod at Joscelyn, and take himself off to bed, leaving the two women to drink coffee and continue their discussions.

Joscelyn related the argument over the MacAteer script in some detail. "He's giving up; not giving up work, he's still very busy. But that real determination to succeed; he's just giving up on it."

"That's his problem, though," said Philippa. "Isn't it?"

"And mine. I'm his wife. I share his problems."

"Joss, if Paddy was going to be really happy by deciding to shift his career down a gear, not be so ambitious, but just make a living, you'd support him in that, wouldn't you?"

"Of course, but this isn't going to make him happy. That's the whole point."

"Well, he must make that decision. Not you."

Philippa could be calm to the point of being brutal, sometimes, Joscelyn thought. She changed the subject.

"You know that baby shop on the Fulham Road. It's called 'Bloomin' Marvellous'. I cross the road rather than pass it." Joscelyn, as she spoke, recollected having told her friend all this before. But Philippa was listening, all attention, and nodding.

"Probably I should be having a baby myself. But I don't want to do it just because Hilary is. I don't want Paddy to let me have a baby just so he won't feel so guilty. I want to do it for the right reasons."

"I can see that the time isn't right."

"I told you that he discussed it with Barbara, didn't I?" Joscelyn had already told her friend this several times.

"He's never forgiven me for asking him to stop contact with her. And it's not as if he cared so much for her, it's the fact that I made him stop it. There's someone else of course. A revenge relationship; revenge on me, and on Hilary, except she doesn't know about it. A hard-bitten American woman called Eugenie Pendlebury. They meet at lunchtimes in her office's executive flat. She sends him messages with laboured jokes and he keeps leaving them round the house for me to see. It won't last, and she's not the type who would have a baby by accident. She's so horrible that I don't even care about her. Paddy deserves her. If he thinks he'll get me running around after him to compete with her he can think again. But the point is that he's only with her because he's angry at giving up Barbara. That bloody woman is still coming between us."

"Barbara seems to come between you more than Hilary."

Joscelyn thought about this for a moment.

"I think she does, at least as far as I am concerned."

"But are you projecting it all on to Barbara? Those feelings of anger, and anguish, all those real feelings that you are entitled to have, about Hilary and the baby. Are you sure that you are not just putting them on to Barbara?"

Joscelyn thought for a moment. "Perhaps a little bit. But I was really angry about Barbara before Hilary and the baby. And Paddy taking up with her again when I had all that to cope with, it really upset me."

She thought for a moment, struggling to find the words to explain what she knew to be true. Philippa waited patiently, and watched her.

"It was one of those things, Hilary becoming pregnant. It was awful, for me. It felt like the worst thing that could ever happen, and it did. But I just had to live with it. In fact one of the only things I can admire about how he has behaved recently is how he is providing a fair package for the baby. But Barbara was all out to get him. You know what she was like."

Joscelyn looked at her friend, still struggling for the right words to express herself. "The thing was I hated her and I had always made this perfectly plain. And Paddy didn't even care about her. Not really. Of course he was attracted to her, and she would lavish him with sticky praise and tell him how wonderful he was. But when she first went to Hong Kong, he forgot all about her. Then she got back in contact one day when he was feeling low over Hilary's baby, then suddenly she was essential and he had to be in contact and get her gooey messages, and the fact that I hated it meant nothing."

Joss paused only for breath, because now the words were tumbling out fast and furious. "For a while everything seemed OK. He seemed have forgotten her. But since we've had our problems again he keeps bringing it up, making snide remarks. Just like my father used to go on punishing my mother over some ridiculous little thing on the rare occasions when she got her own way over something."

Joss started to cry. "And after I have been so good to him. So supportive of everything, his career, and Hilary, which was such a big blow to me. And I only asked him this one thing and he couldn't even give it to me. Not graciously; not without looking for revenge."

Philippa found some tissues for Joscelyn, who was now weeping copiously.

"And I don't think he even liked her. Not really."

Philippa watched her friend for a moment. Then she said, "But that's how Paddy is. Alistair's the same."

"Alistair?" Joscelyn couldn't quite credit this.

"Yes, in his own way. With him it is work, and not women. He doesn't need to work so much. He doesn't even like at least a quarter of what he does. He won't delegate, and this makes him inefficient, and his junior staff get pissed off about not being trusted and having what they do being interfered with all the time. It causes no end of disputes. But he will work all the time. He will hang on to all those files that his assistant, even his trainee could do perfectly well. He won't give them up."

Philippa looked at her friend. "OK, I know that a litigation file is not the same as the awful Barbara Irvine. It's not the same personal betrayal, and to be honest I wouldn't stand it if Alistair had an affair. But it is similar behaviour. Alistair doesn't want the work, he doesn't need it, his colleagues and I would dearly love him to relinquish at least some of it, but he won't. He just won't. He feels that his whole world will collapse if he lets go of just one case. It's his emotional security - however false and however damaging - just as the Barbaras of this world are Paddy's. They believe they really need the work, or the women. They don't perceive themselves as being able to do without them, even though of course they can."

Joscelyn was now watching Philippa closely as she talked.

"I do fear that it will all collapse one day. Alistair is good at his job; he's on all the committees. He earns his keep, as well. But he really does aggravate people at the office. One day they might just decide to get rid of him. And then where will we all be?"

Philippa looked tortured. Her face was all contorted. She was really distressed. Joscelyn was taken aback. Philippa was such a strong, capable person.

"Of course we'd cope," Philippa said, as if she were reading her friend's mind. "And look, I'm sorry. I didn't mean to talk so much about me. You really do have a problem. You made Paddy give up Barbara when he wasn't minded to. Some men, lots of men, would have chosen to give up Barbara, even if she hadn't been such a nasty manipulative cow, because they didn't want to hurt their wives and that was a real priority for them. But not Paddy. So he's angry and resentful, and he's found someone else to take Barbara's place. If that's not acceptable to you, you will have to decide to leave. Otherwise the only way to keep your sanity is to accept who he is and look after yourself. Make your own happiness. Paddy may make you happy sometimes but you'll never be able to rely on it. Sometimes he'll be a complete bastard and if you are not looking after yourself there will be no one else who will."

Philippa had never spoken so critically of Paddy before, and half of Joscelyn felt that she should defend her husband. But the other half knew that her friend was only speaking the truth.

After she had gone home, though, Philippa felt seriously worried about her friend. Joss had let off a bit of steam, with her, but she had gone back to Paddy and no doubt was going to forgive him all over again. Philippa had always liked Paddy and she had tried not to interfere too much, but she was getting really anxious about Joss. She was looking pale and thin, and as she had more or less admitted that evening, Paddy always managed to get what he wanted, while Joss only got her needs met if they happened to coincide with her husband's.

It was difficult, though. If Joss insisted, as was long overdue, that Paddy started consulting her more and looking after her a good deal better, he probably wouldn't stick around for long. Poor Joss, she would be devastated if Paddy left her.

The alternative, and the one that seemed most likely, was that Joss just kept on with her determined, desperate denial of the full awfulness of her own situation. And the trouble with that, Philippa feared, was that in the end, something would have to go.

She could see herself, not just providing tea and sympathy, but dealing with some real crisis; maybe visiting a desperately ill Joss in hospital. All that punishment, albeit emotional rather than physical, it was going to have to have some effect, wasn't it?

* * *

In the months before, and the weeks after Hilary gave birth, Paddy's affair with Eugenie Pendlebury was about the only thing that cheered him. This was his excuse, in fact, for spending so much time and effort on a relationship with a woman that even he knew he didn't much care for. True, she was intelligent, and good at her job. Paddy had to admire her for that. Also she was attractive, with that glossy dark hair and arresting green eyes. But she hadn't helped him over the MacAteer deal. Nice as pie, of course, but she really hadn't been on his side.

"So, she owes me," Paddy would think to himself, as he left the office early, or returned late after lunch, yet again. Eugenie had access to the company flat; a small and surprisingly shabby place, that was nonetheless conveniently situated in central London and possessed a sturdy double bed. She would contact him at the office, on the days when both she and the flat were available, and they would arrange a rendezvous. They liked to use a jokey and very obvious code; although as time went on they both started to run short on alliteration with lunch (lust, lecherous, lascivious) or sandwich (saucy, sexy) and sometimes Paddy had to resort to Roget's Thesaurus for inspiration.

He let Joss know about the affair, but she reacted to it, as to so much of what he did these days, with a hurtful indifference. He left messages from Eugenie, in her large flamboyant handwriting, first in his study, then the living room, kitchen and even bathroom of the Fulham house.

Joss normally put them in the bin.

Once or twice, Paddy resolved to put a stop to the affair. It took up too much of his time. The pleasure, such as it was, was much more in the anticipation than the reality. It probably hurt Joscelyn; she certainly looked very sad these days. But somehow it didn't quite happen. He would get a message, with its invitation to an hour of recreational sex, along with a sandwich and glass of wine, and somehow it always seemed worth it just one last time. Especially as he and Joss hardly had a physical relationship these days.

After Hilary left hospital, Paddy went to see her and the baby a couple of times. Hilary looked tired and was positively unwelcoming. The baby usually cried, or needed feeding, something that Hilary, who was breastfeeding, was obviously reluctant to do in front of him. He still felt nothing for his daughter; and would come away from the visits feeling absolutely awful. He then stayed away for a while, but that seemed awful too. So he made himself feel a little better by sending small parcels of this and that; some honey (which Hilary liked) or soap, and sometimes a postcard with a cheery message. Hilary made use of the presents, and was, in her emotionally blunted state of exhaustion, grateful enough for them. But the cheery messages irritated her beyond belief, and she mostly threw them away as soon as they arrived.

Her mother stayed with her for a few days after she left hospital, and was interfering and fussy, but Hilary missed her terribly when she was gone. Sophie seemed to stay awake all night, and finally sleep a peaceful sleep between nine and twelve each morning. These were exactly the hours when her local new mother friends had their coffee mornings, and five weeks after Sophie's birth Hilary had not managed to attend a single one.

In the mornings, when Sophie slept, Hilary would sometimes struggle to do the various household tasks that seemed never to get done, or she might try to sleep. Her rest would invariably be interrupted by either the telephone, the postman with a parcel from Paddy, the midwife, or a plumber come to mend the pipes in the upstairs flat. The rest of the time she felt exhausted, incompetent, disorganised and depressed. She did love Sophie, in a desperate and confused way, and spent virtually every minute of the day (even those precious minutes when she slept) thinking and worrying about her. But Hilary believed, completely, that she was now destined to be disordered and distressed for the rest of her life.

The one activity that was manageable and therapeutic for both Hilary and her baby was walking. Hilary did the walking, and Sophie was pushed in the pram. The exercise made her feel a little more alert, and a little less depressed. Sophie would often sleep, but otherwise would be content to look at the plastic toys on her pram in an interested way.

Hilary normally walked down Putney High Street, looking at the shops as she went, and then down to the River Thames. The sight of the water, slowly flowing, was restful. One day, anxious for more exercise, she crossed Putney Bridge, and went on walking past Fulham Palace, and onwards, for a good long time.

In time, she was in Fulham High Street. Hilary had never been to Paddy's house, but she had the address in her address book, and had even looked it up on her A to Z. She knew, therefore, and surprisingly easily, when she reached the right turn off towards the house. Not quite trusting to her memory, and telling herself that she might be mistaken, she went in the direction of number 24 St. Anthony Road. Sophie was asleep, and Hilary was quite happy to keep walking.

She found the road quite easily, in fact. For a moment, she looked at it and told herself that it would be best to turn back. But curiosity was a stronger pull, and she pushed the pram across the road, and down to number 24.

It was all very neat and clean looking, with its new paint and tidy, if tiny, front garden. Peeping inside, she saw smooth walls, nicely painted, smart-looking furniture, and an Indian carpet. All very affluent-looking, which was very Paddy, but also clean-lined and cared for in a way that was somehow not Paddy at all. So this must be Joscelyn's influence. Suddenly, the realisation that Paddy was not just Paddy, as she knew him, but part of a partnership with Joscelyn, was borne in on her, as it never had been before. Even seeing them together, as she had in the past, had never made this impression on her. This was where Paddy ate, and slept, laughed and played, and all with his wife.

Hilary stood, suddenly rather unsteady on her feet. She felt tired and thirsty, and aware that there was now a long walk home.

She stood for a moment longer, feeling unwell, and closed her eyes.

"Are you all right?" It was a woman's voice. Hilary opened her eyes, and saw Joscelyn.

It clearly was Joscelyn. Hilary would have been hard put to describe her. But this neat, clean person, dressed in jeans and a slightly faded pale blue shirt, with long tawny hair, was definitely Paddy's wife.

"Yes, thank you, I'm fine. I came out for a walk. I seem to have come a long way. The baby likes riding in the pram. She hasn't been sleeping well, and the movement soothes her."

"You look as if you haven't been sleeping well. Come in."

"No, no," said Hilary, slowly manoeuvring herself and the pram to leave.

"I really think you should. You don't look well. I'll make you a cup of tea, and run you home if you like."

Still protesting, Hilary found herself taking the pram with Sophie in it into the hall, being sat in a large comfortable sofa, and accepting a cup of coffee. The coffee, when it came was warm and smooth tasting, in a cafetiere, and offered with a plate of little biscuits. She drank, and ate, and Joscelyn sat near her, and said little, but exuded a pool of calm and warmth around her. For the first time for weeks, if not months, Hilary felt cared for. She, who these days spent her whole time caring for Sophie, and afterwards when time allowed, for herself, was being nurtured.

"I could stay here for a week," she found herself thinking, only vaguely aware of how inappropriate that would be.

Sophie woke up, and was hungry. Anticipating her needs,

Joscelyn ushered Hilary into another room, with a high-backed comfortable chair, brought her a glass of water and left her in peace.

"How amazing," Hilary thought. "No wonder Paddy married Joscelyn. Anybody would; how wonderful to be looked after like this."

After Sophie had fed, she cried a little, and Joscelyn asked to hold her. It seemed a little strange to relinquish her baby to Paddy's wife, but she was too comfortable and too grateful to make any objection. So Joscelyn held Sophie, and carried her around the garden, talking to her, while Hilary went back to the large sofa and more of the delicate-looking almond biscuits.

After a little while, Joscelyn explained that it would be no trouble to take them both home. Hilary didn't quite know how to collapse the pram, so that it would fit into the car, but the two women worked it out, and they drove back to Putney, Hilary sitting in the back seat with Sophie. At no point did Joscelyn suggest that Hilary's visit was at all strange. And at no point, as Hilary realised after she was back in the flat, did either of them mention Paddy.

"You look much better now. Call again if you are in the area." Joscelyn spoke quite naturally, as if Hilary might often walk over to Fulham, and call in for coffee.

"I don't suppose I shall walk so far again. The river and back is my usual route. I rather over-stretched myself today."

"Well, any time you feel like it," said Joscelyn in her amazingly calm way.

Hilary knew that she would love to go back, odd, bizarre even as it might be, and be cared for by Joscelyn again. But it really wouldn't do. Besides, another time she might meet Paddy.

In fact, it was Joscelyn who visited her, a few days later, bringing some nappies and baby lotion that Hilary had left in Fulham. Hilary's first reaction was to take them in, thank Joss politely and say goodbye, but a mixture of curiosity and a strange desire for further contact meant that she couldn't quite do this, so that Joss was left standing on the doorstep, in front of her.

"I didn't have your phone number," Joscelyn said, as she stood on the doorstep, "so I thought I'd drop them by."

It crossed Hilary's mind that Joscelyn could have asked Paddy for the number. And how, if not from Paddy, had she found out her address?

"I knew your address because I pay the rent. At least, of course Paddy pays, but I am the one who goes to the letting agent with a cheque."

So Paddy got Joscelyn to pay Hilary's rent every month. What a bastard he was! Then, Hilary realised that Paddy and Joscelyn must discuss her, and arrangements that affected her. She had never really thought about this before, she had naively always felt that her dealings with Paddy were somehow private. Had Joscelyn told Paddy about their meeting the other day?

"Please do come in," Hilary said, wondering if this was wise. But somehow she had kept Joss standing on the doorstep so long that it would be rude to turn her away now. Then Sophie woke up, and Joscelyn held her while Hilary made some coffee, and then while she did some washing up, and wrote and addressed a birthday card for her sister Victoria, ready to post. After a little while, Sophie tired of looking around her, and smiling at Joscelyn, had closed her eyes again. Joscelyn placed her gently back in the pram, and then left.

"Do call again if you're in Fulham," she said.

Hilary couldn't help thinking how wonderful it would be to visit the Fulham house every day. To sit in that comfortable sofa, drink coffee and eat almond biscuits while Joscelyn held the baby and emanated calm. But it wouldn't do. Besides, after a while they would have to start talking to each other, and what would they say?

Chapter 22

Hilary wasn't quite sure how it happened, but somehow they got into a routine. On Tuesday and Thursday afternoons, Joscelyn would call and collect Sophie. She would have her for two or three hours, and Hilary had the time off.

At first, while Sophie was away with Joscelyn, Hilary just slept. The second or third time she slept so heavily that Joscelyn had to keep ringing the bell to wake her. She finally emerged, half-dressed and bemused, to collect a hungry and bawling baby from the doorstep. After a while she was recuperated enough to use the time for other things: writing letters, paying bills, or doing some shopping without the fear of her daughter howling all round the supermarket shelves.

Joscelyn bought a car seat, to transport Sophie, and would collect the pram as well. Sometimes she and Sophie went out for a walk. Other times they came back to the house in Fulham. Sophie was such a good baby, she was content most of the time to sit in her car seat and watch Joscelyn get on with household chores. Philippa and her children came to visit "Joscelyn's baby" as they insisted on calling her. So did one or two of her Open University friends. Sophie was happy to be handed round to whoever had an arm to spare, and would become quite one of the party.

At first, Joss had looked at baby Sophie carefully, to see if she looked like Paddy. If anything, she looked like Hilary, but of course she also looked pink, beautiful and absolutely herself. She was a little person, completely her own self. Whatever resentment Joss felt towards her parents, couldn't be visited on her.

Although the arrangement was never formally decided on between the two women, the pattern suited them both, and quickly seemed to become more or less fixed. Joscelyn didn't have any course commitments on those days, and kept the time free.

As for Hilary, after that first meeting, in Fulham, Joscelyn found that she had actually quite warmed to her. At first, she had just been curious, and a bit sorry for her, as she looked so tired. Paddy was right, she was a clever person. She had read all Joscelyn's set texts from the Open University, and had something interesting to say about each one. But she was also, just now, very vulnerable. She had visibly relaxed in Joscelyn's care, and her pale cheeks seemed to gain colour just from sitting and drinking the coffee and eating the food that Joscelyn had provided. The huge threat she had posed was now gone.

Neither woman said anything to Paddy. Hilary didn't see him, anyway. As for Joscelyn, she often thought about mentioning it to her husband, but somehow there never seemed any point. He didn't have much to do with Sophie, and the whole business was a difficult issue with him. Besides, Joscelyn felt that he really might not understand. He might be unsympathetic, and try to change things. And there was no good reason why he should.

Sometimes, Joscelyn wondered what would happen when Hilary, as was bound to happen, mentioned their little routine to Paddy. But she would cross that bridge, she thought, when she came to it.

Hilary began, little by little, to take on a few more things. She started going to coffee mornings with her friends from the antenatal classes. She even started to think about how she was going to manage the rest of her life. And the rest of her life was coming upon her none too slowly. In a very short time, the lease of her flat would be up. She would need somewhere to live. She might even (impossible as it was to imagine such a thing) have to think about going back to work of some kind.

So when her sister telephoned telling her about a director's job being advertised in Durham, and ready to start the next autumn, it was hard to make any rational objection to the idea.

"It starts in the September, which would give you a bit more time to get on your feet. And it's a year's contract. I'm sure we could help you to find somewhere to live. I know you weren't too keen to be on Mum's doorstep, but Durham might suit you better. And you'd have me nearby."

"It's a long way to go for an interview. I'd have to bring Sophie with me. I'm not sure I could manage such a long train journey with her."

"I'd help you, if you got an interview. I might even drive down and get you. That might be better."

Victoria was being unusually willing to put herself out. Hilary didn't know whether to be pleased or annoyed.

"I could borrow a car seat," Hilary said, thinking of Joscelyn.

"Excellent," said Victoria, as if it were all settled.

"Look, I need just a little while to think about this," said Hilary. "It's not exactly what I'd planned."

But of course, she had nothing planned. And so she decided to apply for the job. She had to start applying for work, after all. Most likely she would not even be interviewed for this one.

Peter wrote to her again, from Milan; and one evening, with an unaccustomed burst of energy, she sat at her computer for over an hour, and wrote him a long letter with all her news. She even told him about Joscelyn, and how strange but wonderful it had been to be looked after by her. She hadn't mentioned it to her family, except to say that "a friend" sometimes had Sophie for a few hours. Of course this necessitated explaining a bit about Paddy, and she wavered a little about doing this. But Peter always seemed so solid. She felt that he could take it. And if he couldn't, well, he was a long way away. His loss would sadden her, but it would hardly make a large hole in her life.

Joscelyn sometimes had little fantasies, in which Hilary decided that she couldn't care for Sophie. She imagined (of course without *really* wishing her any harm) that Hilary would fall prey to some dreadful illness, which would make her completely bedridden. In these fantasies, Sophie would be handed over to Joss; and she had even worked out the details of the room in which the fostered Sophie would sleep.

Even if this were not to be, she, Joscelyn, would ensure the integration of Sophie into the Gregory household. Paddy didn't seem to see her on his own, but then he wasn't going to need to, the way things were turning out. When Sophie got a bit older she could come and stay weekends. She would be so familiar with Joscelyn that it would be no problem at all. Joss would be in charge and Paddy grateful.

It was something of a shock, then, when Hilary told her that she had applied for a job in Durham, and in fact had an interview. She asked to borrow the car seat. Her sister was to come and collect her and Sophie and they would travel by car.

It was the obvious thing, of course. Hilary would want a job; she would need a job. And of course she would want to be near her family. But this didn't stop Joscelyn from feeling absolutely desolate at the thought that she might lose Sophie.

True to her word, Victoria came in the car, and collected Hilary for the long journey up North. In real Mackay style, she was well prepared. The route was planned with lots of stops to feed and change Sophie. Victoria and their mother had been shopping for nappies, wet wipes, cartons of juice, and there were blankets for Sophie, spare clothes for Sophie, as well as towels and flannels all wrapped in individual plastic bags.

"You and mum think that I can't organise anything," Hilary protested.

"No, it's just that we knew that you would be too busy."

Hilary hardly had the energy to be annoyed. On this occasion, it was best to accept with good grace.

She stayed with Victoria and brother-in-law Glyn. Her mother was designated to be on duty to look after Sophie while Hilary attended the interview. Mrs Mackay came down from Newcastle for the occasion, and spent a good deal of time telling Hilary, in very precise detail, why exactly she had no need to worry, because every possible eventuality had been thought of and planned for.

"I have checked with Victoria's doctor that we could take Sophie round in the event of any real emergency. The receptionist was very helpful. Sophie could be seen as a visitor to the area, which of course she is. There is a special form we'd have to fill in. I should ring the ordinary surgery number during surgery opening hours, and there is an emergency number for out of hours."

Mrs Mackay was looking at her daughter, to ensure that she was paying proper attention.

"Of course we'd only trouble the doctor for something serious. If it's just general advice you need, you can see your own doctor in London."

"Yes, that's right," Hilary agreed dutifully.

It was a relief to get away from her family's concern, and this made the interview quite a pleasant experience. But it was a complete surprise when, afterwards, as she was drinking tea, and chatting to one of the other candidates, a member of the interviewing panel called her in and offered her the job. A year's contract; starting in three months' time, at the end of August.

What do I do now? Hilary had a moment of panic. But it was a job. They liked her, and she had liked them. And it was a job that she would be able to do; because her family would be nearby to give support. That was the rub, of course. Would she be able to stand it?

"I'll just have to be as independent as I can," Hilary thought. "Organise my own child-care, and that sort of thing. Live in Durham." Victoria could never be quite as dominating as her mother.

"I'll have to be strong," she thought, a little wearily, "but then I shall have to be strong anyway."

"Thank you," she said. "I shall look forward to it."

Hilary came back to Victoria's small terraced house, which was very full with Victoria and her mother, Glyn who had come home from work earlier than expected (rather to the annoyance of his wife and mother-in-law) and a hungry and screaming Sophie.

Hilary, starting off as she meant (or at least hoped) to go on, refused to answer any questions about her interview and went off into a room on her own to feed the baby. Her mother kept on coming in with cups of tea, comments and a long and detailed report on the time she'd been away. Hilary tried to switch off and let it all roll over her. When she had fed enough, Sophie, exhausted from all her screaming, fell fast asleep.

"Well, I got the job," Hilary told her assembled family after Sophie had been put down to sleep.

Victoria went straight to the kitchen, and returned, with a triumphant air, and a bottle of cold champagne and four glasses.

"I didn't know you'd been buying champagne," Glyn said, suspiciously, as if he couldn't be sure what on earth his wife would be doing next.

"It was on offer in Tesco's the other day. I didn't even think of Hilary when I bought it," said Victoria, untruthfully.

They all drank, and Hilary noticed that her sister had only half a glass. Victoria was like that. She had probably decided to limit herself strictly to a certain number of units per week, and the half glass fitted somehow into this schedule.

It was a complete surprise, therefore, after Glyn had been sent back to his college to do some more work, and her mother put on the train to Newcastle, to hear that Victoria had her own news.

"I'm pregnant," she said. "About four months now."

She smiled radiantly. Hilary thought that she had rarely seen her sister look so happy.

"It wasn't exactly planned," she said, with complete equanimity, "and I'm afraid Glyn wasn't very pleased about it. I shall have to give up work, or at least take my very maximum amount of maternity leave. He worries about our finances. He only has a three-year contract, of course."

Victoria, from her attitude, clearly had no worries of her own on this score.

"But I told Glyn that if you can do it on your own he and I

can certainly manage together. And now we'll be able to support each other. Actually, I'm really looking forward to it. I have been feeling wonderful; no sickness or anything like that."

So Hilary and Victoria were to be young mothers together, living near each other and looking after each other's babies.

Hilary didn't feel as bad about it as she might have expected.

"It will be OK," she thought. "It even looks as if maternity might soften Victoria a bit. But goodness, I am going to have to be strong."

"I haven't told mum yet," Victoria was saying, "you know how she fusses. I wanted a bit of time to get used to the idea on my own."

"That's probably a good idea," said Hilary affirmatively. It was interesting that, despite outward appearance of total harmony with her mother, Victoria obviously felt her own need to keep Mrs Mackay at bay at times.

Hilary told Joscelyn her news before Paddy. When Joss arrived the next Tuesday, instead of handing a ready-wrapped Sophie over, Hilary invited her in.

"I did get that job," she told Joscelyn.

"Congratulations. Are you pleased?"

"I think so. There's so much to think about, I've hardly had time to be pleased. But it's not at all a bad job. And I shall have my mother and sister around to support me. My sister's pregnant, too."

Everyone but me, Joss thought to herself.

"It's a shame you can't stay in London. Would that be what you would have chosen, in an ideal world?"

"In an ideal world, yes, a job in a London theatre, even a small fringe one, would have been ever so much better for me, at this stage in my career. But it's just not an ideal world, is it?" Hilary's face clouded slightly. Joscelyn left her be.

"I shall miss you both. But we'll still be seeing Sophie, of course. When she's a bit older she can come and stay at weekends sometimes."

"Yes," Hilary nodded, but looked doubtful. For a moment,

both women were silent and sombre, each for her own reasons.

Hilary was thinking that she would actually much rather not send Sophie to stay with Paddy. Not for ages. Not until Sophie herself was old enough to ask to go. Joscelyn, independently, reflected that a much older Sophie arriving out of the blue to stay with her father was quite a different prospect from the baby who was now a central part of her life.

When Paddy received the letter from Hilary, informing him of her plans, he was already having a bad day. He had, uncharacteristically, arrived late at the office, for no other reason than that he had overslept. Also, he had the beginnings of a cold. This, too, was out of character, for normally he was never ill. He had missed an important call by being late, and everything else that was scheduled for the day seemed to be going wrong, in some way or another.

He was also still smarting from the communication he had received from Eugenie just the day before.

Eugenie had been a bit quiet for a while, and so Paddy sent her a cheery note. It was one of his better ones; poetically lamenting the lack of communication, and reminding her, somewhat saucily, that

"There is nothing I like better, as you well know, than a nice fax in the afternoon."

After an hour Eugenie responded. "Very droll," she wrote. "But I think that we both recognise that the strain of trying to be witty is telling on us both. It is no longer born from a natural exuberance and enthusiasm for each other. That, I am sure we both feel, has more than run its course."

"The bloody woman was never that witty, anyway," thought Paddy, crossly. "She was just trying to keep up with me."

"Of course the first weeks were fun at times," continued Eugenie unkindly, "and I'm sure that neither of us wants to spoil a few good memories by continuing to meet out of habit. This would certainly make us seriously disenchanted with each other."

Of course Paddy had contemplated the end of the relationship with Eugenie a number of times, and often felt that it would be a relief. But he hadn't been quite ready for it yet. Also, his recollection of the last time they had met was that it had been very enjoyable. He was hurt.

"Bugger Eugenie," he had said to himself, thinking, as he did so, that this was one of the few sexual positions they had never adopted.

Hilary's letter, dignified and serious, childlike even in its expression, was a rejection of a different kind. He was sad, but also relieved. He had never seen his daughter without a sense of emptiness and helplessness. Now she would be going away. He might still see her sometimes, of course, but only now and again. She was a problem that could be shut away, while he occupied his mind with other things.

That evening, he told Joscelyn his troubles. "Eugenie doesn't want to see me again," he said, looking grave. "She sent me a message, dismissing me. It was rather unpleasantly worded. But then she was an unpleasant woman."

"I really don't know why you ever had anything to do with her. She was horrible," said Joss.

"She had a lot of good qualities." Paddy bridled. "But she needn't have been so unpleasant at the end. I suppose it made things easier for her. It wasn't in any way a serious relationship, on either side, so there wasn't any call for her behaviour. But I was upset by it."

Paddy looked hurt. Joscelyn looked at him, her face expressionless.

"Perhaps my little fling worried you. If it did, you should have said so. Better that than being all resentful now." Paddy's tone was getting more aggressive.

"I've had so much to worry about. One can't get upset over everything. And I don't think you should let it bother you, either."

Paddy deliberately ignored this, and changed tack. "And I had a letter from Hilary. She's going back up North. She has got a job with a theatre-in-education company, and will live near her family."

Paddy looked closely at his wife, and was surprised to see her close to tears.

"I know," she said.

"How do you know?" Paddy sounded as if he didn't really believe her.

"We met up, by accident. Hilary was in Fulham one day, and we just met each other. She came in here in fact. We had a talk, and she told me. Her sister is pregnant, too."

Joscelyn felt no guilt at giving this very much edited version of the truth. Paddy looked at her and furrowed his brow. The two of them must have spoken to each other. How else would Joscelyn know a detail like Hilary's sister being pregnant? And how galling that Joscelyn, who could only have met Hilary two or three times as a casual acquaintance, knew things about Hilary's new situation that he did not know himself.

"I suppose it's a good thing for her. A director's job, and near her family." Joscelyn was still near to tears.

"Of course it's a good thing for her." What odd creatures women were, sometimes, he thought. She must be upset about Eugenie. Hilary's going away could only be a good thing for Joss.

Paddy had just been going to suggest a weekend away in the Bear. He had been thinking about it on his way home. Joscelyn was very miserable just now, and although it was hurtful to him that she seemed to care so little about all his troubles, he hoped to make things better for her by a really good weekend away. But before he did, Joscelyn said,

"I've got to phone Maria, from my course. I promised to speak to her before seven o'clock," and walked off.

Paddy watched her go. Suddenly, there seemed no point in staying at home, where he had so little welcome.

He had plenty of work to do. He gathered up his papers, left a note for his wife, and headed back into town.

Chapter 23

Within a few weeks, Hilary had gone to live in Durham. Joscelyn helped her get everything ready. Hilary had got a bit flustered about all the planning, an anxiety that was exacerbated by the calls from her mother giving detailed advice on everything including which clothes to send ahead and which to keep for the journey.

Hilary had insisted on doing the journey herself, by train, despite the offer of another lift with Victoria. When the day of departure finally arrived, she felt a sense of relief. She'd had very mixed feelings about leaving London, but the move did signal a new phase in her life.

Hilary and Sophie were all ready when Joscelyn arrived to take them to the station. The drive to King's Cross went smoothly, and they were there in plenty of time. Joscelyn stayed with Sophie and her pram while Hilary collected her ticket and a newspaper. When the train was ready, she helped Hilary, Sophie, luggage and buggy to board and settle themselves down.

She stayed until the train left the platform, and waved at mother and baby as their carriage moved sedately out and onto the main line. Hilary waved back, and smiled.

Joscelyn walked back towards her parked car. She felt unutterably sad.

Supper that evening was a quiet affair. Joscelyn had little to say, and Paddy seemed preoccupied. But afterwards Paddy made some coffee, and while the two of them were waiting a moment before pouring out, Paddy said,

"I have booked for us to go to the Bear, the weekend after next. You deserve it."

Joscelyn said nothing, and Paddy went on. "I've been thinking. I was foolish to have that fling with Eugenie. It was a waste of time; time that I should have been putting into my work. And I can see now that it upset you much more than you let on."

He looked at his wife, a serious expression on his face. "You must learn to say when you don't like things. I can't be held responsible if you just put up with something, and don't say. But I can see now how unhappy you've been. And I'm sorry about it."

Paddy looked relieved to have got this off his chest.

Joscelyn looked at him. "I told you about Barbara. And you weren't very pleased about that."

"Joss," Paddy looked stern, "you really must forget about Barbara. That was ages ago. And if you remember, I did break off contact when you asked, didn't I? You've got to let it go now. We've got to move on." He paused, deliberately. Joscelyn looked up, and was again silent.

"It will be good for us to go away, just the two of us. I think we need a bit of a fresh start."

The next day Paddy was off early. It was Tuesday, which had been one of her Sophie days. She had an essay to write, but it didn't have to be completed before Friday of that week. Friday seemed an age away. Otherwise, there was a trip to the supermarket that needed to be done, but basically a long day stretched ahead of her, with no point to it at all.

Joss looked out of the window. It was raining, and so there was no prospect of doing some of those little jobs in the garden which would normally cheer her up. Inside the kitchen, there was a stack of washing-up. Paddy had been the cook the night before. As usual, he had managed to use just about every pot and pan, spoon and knife in the kitchen. Sometimes she found this endearing, and took an active pleasure in cleaning, sorting and making the kitchen bright and tidy again. They had no dishwasher (which were becoming fairly standard in the 1980s) even though Joscelyn often suggested buying one. This was because Paddy believed that dishwashers were environmentally unsound (using too much water) and didn't do their job properly. Sometimes that seemed rather noble, and Joscelyn took a pride in supporting him. But today, as she looked at the greasy piles of plates and pans, she wondered why it was that Paddy's fastidiousness and his social conscience always seemed to operate in areas where she was left to do the work.

She made herself some instant coffee. It was a cheap brand that she had bought as part of a recent economy drive, and tasted awful. There was not quite enough milk, and that made it taste worse. She could have taken a ten-minute trip to Fulham Broadway to buy a carton of milk. But it didn't seem worth the effort, especially with all that rain.

The coffee half-drunk and the books from her course in front of her but still unread, Joscelyn wondered about ringing Philippa. They might meet in a cafe for a cup of nice coffee. Then she remembered that Philippa had started working in the local citizens' advice bureau every Tuesday.

So she picked up the phone, and telephoned Ben.

"Hello," said Ben, evenly. "How are you?"

"Terrible," Joscelyn found the words came out, unbidden. "Absolutely terrible. Ben, can we have lunch soon? I need someone to talk to."

"Of course, when would you like?"

"Well, whenever you are free. I'm not doing anything today."

"Today is fine. You go to Gino's. I'll meet you there. Just after one o'clock."

She put down the phone, feeling relieved and a little bit foolish. Ben had sounded quite calm about it all. But what would he really think of her? He had once said that she was a strong person, who didn't panic. Would he still hold this opinion of her, after this kind of behaviour?

Joscelyn arrived at Gino's a little before one o'clock, and got them a table. She ordered a bottle of wine, a little nervously, in case Ben didn't approve of her choice. Fortunately, she'd remembered to bring a newspaper with her, and so had something to read while waiting.

Ben arrived about a quarter past one, and was polite about her choice of wine, in a way that Paddy wouldn't have been, but also in a way that told her that it wasn't quite what he would have chosen. They ordered a meal. Joscelyn, who normally selected something light for lunch, felt hungry and deserving of sustenance and made a choice of peppered chicken with vegetables. Ben chose pasta with seafood sauce.

"So what's wrong?" said Ben, as soon as their food arrived.

Joscelyn told him. She told him a long, long story, full of lots of details that didn't need to be told, but which to her seemed vastly important; crucial to any understanding of her situation and mental state. About Barbara, and Hilary, about her father's death and the funeral, and how dreadfully sad she still felt and how Paddy had never said one kind word about it.

"My dad was a difficult man," she said, with tears forming, and beginning to fall. "But I feel quite bereft now he has gone."

Joscelyn, even as she spoke, wondered why she had used the word "bereft" which was not at all part of her usual vocabulary, but which seemed right, somehow.

Ben seemed unperturbed by her tears and ordered more wine. It was a different wine, she realised, from the one she had ordered. A little more Ben; with a more distinctive taste.

And then she told him about Hilary, and baby Sophie, and how she had so loved looking after the baby. How she hadn't told Paddy about it, because she didn't think he would understand.

"I felt a bit guilty about it," she confessed. And she told Ben how much of a bully her father had been. How really the only way to circumvent him had been to deceive, to pretend to do his bidding but actually do something different. How she and her brother used to be party to deceit, and how her mother always used to say: "We shouldn't do this really. But it's the only way with your father."

She told Ben the story of the letter that her father had once insisted her mother write.

"Mother was supposed to cut off all contact with one of her cousins. We called her Aunty Vi. She was a jolly soul, but she'd displeased Father by speaking her mind too much in front of him. Father said that Aunty Vi was a foolish and ill-bred woman who could only be a bad influence. He told Mother to write a letter.

"'Tell her that I am very offended by her attitude, and that out of proper loyalty to me you can't be in contact with her anymore.' That's what Father said. I can remember it quite clearly even now. And Mother went to the dining room and wrote a letter. Then she called me in and asked me to ask Father to look at the puncture on my bicycle. Father did agree to take a glance at it, but his mind was on Mother and her letter. He came back in and demanded to see what Mother had written, and he went with her to the post-box to watch her post it. It seemed so humiliating. I remember feeling so upset for Mother. She took it so meekly.

"Afterwards, when Father had gone to mend my puncture, James said to Mum,

"'Why don't you stand up to him?' And Mother confessed. She told us that she'd written two letters. She put them both in her pocket, walked down to the post-box and posted, not the one that Father had seen and approved, but a different one.

"She said, 'It's not the right thing. It's deceit, of course. But with your father it's the only way.'

"I never wanted things to be that way with Paddy. I wanted to always tell him the truth. He seemed such a different man from my father. But recently that's been how it is.

"Even today, I should have told Paddy about meeting you. I always used to. Really, I shouldn't be here now."

Joscelyn was aware of having drunk a little too much, and of not wanting to let go of Ben's comforting presence. They had both finished their meals. Ben had said very little during lunch, and now she dreaded the words, "I'm afraid I really must be getting back now."

But, instead, he said, "Why don't you come home with me? It's not too far. I'll order a taxi. We could talk some more."

Joscelyn had often wondered what Ben's flat was like, and as she sat, feeling drunk, surprised and confused in the taxi, she speculated afresh about his choice of domestic environment. It turned out to be very small, central, immaculately decorated, with original pictures on all the walls, and a minimalist approach to furniture. There was one sofa (with a bright white cover) and one table in the living room, as well as a lot of shelves for books and some delicate china. The kitchen was tiny, bright and built-in, immaculately ordered.

Joscelyn felt rather nervous about sitting on the sofa. She would make a dent in one of the beautifully plumped-up cushions. So she stood, a little awkwardly, in the middle of the small room. Ben stood beside her, and then he put his arm around her. He felt strange and slight, quite unlike Paddy. He kissed her on the cheek, and Joscelyn was startled, but made no objection. She wanted to stay with Ben. She wasn't sure that she wanted this, but she wanted to stay, and be with Ben.

Ben let her go, and gestured towards the immaculate sofa. Joss sat down in it, and Ben sat on the floor in front of her.

"He's going to make a pass at me," she thought, and although the prospect was not entirely unwelcome, her heart sank. Things were going to get so messy.

"You are a very special person, Joss." Ben was speaking to her. He was holding her hand.

"And so are you," Joscelyn heard herself speak, and was a bit surprised at the words that came out of her mouth.

"But," she continued, gathering her wits about her, and putting on a calm, serious voice, "I'm not at all sure that I should be here with you. You've been a wonderful friend to me, and I value that. And it's not just because you've been a good listener over my troubles with Paddy. I like you and I enjoy being with you. But perhaps coming here was just overstepping the mark a little - I mean I hope that I haven't been giving out the wrong signal...." She tailed off a little, hoping that Ben would not need her to be any more specific.

She thought that Ben was looking a little disappointed. There was a moment's pause, and then he said,

"Joscelyn, I care about you. We've been friends, and perhaps that's all we ever should be. But I have felt closer to you, these last few months." Ben looked at her, and Joss, bemused, could think of nothing to say in reply.

"Joss," Ben said firmly, "I want you to know that whether or not you decide to leave Paddy, I am here for you."

"Leave Paddy?" Joscelyn heard the surprise in her own voice.

"Things aren't good between you and Paddy. Only you can decide whether to continue in your marriage or not. If you stay, we can have lunch sometimes. But if you do decide that your marriage is at an end, I am here for you."

Joscelyn felt stunned. This simple, clear declaration was a complete surprise to her, but Ben must have been thinking about it for a good while.

"I don't know what to say."

"You don't have to say anything yet. In fact it's probably better if you don't."

Ben made them both some tea, which he poured into beautiful bone china cups. He told her about the pictures in the flat, when he had bought them and where. "I brought that one home in my suitcase after one trip to Paris." Ben indicated to a large, brightly coloured picture depicting a North African scene.

"It must have been a big suitcase," Joscelyn observed.

"Fortunately, it was. But I did have to leave most of my clothes behind."

Joscelyn laughed, relieved that they could still talk as they always had done to each other.

Chapter 24

Joscelyn got home about six o'clock, only about fifteen minutes before Paddy. She was, in fact, still doing the washing up when he got home. She started, rather guiltily, to explain that she had been out all day, but he wasn't interested.

He was buoyant, having had a good day. One of his projects had definitely been sold, and another was looking promising. He was full of all the details. He had booked their weekend away, as well.

"We're going to have a wonderful time there. I know we are," he said. "I feel that I'm really entering a new phase in my life. We've had so many troubles." He looked up at his wife. "But I really think that we're coming through them. You deserve it. You've been so good. I was thinking about it only this afternoon."

Paddy opened a bottle of wine, and was hardly interested when Joscelyn tried to tell him that she had had a little too much at lunchtime. He looked around for some peanuts, and as there were none, went out to buy some.

"Please will you get some milk as well?" Joscelyn asked.

"Of course." Paddy breezed out, leaving Joss on her own.

Before returning home, Joscelyn had taken herself for a long walk, all the way down to the River Thames. She had, increasingly often of late, thought of leaving Paddy. But the moment Ben had said "If you decide to leave," she had realised that the time really had come: she had to make a choice to stay or go.

And Ben, when he had said, "I will be here for you," had he really meant that if she were free, he would want her to be his partner in life? That was how she had understood it at the time, but it had been an emotional day and perhaps she had misunderstood. But the life she wanted, with children, and the domestic disruption and disorder that came with them, how would that blend with Ben's elegant lifestyle and his precise choice of wines?

Besides, that unexpected and very clear declaration had been quite scary. Why did Ben feel that way about her?

Ironically, she realised she had never doubted the success of her marriage to Paddy. They had loved each other, of course, but Paddy had also needed her so much. And she, Joss, was so good at being needed. It had been the perfect match - except, of course, that it had all gone so horribly wrong.

Ben, on the other hand, was alarmingly self-sufficient. She saw and felt that he did want love and companionship, but even so his life seemed complete without it. What would her role be, with a man like Ben?

A slow walk finally took her home. And within a few minutes Paddy had breezed in. He was so happy and bouncy, and above all so very Paddy: large, and familiar in a comforting way. It seemed impossible that she should leave him. And he was talking about the future, for the two and them, and even more importantly he was at last saying that he had noticed her suffering, and cared about it.

This, she decided, was the moment to be truthful. She had always wanted to be honest in her marriage. Paddy was showing concern for her. He would understand. He would see that what had just happened was born out of all her troubles. He would feel sorry for her; he would want to put things right.

This might, Joscelyn thought optimistically, be the best thing that could have happened to them.

Paddy came back with milk and peanuts, and busied himself finding exactly the right bowl. And then he resumed his flow about his new project, while Joscelyn felt the words wash over her. Then she interrupted.

"Paddy, I have some news as well." Joscelyn tried to convey seriousness in her tone, without being over grave.

Paddy stopped for a moment.

"Yes?"

"It's about you and me. About what you were just saying. About what a hard time I have had, and how we need time together."

Paddy's attention was focused on her, but she didn't feel very encouraged by his expression.

"I had lunch with Ben, this afternoon."

"And what has Ben got to do with our relationship?" he said, bordering on the hostile.

"Paddy," Joscelyn started to falter, "I went back to his flat..." She tailed off, not knowing quite how to explain. This would have been better rehearsed.

"What happened?" Paddy glared at her and shouted.

"Nothing happened. We talked. He knows that things have been bad between us. He cares for me. We've grown fond of one another. A little more than either of us quite meant to. It made me realise..."

"What exactly are you trying to tell me? And I do mean *exactly*." Paddy's voice was heavy with sarcasm.

"That I realise how bad things have got between you and me. I still want things to work out between us. I've tried so hard, but I did see that we might not make it. That we might be better off without each other." Joss had almost said, "that I might be better off without you," but changed the words before they came out of her mouth.

"What do you mean 'still'? Aren't I planning our future together while you are getting into some kind of foolish involvement with Ben of all people? The man I asked you not to see. The man I share an office with!"

"Paddy, you have had affairs. I am not having an affair with Ben."

Paddy looked at her, his face clearly showing disbelief.

"Well, even if you are telling me the whole truth, the difference is that I have never got mixed up in any way with someone you were close to. I wouldn't have an affair with Philippa, for example. My other relationships, physical or otherwise, have not threatened our marriage. But yours seem to, from what little you are prepared to tell me. Now what am I expected to think?"

Paddy was red-faced and furious.

"Paddy, that's the whole point. I've been so unhappy. Over Hilary, the baby, and over Barbara. Especially bloody Barbara. When my father died, and you didn't even come to the funeral. I was telling Ben about it all. I wouldn't have wanted Ben in that way if it hadn't been for all my troubles, or even if you'd been able to be a bit more sympathetic; able to help me a bit more."

"So there is something between you and Ben, you just haven't been brave enough to be honest about it. And another thing I don't do is to complain to my women friends about your shortcomings, real or imaginary. I am always impeccably loyal. But that seems to be the basis of your 'friendship' with Ben."

"This should be an opportunity for us. It happened because of all our troubles. I want to put them right." Joscelyn was struggling now.

"I don't see it that way." Paddy looked grim. "Whatever this thing with Ben is, it certainly needs a clear end. You will write to Ben now, and say that seeing so much of him on your own was a mistake. That you have told me that and by far the best thing is if you do not see him or be in any contact with him ever again. Of course I shall have to find another office and once that small matter is sorted out there is a chance that we can get on with our lives."

Joscelyn looked at Paddy. She felt numb. Obediently, she went to the study. She sat down, and wrote a letter:

"Dear Ben," she wrote, *"I told Paddy in a rather confused way that we had been getting fond of each other. I told him that nothing had happened, but he wants an assurance that we won't be in contact again, and he feels that this is the only way that our marriage can continue.*

"I am so sorry. You have been a good friend. Joscelyn"

She re-read her words on the page. And then she wrote a second letter. It said:

> "Dear Ben,
> "Our conversation today and what you said to me concentrated my mind. I now know that I must leave Paddy. Things are very bad between us and I have come to realise that they will never get better. I have not yet worked out any arrangements. I may stay with Philippa. I will let you know.
> "This is such a big step for me that I don't know what my life will be like afterwards. Perhaps you and I are right for each other. I think that I hope so. But I just don't know. I shall be in touch and shall value your friendship more than ever."

Paddy followed her into the office, just as she finished the second letter, which she quickly put underneath a pile of papers.

"Aren't you done yet?"

"Yes, I'm done."

"Can I see the letter?"

"No, Paddy, it's private. I didn't see the letter you sent to Barbara. I have said that you have asked for all contact to end, if our marriage is to continue."

"That doesn't sound very final. Aren't you going to take some responsibility for this decision?"

Paddy's voice was sarcastic again.

Joscelyn wavered. Then she said, "Please don't stand over me."

Paddy left the room, and Joscelyn looked at both her letters again.

Just supposing, she thought, I deceive Paddy. Take a risk, and send my second letter. She signed both letters, folded them both, and put each one in an envelope. She wrote the address on each one, in her best writing.

Paddy came back into the room.

"I see you've done," he said grimly. "I've got a stamp you can have."

Joscelyn stuck on the stamp, and put one letter in her handbag.

"I'll come with you to the post. I need to buy a film for my camera, anyway."

"I'll be right down."

For a moment, it seemed as if Paddy was going to watch over her every move. Then he went downstairs. Joscelyn stuck a stamp on the second letter. She put that one in her bag as well. The first one - the one that ended things with Ben, was in the front pocket. The second was in the back.

* * *

Hilary had had a letter that morning. It was from Peter in Milan. It was in response to one she had sent to him, giving her news.

> "I am sure that you will be grateful for your family's support at this time," he wrote, "although I can understand that it may feel like a retrograde step in some ways. At least you will have your job. This is yours and only yours, and can be your area of independence. But as it is only for a year, who knows what you will be doing next or where. Perhaps you should look on this as a year to really get on your feet."

He went on,

> "I have grandparents in Durham. I'm sure that I'll be coming to see them sometime. When I do, I'll be in touch. Perhaps we might meet up."

A year is a long time, thought Hilary. Would Peter really wait that long for her? And would he want her, baby and all?

It did seem to be a possibility, at least.

* * *

Joscelyn and Paddy went together, towards the post-box in

Fulham Broadway. Neither of them said anything, and neither of them looked at the other.

When they got there, Joscelyn opened her handbag. Paddy stood next to her. He wasn't going to leave her to do this on her own.

Joss took the second letter out of the back pocket. After holding it in the air for just a moment, she posted it.

Ben would get it tomorrow. She would speak to him then.